I0772006

Savantia and Other Speculative Stories

A Collection of

Short Stories

Volume IA

By Justin T. Cole

Cover Art: Astral Travel by Pavlo Kandyba
Cover Design: Michelle Kapschull

This book is dedicated to the many people who read the initial drafts of the stories contained within this volume.

Your encouragement and support have motivated me to use this as a stepping stone to what will be something much grander.

Special thanks to my parents for making this book, and any that come after, happen.

Slip N Slide 1

Savantia 13

Quarantine 43

Championship Match.....................99

Syrup Harvest 143

Lecture 143

Syrup 154

Harvest...171

Transport and Holding 182

Syrup 191

Accompanying Artwork 200

Story Notes 220

About the Author 221

Edition Note:

This is the second half of Volume I.

The overall volume was broken in twain to make this book an easier format for portability and on-the-go consumption.

Preface

I have always enjoyed a good story.

When I was in college I found that, on occasion, words would just come to me. A decade later this became such a problem that, on occasion, I would have to pull over when driving to jot down a story that was manifesting to me at that moment. Another decade later, and at least 250k words of various stories written in various places, I began to exercise my writing by posting shorts online in various places to see if they were enjoyed... or to discover that I was writing garbage.

They were enjoyed. They were far more successful than I expected. This book is a volume that includes some of those stories, compiled with others, to showcase some of my works.

Slip N Slide

The automated alarm tripped a traffic congestion warning on the monitoring panel, the cyan glow displaying fiercely against the normal amber "all good" status indicators.

The dutiful employee that he was, Mrelnik examined the warning and collected the automatically generated ticket into his service queue, thinking it would be a quick and easy investigation that tied back to a traceable boost in traffic from one of the thousands of worlds tied to the matter-transmission network.

Mrelnik was mistaken. After multiple work-shifts, there was no clear source for the increase in traffic through the network: no source and no destination. There was, however, a significant increase in the flow of mass being ported through the slips. Mrelnik, having exhausted the level of his expertise, escalated the ticket to the Tier II Slip support team.

Jaxon saw the unusual ticket in the escalation queue and, immediately, presumed that the originator, a "Mrelnik" must be an idiot who doesn't know how to do a mass-source trace through the network, so Jaxon began the process. The mass trace, as indicated in the ticket that Jaxon did not bother to read, returned errors: no source could be located and no destination was found. The extra mass had no record of entering the Slip system and no record of leaving it, it just WAS. After a considerable number of work-units invested in trying to unravel the mystery, Jaxon, too, admitted defeat and escalated the ticket to the Tier III Slip support group.

Jessaxine found the mystery mass ticket to be fascinating. It is clear that Jaxon holds those in Tier I support in contempt and did not bother to read all of the notes that Mrelnik included about all of the tests done. Jessaxine, however, does respect the lower tiers of support as they handle all of the routine tickets and keep the entire system running. Their work allows her to handle only the most fascinating of problems, fascinating problems like a mystery mass clogging the entire Slip system.

After a significant number of cycles of diagnostic tracing, Jessaxine discovered that the mass was not being introduced at any of the registered SlipGate locations, but it was randomly traversing through all of them, seeking a valid exit point correlation before vanishing again. Verifying that the mass was randomly entering the network and being relayed around allowed for triangulation of the origin point and exit point through a long-running analytical diagnostic that ruled out millions of permutations of possibilities.

It took a half year for Jessaxine to further the mystery of the mystery mass, isolating a boring yellow star at the outer fringes of civilization. Extensive research into the archives revealed that a SlipGate had been deployed there, thousands of rotations ago, on the backside of the tidally locked natural satellite of the most promising planet in the system. It had been placed as a means for future research teams to have access to the world to do anthropological studies on the rapidly advancing sentients that had evolved on the world. It was placed and forgotten. It was never updated, and while it could connect to the network, it could not register with the current coordinates system, so anything it transmitted went on a full-system relay, searching for the matching destination coordinate before being returned to the loopback address, depositing whatever was transmitted back where it started. The entire journey would span several hours from the perspective of the Slip operators, but the subjective time spent by the contents transmitted would be significantly shorter.

Jessaxine compiled her report, filing it with an urgency flag as the only means to resolve the mystery mass would be to travel to the long-forgotten Slip and run the required firmware and software updates to it, allowing it to connect to the remainder of the network correctly.

The sentients of that world had, clearly, advanced enough to reach into their local neighborhood and had discovered the Slip and were trying to use it. Their efforts would have to go uncorrected until such a time that the update vessel could reach them.

Universal Grand Tours was the most successful tourist attraction in the history of humanity despite being the most expensive. People bankrupted themselves to reach the lunar colony that had grown around the tourism business so that they could take one ride through the cosmic SlipNSlide. People booked their individual rides YEARS in advance, each eagerly waiting for their opportunity to witness the splendors of the universe sliding by them at a speed bordering on incompatibility with the human mind.

As the time approached, each rider would sit through the liability video and sign their danger waiver, freeing the SlipNSlide operators from any wrongdoing should they not return or come back altered in any way. No one bothered to read the papers everyone signed them. No one had vanished or come back altered in any way other than having a newfound awe for the universe.

Each rider ascended the stairs and got settled into their group raft as the water started to pour down the slide, lubricating it for the raft's departure. The ride operator would yell, "Go" and give the raft a solid shove off the platform, allowing it to gently slide, with slight acceleration, down the steep slide and into the silvery surface of the Slip. Momentary swirls of rainbows, spanning colors humans had no words for, whipped and spun around the raft for an infinitesimal eternity before a strange world of aliens bustling about in a travel port of some sort blasted across the conduit, to be replaced with another moment of colors and another location being presented. Hours of riding the wave of water past thousands of glimpses of the life across the galaxy streaked by the rafters as they continued their "downward" trajectory before erupting back through the gate and sliding into the recovery pool in the lunar facility.

For nearly a century the lunar cosmic SlipNSlide operated, sending out billions of people throughout the heavens, giving humans untold numbers of existential crises about their place in reality but, also, inspiring untold innovations toward achieving the ability to traverse the stars on their own. For nearly a century the Cosmic SlipNSlide was the pinnacle of humanity's aspirations, everyone seeking to have their one day of wonder before mortality caught up with them.

Then the update ship arrived and the SlipGate failed to open, causing an entire raft of people to simply bounce off an impermeable membrane of fluidic silvery material and rebound into the recovery pool.

The Cosmic SlipNSlide was replaced, ending its life as THE tourist destination and beginning the life of its original intention, allowing humans to join the intragalactic community at large.

Savantia

Savants, people with extraordinary powers in one very specific thing, have been known to humanity for as long as records exist though they are not often diagnosed as such. Most cases bring a form of balance to the savant by stripping some other critical functions from the mind of the afflicted. One of the earliest examples which is labeled as a case of Savant Syndrome was Gottfried Mind, whose talent for drawing cats is considered unparalleled, as was his social interactions with his beloved feline companions. Gottfried's appearance follows roughly twenty years after The Royal Society validated the uncanny mathematical abilities of Jedidiah

Buxton, who was proven to be able to complete complex mathematical calculations with ease to the thirty-ninth decimal place. Mirroring Buxton's placement against Gottfried Mind was an American named Thomas Fuller, whose extraordinary ability to count manifested in a talent for converting the current age of any person into the correct number of seconds they had lived. In 1887, the term "idiot savant" was coined to describe this pairing of extreme skills against the inability to function normally in society; the term persisted for more than a century before slowly being phased into other forms of clinical labels.

Fascinatingly, not everyone who was, or is, a savant presents a corresponding handicap severe enough to impact their daily lives. Some carried the genius without an apparent detriment to their ability to function in normal society though many suffered from other forms of mental illness.

The history of fascinating abilities would be, merely, an inventory of oddities if not for a few specific examples, examples where the savant's abilities were introduced by illness or injury instead of being inherently present for the entire duration of a person's life. These examples bring the reality to light that every mind may contain the potential to have superhuman mental powers. People like Tommy McHugh who became a compulsive painter and poet after a brain injury. People like Alonzo Clemens who was able to sculpt any specific animal after seeing it once since he suffered a brain injury as a child. People like James Henry Pullen whose carved wooden ships are accurate to the number of rivets. Both George and Charles Finn who were able to calculate what day of the week a particular date would fall on, or fell on, for 40,000 years in either direction. History provides many more examples of such extreme talents, proving that the potential is there.

The potential of creating a key that would unlock this potential in every human drove a vast industry of research for decades. It fueled multiple efforts to improve people, to make them stars in the arts and sciences, to spring humanity forward by exploring what we could be. Often, though, these efforts to achieve potential came at the expense of what we *already* **are**.

Doctors and scientists of questionable ethics tested their hypotheses on animals with mixed results. Some subjects had significant behavioral changes while others seemed completely unaffected. The liquidity of results proved only one thing to the research community: animals were not complex enough to see if it worked. So, the more ambitious, and less ethical, began illicit activities to validate their work. Research laboratories in remote regions accepted political prisoners, the mentally ill, and even desperate volunteers for experimentation. The world saw the successes of these subjects but was shielded from the failures. The successes flaunted their new found skills openly, and lucratively, in tours and talks around the globe. The fervor for unlocking the hidden potential within us grew while the bodies of the failed were quietly, and efficiently, disposed of in their remote facilities.

The dark experimental labs refined their techniques until the survival rates rivaled that of any routine surgery. Survival, though, did not guarantee a savant ability. Survival did not guarantee the preservation of the person who entered the operating room. Survival meant only that the **_body_** survived the procedure. Survival was defined by the clinical definition of life as applied to a human body. Survival was enough to bring the research into the light of the formal medical community, but because of the dark secrets of the experimental phase, adoption of continued trials was placed on hold for thirty years while additional study of the brain, and the mind it contains, was completed and the horrors of the initial research faded from the collective consciousness of the general population to become a myth of "mad science gone awry."

My great-grandparents told me the stories of their youth, when it became acceptable for adults to take on the risk of an elective Savantiotomy in an attempt to unlock their buried potential. Everyone knew the risks, and those undergoing the surgery accepted them freely. Those who unlocked their abilities rose to stardom as their newfound talents wowed the world, which was a vast reward for the small price of slightly diminished capacity in other areas of their lives. Those whose procedures failed risked their diminished capacity and lost their gamble. Very few patients suffered severe brain damage, and fewer still died. Society considered the procedure an acceptable risk for adults to take with their own lives.

As with the unethical origins of the treatment, certain practitioners would perform the procedure on anyone for the right payoff. At first, these practitioners confined themselves to countries with loose regulations, but their presence spread around the globe, and they planted their operations in the shadiest of locations throughout the known world: mobile surgery suites, "back-alley cuttings," or even after-hours work in dentist offices (sometimes even without the knowledge of the dentist, it turned out). The proverbial genie was out of the bottle as the overly ambitious parents of the world sought to have the brightest and best children. "Helicopter parenting" and "dance mom" behavior was an insignificant, infantile cousin to parents who would butcher their children in the hopes of creating a star.

Society learned, rather quickly, that failed savants became a burden on society when the families of the unsuccessful attempts cast them aside. By the time my great-grandparents reached college, the world rebelled against the barbaric methodology completely.

Artificial savants became pariahs and outcasts, and the demand for the barbaric methodology evaporated in a matter of months.

But the research into the savant phenomena never ceased; it just changed direction.

The Savantia drug was discovered and it changed everything.

The drug was an accident: a waste product from developing another product. I can't even remember what the other product was, most likely some sort of drug. No one cares what it was, so no one remembers. Savantia is all anyone remembers from that point in time. It's all anyone needs to remember.

The story is an interesting one. The scientists working on the project discovered, quite accidentally, that exposure to the waste product induced an artistic flair in them that they HAD to abide. The compulsion would steal days from them. The effect was always temporary, but they produced beautiful drawings, paintings, sculptures, music, or other works of extraordinary talent. Each time they accidentally were exposed, their compulsion to work on their artistic medium was activated, and it drove them for a few days, occasionally impairing their ability to perform their normal duties to the extent that they received disciplinary actions at work.

It was after noting the correlation that they began controlled studies of the substance and discovered that there was a direct cause and effect where the waste product induced a massive shift in brain activity. Brain scans of the experimental subjects showed fireworks in the frontal lobe, super activity in massive bursts that appeared to wake their potential talents. The best part was that it did this without damaging the other regions of their brain. There were no failed attempts that left mentally crippled survivors. There were no apparent side effects. The worst-case scenarios seemed to be no bursts of talent or insight coupled with some low-grade headaches.

The product was rushed through the testing phases and to market.

At first, those who had the artistic spirit but no true talent sacrificed everything they had to afford the drug, and they became masters. Their works, sometimes in mediums they had never considered, became known world wide as the epitome of the modern artistic world. They paved the way for widespread deployment of Savantia. They drove us forward by proving what the drug could deliver to those who already had the drive. Those who could afford the drug (or who would mortgage their future to try it) took it.

When Savantia dropped in price enough that the regular people could afford it, we began to see people suddenly developing obscene skills in mathematics, faster than even the quantum computers. We experienced people developing logic skills and military strategy skills and mechanical aptitudes that exceeded anything the world had seen before in a "normal" person. Suddenly, humanity was harnessing their inherent talents while still being able to function as autonomous adults.

The more people who took the drug, the more variants in savant-like abilities emerged. The more nuanced abilities that manifested, the greater demand grew for the drug.

The explosion of new arts and sciences was immense, radically expanding the library of cultural works and overall comprehension of the universe. Production of all of the works of humanity increased one thousand times over, and the production of low-quality works floundered, diminished, and died off as people's particular savant talent drove them to something that they were successful in rather than something that they had a mediocre, at best, talent with.

It was known that the depression that set in when one stopped taking Savantia would cripple a person. Losing the talent they had experienced was worse, for many, than death. In fact, many who had to stop (for whatever reason) taking Savantia killed themselves shortly after their talents ended. The crushing weight of mediocrity was too much for them.

This pressure led to a massive effort to ensure the supply of the drug was maintained. As a result, no one was denied the ability to have it. Humanity flourished more, and demand rose further and further. The entire population of the world was, effectively, addicted to this drug so that they could produce at the peak potential of their brain.

Then a funny thing happened. A scientist whose talent was studying the brain discovered that if one was on a high enough dose of Savantia for a long enough period of time, there would be a subtle but detectable shift in their brain activity. This subtle shift happened when the effects became permanent.

He tested his hypothesis on himself by terminating his use of Savantia and discovered no reduction in his medical talents. This man was killed by the makers of Savantia. It was only through the ingenious investigative skills of a detective on the drug that the truth was uncovered and the story released to the world.

The news was tremendous. Suddenly, the world was open and no longer dependent on the ongoing supply of this wonder drug. Suddenly, the very idea of a world in which humanity, as a whole, could be made better was a reality. Suddenly, too, it became apparent that there were vocational effects to the drug instead of just in the arts and sciences. People could become genius investigators, or intuitive electricians, or plot the fastest, most efficient routes for trash collection.

Children were given the drug at younger and younger ages, and their scans were watched closely. The same subtle shift happened in them, and like the adults, the gift became permanent.

There appeared to be no age correlation with what gifts people would get, and it became accepted that every child would be given the drug as soon as they were old enough to enter school. Why deprive them of their gift?

The world was filled with child prodigies and adult superstars in their fields. Everyone was special and the epitome of human performance at their thing.

After a generation of this thinking, the problems began.

A generation of people whose entire lives held a special gift altered the way the world thought about everything.

A generation of people taught to embrace their impulses and special talents because they were a gift of science.

A generation taught, rightfully so, that EVERYONE is special and EVERYONE has a brilliant talent that will make them one of the best in the world at their talent.

A generation taught that impulses were good and that they were to be indulged rather than controlled.

A generation of narcissistic sociopaths who believe that their talent is the peak of humanity because it was.

At first, it was a subtle shift that no one could figure out.

People were uncertain if they were even seeing a shift at all, but they all felt that they were.

It took the savant abilities of several mathematicians to correlate all the data and determine that there was, in fact, a shift in progress.

Then the shift exploded.

Thefts rose.

Assaults rose.

Rape rose.

Murder rose.

Any antisocial behavior driven by narcissism and the belief that the world should honor "me" rose because an entire generation had reached adulthood believing that they truly were the most special and privileged person in the world because, in one specific sense, they were. The very reality of everyone being special created a world where no one was special because everyone was lost in a sea of excellence.

This upheaval lasted for a few short years because all of the talents that aligned with the social sciences were brought to bear on the task. The majority of the troublemakers were rehabilitated into a world where everyone was unique and special but in which no one was MORE unique or special than anyone else.

What everyone failed to notice was that Savantia had also awoken talents that remained hidden from everyone except those affected.

The end of the rehabilitation period started the "Dark Horror" as the smallest percentage of that generation utilized their special talents in concert.

Talents for crime.

Talents for violence.

Talents for traceless murder.

Talents for torture.

Talents in brutality.

Those with the talents to hunt crime were able to correlate out the criminally savant who possessed no other talent, but some have multiple talents and which are impossible to detect. There are also some whose abilities lie in hiding from detection.

We are now hostage to our fears as an unknown number of mastermind violent psychopaths roam the planet killing their targets.

Sometimes, the victims just disappear; sometimes, their remains are found.

Sometimes, those remains are found laid out in a brilliant masterwork that demonstrates that the killer has a brilliant artistic flair as well as psychopathy. If they were not so gruesome, the art would be profound and beautiful at the same time, but the vestigial thought that it is the remains of a murder victim is just enough to kill the acceptance of beauty in it.

The world is terrified, and no one knows what to do. No one knows how to proceed. No one knows how to determine if this price is worth the gains.

No one knows how to stop it.

No one knows how to stop _**me**_.

That is how I like it because my art comes with the blood of others, with their screams. My art lies in hiding the evidence, in making people vanish from the world. My art requires the sacrifice of others. My art mirrors the beauty of Lawrence Bittaker and Roy Norris though they were infantile in their execution. They are to me as a pre-Savantia child was to Monet.

I've told you all of this because I like my palette to know the story of how they came to be here before I cut into them. I want them to see the lack of hope, the horrors of what society did to itself, to imagine how I might hurt them. How I can keep hurting them? How long will the pain go on? I want them to know that I am the Tom Wiggins of murder, the Gilles Trehin of torture. I am the Stephen Wiltshire of covering my tracks. My history with hitchhikers exceeds that of Edmund Kemper.

So, now I ask you, how do you want to go? Should I put you in a Brazen Bull and feed your roasted meat to guests at my next house party? Perhaps you should take a bath in "the tub" and I can use your remains to fertilize your parents' garden. I'd put a Heretic's Fork on you, but I have grown bored of that device, at least for now, and impaling holds no fascination for me any longer. I think, perhaps, we will start using thumbscrews to crush your fingers and toes one at a time. Crush the bones and then I will remove the pre-tenderized parts and cauterize your flesh. I will then use those parts in your meals. I will work my way toward your body, and when you are nothing but a torso and head, I will either put you into my brazen bull or the tub to finish you off. I hope you don't mind. This is, after all, to appease the greater good of giving Savantia to everyone. This is a price society is willing to pay for everyone to be special.

No, don't fight it. I WILL get your fingers in here. There is nothing you can do to stop it.

There, now. Scream for help all you want. No one can hear.

Let's begin with the first crank of the screw. Let's see how long you can hold out before you have to scream from the pain. Let's see if you can beat my guess of seven full turns of the screw. Ready or not, here we go.

One.

Quarantine

Trapped.

There is no other word for it.

We are trapped and unallowed to leave.

We can't even be sure how many years we've been trapped. We know it's at least seven, but some of us insist it's as many as ten. You lose track of the years when every day is a struggle to survive.

When The Wall went up that was it. No one else was allowed out. For a while they sent supplies, but then those stopped, too.

We've been trapped and abandoned since.

A couple years after The Wall went up, people collected into little "clans" to survive. Some, like us, built our own wall from whatever we could find. Even with our wall, it will only be a matter of time before something happens and we are all exposed because our wall, unlike theirs, separates us from the resources we will need to survive. They have the luxury of letting us die and rot in here while they stay safe out there. We have to scurry around outside our wall

hoping to find something to help us survive one more day.

It's always about ONE. MORE. DAY.

We don't have a future. We have only tomorrow, maybe.

Each and every thing we find carries a risk with it. We might desperately need warm clothes, but that jacket might be infected. We have no way to tell. Every find is an alloy of fear and hope. We need to hope it's not carrying the infection, not carrying our death back into the camp. We have no other choice but to hold that hope EVERY TIME.

We think THEY know what the infection is and how to avoid it, but they will not share what they know with us. They will not communicate with us in any way. They will not let us out. To them, we are already lost. To them, we are expendable to protect the "greater humanity." To them, we are an "acceptable loss" to save everyone else. To them, we are nothing.

FUCK GREATER HUMANITY!

I am a person. Anna is a person. Steve is a person. Bob is a person. WE ARE ALL PEOPLE! We are NOT "acceptable losses." They sit out there living and protecting their HUMANITY *by LETTING US DIE AND ROT **<u>IN HERE</u>**. What good is their fucking humanity if they can live with that?*

We are certain the robotic drones that move along the top of The Wall can see and hear what is happening in here. Otherwise what would be the point? We all have our bouts of futile hope where we run out and beg to the heavens in the hopes that a passing drone will take notice. We have our moments of hope where we imagine that there is a safety zone ready for us outside The Wall where we can have food and shelter while we wait for

them to know we are safe.

The drones never reply. They never acknowledge. They never deviate. They're probably just robots that are programmed to observe, ignore, and report.

Our pleas go unanswered. Every last one. Every time. If anyone watching, their hearts are numb to our pain and suffering.

We try to minimize the number of people we send, and the number of

times we venture, into the danger of our world, but we cannot eliminate it. Yesterday, Don went out to find food and water. Don did not come back. Maybe he is still out there. Maybe he is dead. Maybe he got infected and is sick and dying. He's not here and neither are more food and water for us all. He will have until tomorrow before we assume he is dead. We will not search for him because we cannot afford to risk anyone on the hope that someone is out there and alive. Each successive death brings us closer to being unable to sustain ourselves in the meager life that we are achieving in the shadow of THEIR wall. In the shadow of the disease. We live in the shadow of death every day.

Our little encampment is named "Purgatory." Some of the older people here decided upon the name. About half of the people understand what it means. The rest of us had to have it explained. I still don't fully understand it. All I understand is that it is a waiting place, a place where you are judged before moving on.

Tomorrow we will send someone else out to look for food and water. We used to send two at a time, but we no longer have enough people for that. Every journey is a solo mission.

Our only real hope is that they will see our plight and help us before we all die.

Jess went missing but came back. We were sure she was dead. She said she was hiding from some others. She says they did not see her. She says they found a stray person and did horrible things. She wouldn't tell us what those things were. She couldn't because the sobs and crying prevented her from it.

She begged us not to put her in the quarantine tent, but those are the rules. EVERYONE has to be quarantined if they are gone too long. It's for the good of us all. It's the one lesson that THEY gave us with The Wall. But, unlike them, we let people back out of quarantine after two days. Isolating Jess was hard because we all heard the screams from her nightmares. Whatever she saw was brutal.

We saved some of the food and water Jess found for her. It's her right to have some of it since she risked her life for it.

We've lost three more people. Don never returned. Anna came back sick. We had to refuse her entrance back

into the camp. Her death was horrible. We all had to watch it because she wouldn't go away. Her death is what THEY are scared we will bring to THEM. We know the disease increases the rate of perception, so what passes as a few hours to us seems like days, or even weeks, of agonizing pain to the infected. It gnaws at the nerve endings and replaces everything with excruciating pain. It usually starts in the fingers and toes and spreads toward the brain, burning every nerve along the way. The luckiest burn up and die quickly before the disease gets in their brain. Most people convulse and twitch from the pain. Some, the unluckiest, become paralyzed, so only their eyes can reflect the pain that they endure for whatever eternity their brain creates for them in their final hours.

This is why the disease is so terrifying. Once it's in you ... the end has come. The reaper has found you and walks toward you slowly. Most people afflicted chose to kill themselves rather than be ravaged by the disease. Why Anna did not choose this we will never know. When she was denied readmittance, she sat outside and would not speak. She sat for the hours it took for the pain to become intolerable, and then she screamed. She screamed for hours until the part of her brain that made the screaming happen was eaten. The silence was no reprieve because we could still see her face contorting in agony as muscles spasmed underneath her skin. We could not help but watch as her body convulsed hard enough to break her bones while she died. Joseph couldn't handle it, so he went out to her. We didn't let him back in either. He chose to comfort Anna's empty body in its final moments and paid the price for it the following day, caught in the same agony that had killed her. He cut his own pain short with a knife through his own eye. We all sighed in relief as his screaming was silenced and his blood poured onto the ground.

Including Jess and myself, there are five of us left. How long before we *starve? Will we make it long enough to worry about freezing in winter? Resources are harder and harder to find and fewer bodies to huddle with means colder nights. Our little garden cannot sustain us in the winter, and we haven't seen any canned goods in months.*

We've decided to take what we can carry, which is pretty much everything we have, and walk the inside perimeter of The Wall. Maybe we will find a better place to survive for a while. Maybe we will find another group like us. Maybe we will find a more forgiving gatekeeper to the

outside world. Maybe, maybe, maybe. Staying here is no longer an option, maybe moving together will be our salvation, maybe it will be our undoing.

Only time will reveal to us the answer.

I am leaving this account, limited as it is, for whomever may one day find it. I want our plight to be remembered. I want people who never had to see the disease ravage their loved ones to know what our deaths

looked like. I want the future to remember how those trapped inside were discarded by society out of fear. I want humanity to do this better next time … if there is a next time.

The tag for the exhibit is labeled "Journal Fragment of Unknown Plague Victim."

The book, or rather a portion of one, is encapsulated in an environmentally controlled, transparent square. When activated, the surfaces of the square display the pages to each observing museum patron at a pace that they control; each entry is available for viewing while leaving the original book completely unmolested by anything outside the nitrogen-filled polymer-metal alloy display case.

Adjacent to the journal fragment is a rudimentary holographic demonstration of the disease progressing through a human body in the most basic of detail. The hologram is almost cartoonish in the way it represents the progression, changing the nerves from a deep forest green into a blazing fire engine red as it creeps, at an accelerating pace, toward the brain. The hologram provides enough basic context for the journal entries to have meaning without imparting the gory details of the plague to those who refuse to enter the larger exhibit.

Behind the holographic display is a door. Above the door is a sign that reads "The Great Neuroplague," and a sign accompanies it on the door that reads "The contents of this exhibit hall are extremely graphic. The terrible time in which humanity had to take drastic actions to stop the Neuroplague to save ourselves from extinction is portrayed in great depth and detail. Enter with great discretion."

Passing through the doorway and into the full Neuroplague exhibit is an experience in itself. The doorway is a polarized holographic field that immediately blocks out the light of the happier portions of the museum, plunging the museum patron into a morbid dimness which is a prelude to the utter darkness of the times being portrayed. A scanner notes when the patron's eyes have adjusted to the darkness, and a recorded voice is directed, using a hypersound beam, at the patron. "It has become appallingly obvious that our technology has exceeded our humanity," starts the tour in Albert Einstein's voice. A soft light exhales from a hidden apparatus to indicate to the patrons the direction of their journey.

The voice conducting the audio tour is a much darker, deeper, and stronger voice than Einstein's. It carries a hard authority with it, an authority that lacks all compassion. It instills a sense of necessity and stubbornness that can only come from those who "did what they had to do" to survive. The voice's hardness is an edge that cuts straight into the minds of the patrons to impart the grimness of the decisions they are to witness.

The voice narrates the first station of the exhibit. "The Second Great Depression regressed many of the 'first world' nations and left ruins spanning their borders." The station's three-dimensional model warps and alters to represent the descent from a prosperous city into one gripped by the plight of the economic horrors of the Second Great Depression. Buildings crumble and decay. The number of homeless people increases dramatically. People hurl themselves from buildings and into traffic.

Homeless people die and rot in back alleys, with no one to clean up their corpses. The city decays into ruin, and the light fades, mimicking a mournful sunset. Accompanying the lighting effect are the words "for many the Depression brought the end to their lives; for most, hope died and never had a chance to come back. It lapsed into an unending slumber, bringing the sunset of civilization upon the populous."

As the setting sun effect is completed, a transitionary sunrise begins to bloom along the opposite wall, enticing the patron to move forward. Photons pour, lightly at first, with increasing ferocity, from the next presentation. Light rises on the city as it was left in the previous station. "Fortunately all sunsets bring but a single night before the dawn of the next morning. For humanity, this dawn was brought by drastic actions." The lighted area around the city begins to grow, revealing a countryside that is barren and littered with abandoned farms. "The cycle of economic despair had destroyed the ability of farmers to make food and of anyone to acquire money. Each passing day shrunk the economy more and more as less and less money changed hands. So, the government acquired the farms." The lighting reaches its peak, and the holographic display shows the process of government workers taking control of farms across the entire plain and into the horizon where neighboring cities were barely visible to the museum patron. "There was no money to pay workers, so robots were created to seed the fields and tend the crops." Giant robotic machines are seen planting followed by the time-lapse of crops growing and ripening to be harvested by the robots, then shipped into the cities. "Harvests were trucked into the cities and the food given to all for free; their taxes would pay for the food so they owned it." Massive riots are seen to break out initially in the hologram "At first the free food sparked riots as desperate people fought one another to take as much as possible from what they believed would be a singular event. When the trucks returned, time and again, the riots gave way to peaceful lines and, eventually, normal patterns of food distribution that replaced the prosperity enjoyed by nearly all before the economic crash." The hologram mirrors the words and reaches a point where people, still homeless, are able to enter grocery stores and take what they need to survive without concern. "With the food shortages resolved, attention turned to easing abject poverty and lack of housing. The government absorbed abandoned buildings, and people were employed to restore the buildings. The finished buildings were provided as housing on an as-needed basis." The holographic model displays more and more homeless individuals entering buildings to reemerge clean and properly clothed. First one building, then another, then two more; the geometric growth of the program consumes all of the empty buildings and all of the people. A form of prosperity for everyone displayed in the projection is clearly apparent. "The rebound growth lasted for a generation." The hologram fades into the darkness.

The third station is timed to draw in the patron as the second station releases their attention. The voice returns amidst the coalescence of the hologram. "It was those who were born into the reformed world who began to reject it. They hungered for more than the mere survival which their parents had been pleased to have. They hungered for larger homes and more things. They, more quickly than the survivors could imagine, forgot the lessons of poverty and hungered for more." The city shifts and the emergence of things, useless trinkets and toys, gadgets and distractions, become visible in the possession of more and more of the younger generation in the hologram. "Soon they hungered for more information, so they restored the internet and rebuilt the vast array of information that could be shared across it." The accompanying holographic display perfectly illustrates the idea of restoring the massive information platform that existed before the great crash. It highlights the paths between people and homes with an illuminated grid of lines, tracing how the information flows. "The network regrew rapidly. With each new node being attached, more information became more available, and more work could be done faster. It took five years to restore all operations of interconnectivity to the world." The holographic display of everything except the network retreats, fading into nothingness. The network warps and bends until it is apparent that the patron is seeing the interconnected paths of the global network as it spans a spinning globe. Satellites are seen to come online, one after the other, allowing for the communication beams to reach around the globe. Then, the entire blue-green luminescent map distorts and appears to be pulled into a funnel, much like a planet that touches the event horizon of a singularity, the light streaking through the darkness to the next station where it swirls into a single point.

The display presents the outline of a smartphone as the core access to the world network, data pouring into its little screen and bleeding outward, forming the rest of the phone, then the hand holding it, then the arm, and washing into an entire scene of a busy street

with hundreds of people of many ages. A generational gap is hinted at, showing a divergence in mobile phone usage between the youngest and the eldest of the people. "The network allowed for a restored level of connectivity with those who are far away and a renewed ability to be isolated from those physically near us whom we have no affinity for." The display zooms out and the world spins away from the patron. The people shrink until they are no longer visible, but it is clear that they are, in all the cities, going through the same reawakening. "We brought prosperity to the entire world as we rebuilt it. The destruction of society made it possible to build a newer, better society with a greater level of equality and a higher standard of living for everyone." The world slowly stops spinning, and one individual walks out of the hologram toward the patrons, growing in size at a rate that gives the illusion that every step spans miles of distance. When the hologram steps out of the exhibit to join the patron, the station goes dark, and the hologram walks down the hallway, indicating that the patrons should follow it.

Matching the voice's words, the imagery morphs around the patrons.

The corridor's walls begin to show the imagery that corresponds to the voice's words. "Humanity's hunger proved, again, to be unending. The lessons of poverty and starvation never last, so we hungered for more. We followed the previous technological revolution from before the Second Depression by building our gadgets smaller and smaller until we began to implant them directly. At first, the implants were functional, designed to help people who were deformed or defective or had been seriously damaged. But that wasn't enough. We moved from medical implants ... to unnecessary replacements ... to convenient replacements for artistic expression in the form of replaced and altered body parts." The display reflects a sea of people about two-thirds of whom appear fully human; the remainder have various modifications that bring them past human into the realm of transhumanism. There are men and women with tentacles instead of arms and individuals whose faces are completely replaced; there are people with replacement eyes and ears, people with robot arms; the variations span the depths of the imagination of the programmers of the holograms. The hallway appears to reach a dead-end, and the holographic guide stops and turns around. "We had ceased to be all-human; we were now a divided culture. Cyborgs and mankind living beside each other, intermingling.

Conservative fear sparked and grew, consuming the unmodified humans. A radical movement sprung up to voice disdain over optional Cybernizing. It sparked editorials and sermons, protests, and attempts at legislation. When none of these stopped the tide of people upgrading themselves, the violence began." As the last sentence surrounds the patrons, a new hologram steps through the wall to the right and begins to beat the Cyborg guide. The Cyborg fights back, and others join the fight. The fight pushes through the wall to the left and reveals that the exhibit continues that way. The regular humans overwhelm the Cyborg and beat it into submission, a broken pile of parts soaked in blood, its face unrecognizable as anything more than a bloody mass of destroyed flesh, bone, and cartilage, leaving the one biological eye hanging by the optical nerve to stare at the ground and the river of blood pouring across the pavement. A hologram of an unmodified human stumbles forward, highlighting the path that the patron is to walk, before collapsing and spilling the remainder of its blood on the floor. In the momentary pause provided by the exhibit, the human's injuries are visible; it is clear that the modified people fought back hard, inflicting massive damage to their attackers. "We humans have never been good at learning the lesson of violence. The violence against the Cyborgs begot retaliatory violence that, in turn, escalated the situation. The violence grew and grew. Despite some unenhanced humans defending the Cyborgs out of principle, the violent tide washed upon the shores of humanity and brought, again, warfare fueled by hatred." The holographic exhibit generates the illusion of the dead human shrinking, as though moving away rapidly, at an alarming rate to become a small part of a city block in the middle of a riot. Fighting between the two groups is happening in various places. Graffiti present on the walls depicts both sides claiming the superior moral stance. "The fighting was not contained by any political boundary. It spread rapidly. It spread around the globe in a matter of days as the extremes from each side sought to avenge the atrocities committed by the other. Like so many situations before this became a war of terrorist tactics where each side flailed against the oppression of the extremists on the other without any regard for the people trying to stay out of the conflict."

The pattern of violence shifts in the display, generating what appears to be a "front line" of battle. "Neither side could be victorious, and everyone knew it." The fighting in the streets fades to a variety of scenes with energetic representatives of each faction arguing and talking over conference tables.

"The extremists from each side concluded that segregation was the only solution for peace, and so it began. Tired of the fighting, soldiers of the warring groups resigned themselves to separation for the greater good." The display shows region after region of segregated zones with empty "no man's land" zones in between. Few people cross through the central strip, and most are left undisturbed so long as they leave violence behind them.

"The uneasy peace was not enough for those who wanted to preserve 'God's creation.' Their religious messaging persisted even though the majority of the violence had stopped." A perspective shift brings the patrons from an overhead view of the segregated zones into the heart of a protest group within an unmodified zone. They hold signs that carry antimodification messages of varying strengths. Phrases such as "God gave arms, not tentacles" and "It's a sin to throw your body away" shared space with messages of continued violence to "wipe out the soulless Cyborg" and "cleanse the earth of technodevils." The text on the signs detaches and floats into the air around the patrons to be joined with hundreds of variations of the anti-Cyborg messaging. Those formless letters turn into a fluttering of pamphlets as the voice continues.

"No one knows, for sure, where it came from nor do we know, for sure, if it was actually engineered. What we do know is that there was a concerted worldwide message of anti-Cyborgism followed closely by the first appearance of the Neuroplague." The pamphlets settle, creating an image of Rome, with the Vatican clearly visible in the center of the display. "The first cases appeared in Rome." The city display rotates and whisks the viewer's perception inward and around corners to a specific coffee house where it fades into actual footage from the CCTV that witnessed the event. "The infection happens quickly. First, the victims have a burning sensation in the extremities which clearly grows in severity. This is caused by the nerve endings at the edges of their implants lighting the pain receptors in their brains. The agony grows as the infection spreads such that spasms wrack the musculature of the victims, distorting their faces and bodies. This footage, taken from the security cameras of Incident 0, shows how quickly the infection spread from the site of the implants into the remaining tissue. A few seconds casts the victim from initial symptoms to the convulsive death throes. You can see that humanity is not entirely dead as it is apparent that some rush over to help the victims while others run. The most horrifying part is that the cyborgs that attempted to help became infected themselves. It is from them that we determined the incubation time for this disease." The CCTV footage retreats down the walkway, enticing the patron to follow. Each cyborg that attempted to help is captured and a still of their image is pulled away from the rolling film.

"Four days later, the Cyborgs that attempted to assist Patient 0 collapsed in writhing agony where they stood." Four additional screens appear, each showing one of the four, adjacent to their still image, falling where they stood and being consumed by the raging pain. "Their suffering elicits the attention of others who attempt to help, getting infected in the process." The original video fades into nothing. Each of the Cyborgs that attempt to help are pulled out of the video and spun off into their own display, and those displays split to show the next tier of the infected. "The spread was unprecedented. This pandemic was 100% fatal. Every exposed cyborg had their neural tissue devoured from the implants toward the brain until only death halted the progression."

All of the screens go dark at once. "For two years the best scientists in the world studied the disease in an effort to find a means to stop it, treat it, cure it. Anything. Two full years the world existed in the dark time created by the CyberPlague." A tiny dot of light appears, accompanied by hopeful words "Eventually the study bore fruit. The pathogen was isolated, and all of the infection vectors were determined. We assume that it must have been engineered because it worked too well, too efficiently, too fast, but no individual or group ever claimed responsibility for it. The root cause of the CyberPlague was a tailor-made retrovirus. As communicable and resilient as a general 'cold' virus but invisible to the immune systems of the Cyborgs because of the special exterior coating that it produces for itself. This coating ...," the hologram grows and highlights the various anatomy of the virus as the narration outlines the functions, "mimics the biological response to where the flesh meets the implants. The body sees the virus as part of the implants and, therefore, 'self' so it ignores it."

The hologram slides the hand-sized virus cell closer to a giant body which spans the wall and hallway ahead.

"When the CyberPlague virus enters the system, it seeks out cells of the body that are part of the immune system." The viewer is enticed to follow the cell into the body and down the hallway by the changing hologram. "Upon locating a victim cell, it attaches to it and rips out the cell's DNA. The CyberPlague worked within its victims in much the same way that the HIV virus degraded the immune system of its host in the late 20th and early 21st centuries. The newly emptied cell has virus DNA copied into it before the virus detaches and floats along, seeking a new cell to infect." The holographic display shows a second immune cell being infected and the virus detaching again. The immune cell is made the focus of the hologram, and the patron is led to follow it along. "The cell creates a hard coating which the blood will dissolve, a process that takes four days. During this time the cell is programming itself to attack the very biological element that prevents its detection in the first place, the same element that prevents the body from rejecting implants. If that were all it did, the death toll would have been very small. Instead, the virus continued to act. The first stages of the sickness are the uncomfortable itching sensation as the reprogrammed immune cells attack the places where the implants meet the flesh. This discomfort grows exponentially as more cells are infected and call for more cells to fight the infection. The immune response cycles into an uncontrollable feedback loop of inflammation and tissue damage."

The hologram shifts to real footage of the medical processes being described. "The critical danger, though, comes after. When the tissue that is married to the implants is fully under attack, the remaining immune cells shift to the nerves that connect to the implants. We do not know, and likely never will know, if this was intentional. As each successive nerve ending is compromised, the immune cells continue to move along to the next. The CyberPlague moves in this fashion throughout the body, tracing the entire neural network from the implant site, past the brain stem, and up into the cerebral cortex. Few sufferers managed to remain coherent during the process of consumption; each provided a description of the sensation. The activation of the nerve endings for pain induced an experience that they, universally, described as being immolated. Upon the destruction of the upper brain functions, the disease continues to devour the neural tissues until the autonomic functions cease, letting the remainder of the body expire from lack of any brain tissue."

The hologram fades and a series of videos of people actually dying from the disease become the beacons for the patrons to follow. "During the two years it took us to isolate the CyberPlague, nearly 3 billion cyborgs died. People with medically necessary implants also died. Unenhanced humans did not contract the virus. Cyborg communities walled themselves off and refused admittance to any strangers with an implant to ensure the safety of those already inside." The videos change back to a hologram showing the erection of walls around communities. "At first this worked. Three years later, though, a change occurred: unenhanced individuals had begun to carry the virus without being infected. A single infected, non-enhanced person entering a Cyborg community could kill them all within a week. Word of this spread around the globe within days of the first incident occurring: an incident in which a delivery driver carried the Neuroplague into a community. The Cyborg community was devastated. Their efforts to survive were no longer effective. Any stranger was suspect." The hologram shows the delivery driver entering a community, unloading supplies, exchanging payment for the supplies, and leaving. He drives to the next town while the Cyborg community thrashes in pain and all die.

"The real threat to the existence of all humanity came a year later. An unenhanced human, known to be a carrier of the CyberPlague, was involved in an accident where metal became embedded in their arm and required extraction by medical professionals. The emergency room staff sedated her and began the work of extracting the metal when she woke up screaming." The hologram switches to the security feed from the hospital. "The injury had triggered the virus, and it was consuming her nerves from the injury upward toward her brain. The fire of the pain burned through the anesthesia and woke her. As you can see, the pain was traumatic and her body thrashed about the table uncontrollably. She was the first unenhanced human to jump from being a carrier to being afflicted by the CyberPlague. She was not the last." The hologram splits and shows another, and then another, and then another, each splitting multiple times as the CyberPlague traverses the unenhanced population at the same rate that it ripped through the cyborg population.

"The CyberPlague had mutated. It was now a NeuroPlague that required no implants or foreign bodies to attack humanity. The NeuroPlague had become the single-greatest threat our species had ever witnessed."

"I am Brigadier General Alexander Coombs. I am the one who made the decision to wall the safe places off and exclude entry by anyone. I created the inverted quarantine zones. I saved tens of millions of people. I also ordered the construction of the quarantine zones and walled tens of millions of people whose infection status was unknown inside them. I may have saved tens of millions of people, but I left tens of millions to die from the NeuroPlague to do so. I did it to save our species from death at the hands of this terrible disease, this weapon. This instrument of hate would have wiped every last one of us off the Earth had drastic action not been taken. I knew then that I would be the most hated man on Earth for the hard decision I made. I also have faith that, someday, history will acknowledge the heroism in my decision and give me the forgiveness that I will never be able to give myself."

The hologram dissolves and the floor loses its opacity, revealing a scene below. "What you are now standing over is the encampment where we found the journal you saw encased outside the full exhibit. Twenty years after the last case of the NeuroPlague we allowed anthropologists into the abandoned lands and the quarantine zones to see what they could find. We found thousands of these encampments spread across the land. Many had the remains of people scattered about them; some had obviously died writhing in pain; others had died at their own hand. We even discovered walled-off villages with a few survivors whose anger and hatred toward us made it impossible to approach them. The disease, it appears, has exhausted itself. Humanity is safe, and we, once again, are free to roam the surface of the world."

The floor regained its opacity, and a doorway slowly illuminated, presenting the hallway where the exhibit exit was to be found.

The pair of patrons exited the exhibit and stepped back into the hallway. "Fascinating," the taller one states, "this species appears to have exterminated itself in a war over whether or not their mythology would approve of merging with their technology."

"Agreed. This truly is fascinating. Our report will make for a very interesting experience. If only we could transport this entire shrine to their survival with us when we return. It is a much greater experience than our recording of it can be," the shorter one replied.

"Agreed. We will have to accept only the recording and the other evidence that shows that the NeuroPlague was not extinct as the exhibit outlined. Finding this shrine is fortuitous as it would have taken decades to determine the cause of their extinction without it. We shall make it a cautionary tale for other developing worlds in the future."

With those final words, the two beings of gray skin and black eyes touch buttons on their wrists and flash out of existence. The sounds of nature, uninterrupted by the extinction of mankind, continue outside the walls of

the indomitable structure of the
Museum of Modern Human History.

Championship Match

"Well, Marv, we've got a good lineup ahead of us tonight. Each of these contestants has had a full night of table-service as their requisite warm-up for tonight's big event. Rochelle is the leading contender. She has been known to roll 50 silverware rolls in as little as a half-hour to get out the door. Mark, though, has had a long-standing reputation for trading rolling with his teammates, so he has built up endurance, often doing 150 rolls in one night to get a couple of nights off. Brian and Sue both have extraordinary rolling prowess and have been known to beat their coworkers out the door by as much as a half-hour regularly."

"Gary, you're absolutely right, here. The fan favorite this evening seems to be Brian. I think it's the underdog scenario that draws everyone to him. He always performs strong but has never won any awards for his rolling skills, so people want to root for him and be part of it when he finally wins his first professional round. The obvious loser in the fan polls is Mark as many consider his training method to be cheating. He argues that there are no rules against it and, therefore, doing endurance training every third night is a great way to build up the muscles needed to keep a pace to be on target for hitting 300 first. He says this is like a marathon, not a sprint, whatever that means."

"Yeah, Marv, I think that Mark is referencing terms used in running. If I'm not mistaken, a 'marathon' is a long race and not just a place in Greece. A sprint, I believe, is when a runner uses all of their energy in an explosive, but short, foot race. It seems, if I'm right, that this is an apt analogy to what we have in front of us this evening."

"Gary, it seems you're right. I took a moment to look up the terms, and they are exactly as you describe them. Perhaps some of our fans already knew this."

"Marv, I'm sure they did. Running is a fairly obscure pastime, but the people who participate in it number in the low millions. Some of them must also enjoy more mainstream sports, too."

"Gary, I'm sure they do."

"Looks like the playing field is getting set. Each of our contestants now has three tables in place, and soon, the crew will bring in the bus tubs filled with silverware. In the amateurs, each contestant gets one run for each of the silverware types, but as you know, this is the league competition. Here, the roller has to sort the silverware before it can be rolled."

"Gary, it sure does. This adds an extra element to the competition and allows for a greater level of strategy.

It's a bit of a Kobayashi Maru in the initial stages since there is no way to win the sorting game."

"Marv, I don't know about that analogy here. I see where you're coming from, but if it were true, none of the contestants would be able to finish the event."

"Gary, maybe you're right, but we know that there is no best way to handle this. Either they have to presort or they have to sort on the way. Either of these methods has their own benefits and drawbacks."

"Marv, you're absolutely right. And how the scoring is done determines which technique is best. In tonight's competition, we have a long-run scoring technique. Each contestant goes until they complete their 300 rolls or relinquishes their spot in the competition and forfeits. I don't think we will see a forfeit tonight, though."

"Gary, I don't think we will, either. I'm thinking Mark will invest the time to pre-sort his silverware while letting everyone else get ahead, then he will race to catch up and, probably, surpass them all in the final part of the competition. This is where his training will help him come from behind to win."

"Absolutely, Marv. Brian, on the other hand, strongly favors the sort-as-you-go approach. This method is best when the scores are tallied when the first person hits the goal, whereas the other method puts contentment as a severe disadvantage if the winner clears their number fast."

"Indeed, Gary, indeed. Let's take a moment to talk about Rochelle and Sue. These ladies have a consistent performance level in their daily efforts and have a strong chance of beating either Mark or our fan-favorite, Brian. The real question will be endurance. Can they keep pace with Mark once he's hit the 225 mark? That's really the part of this contest that will make-or-break each of our contestants today."

"I guess only watching the competition can tell us the answer to that, Marv."

"Indeed. If we could tell ahead of time, we'd be able to win big and let someone else do this job."

"Don't I know it! But, since we can't know ahead of time, we will have to keep working this job and letting all professional rolling fans know what's happening in the upcoming play-by-play. I know our fans really appreciate it. Our fans are the best, Marv."

"Gary, don't I know it! Let's take a moment to let our fans know about the good sponsors over at Tony Robin Steakhouse, where your steak burgers are fresh and made to order! They're waiting for you!"

"Marv, that sure does always make me hungry. I guess I'll have to sate myself with this ice-cold Pepsi and a bag of Doritos as a pre-game snack. {crunch!}"

"Gary, you'd better share some of those with me."

"Of course, Marv, but you have to get your own Pepsi!"

"One of the support staff has entered the competition area with the bus buckets, indicating we're five minutes out. Looks like we're getting ready to start. We should see our contestants shor ..."

"Here they come, Marv. Brian is entering to applause from the studio audience followed by Sue."

"Gary, from the sounds of it, Sue has some adoring fans in the audience."

"It sure seems that way, Gary, but not as many as Rochelle. The audience is erupting for her!"

"They certainly are, Marv. But where's Mark?"

"We're waiting for the doors to open one last time ... and there they are! Mark has entered the competition room. About half the audience is going wild and the other half is absolutely silent."

"That's right, Marv. Mark is not universally liked. As we said earlier, his training technique is considered to be cheating by many."

"As expected we are seeing Brian toss away the empty tubs. He's going to forgo the pre-sorting method."

"This is no surprise to me, Marv. I don't think he's ever used the pre-sort method. Why would he start now?"

"Gary, that's a good question and one that doesn't need an answer because he isn't going that route. Mark, on the other hand, has laid out the three sorting tubs on the table to his left. He's obviously going for a right-handed approach to rolling."

"Interestingly enough, both Sue and Rochelle have laid out their sorting tubs. This is an interesting turn of events!"

"It sure is, Gary. Neither of these ladies uses a consistent method. They seem to flip between pre-sorted and in-line sorting with great fluidity. That they're both going with the presort today is worth noting. I expected one of them to choose each way."

"Well, the odds were 50/50 for each of them."

"Yup, making this development a 1 in 4 chance. I wonder what the Vegas odds were on it?"

"I don't know, Marv, but I'm sure there are some happy gamblers out there right now!"

"The clock has been turned on. Looks like we're ready to begin. Brian's wrapping in black, Sue in blue, Rochelle in green, and Mark has chosen to wrap in red bands."

"The anticipation is mounting as we all wait for the buzzer to signal the start of the competition."

"Gary, you're right! And there's the buzzer! They're off!"

"As we expected, Brian is off to a strong lead, grabbing matching sets of silverware from the tub and laying them out on napkins and Mark is sorting the various types into their isolated bins with lightning speed. The real focus, at this stage, is what are Sue and Rochelle doing?"

"Well, Gary, there is definitely an interesting development here. Sue appears to be sorting, which is consistent with having the tubs laid out in front of her. But, you're right, Rochelle is definitely doing something odd."

"It looks, Marv, like she's rolling silverware directly. But why? Why would she have carefully laid out the three tubs to not use them?"

"Wait, she just dropped a fork into one of the tubs. And, now, a spoon! Gary, we may be looking at something revolutionary here; a brand new strategy!"

"Marv, I think you're right. Look at her go! It appears she's rolling as her primary activity, but unlike Brian, she's dropping every other piece she touches into a sorted bin!"

"Brilliant! Gary, this strategy should come in handy later in the endurance part of the competition!"

"I think so. It will certainly spice this entire competition up!"

"Brian has reached 15 properly rolled silverware bundles. He's the first to hit the bundle, but Rochelle is not far behind."

"Marv, you're right in that since she's just ... now hitting the 15 mark herself! But she has an advantage with her pre-sorted items!"

"Gary, take a look at Sue! She's changed it up! She's starting to roll and she's rolling up a storm!"

"Marv, could this be that we're seeing be the dawning of not one, but TWO, new strategies here? Is this some other new method, or did she just change boats mid-stream?"

"Gary, I wish I knew. We'll have to watch and see if she changed it up or is doing something completely new."

"It looks like, as Sue is approaching her first 15, she's not terribly far behind Brian and Rochelle. Meanwhile, Mark hasn't rolled a single roll yet. If this were a timed competition instead of an endurance one, he'd be in serious trouble right now."

"It's a good thing he's not going for early speed then, isn't it?"

"It sure is, Marv."

"Gary, I'm getting word we need to take a break for our sponsors to deliver an important message. We'll be right back Rollers! Stay tuned to see who's in the lead after these messages!"

[2 minutes elapse as commercials selected by the local broadcasters play]

"Aaannndddd we're back! Brian and Rochelle are still 'neck and neck,' but Rochelle's pre-sort tubs are filling where Brian has nothing to answer it. To me, that means Rochelle is in the lead at the moment."

"Gary, that's a good call, though Mark is still an unknown quantity here. It looks like he's sorted about half of his silverware but he hasn't started rolling a single roll yet."

"Totally true, Marv, if I didn't know better, I'd be worried. I expect that he will have his silverware completely sorted before Brian or Rochelle hit 75 completed rolls."

"Gary, look at that! Sue's gone back to sorting! It looks like she sorted 50 units worth, rolled them and is back to sorting again!"

"Amazing! It IS a new strategy. It's completely different from anyone else on the floor here."

"Indeed it is. We'll have to keep an eye on her for the rest of the match!"

"Gary, I think it's a good moment to give a quick recap and rundown, what do you think?"

"Marv, that's an excellent plan! For anyone joining us late or who has lost track, we've got Brian, Sue, Rochelle, and Mark rolling today. Mark has chosen the sort-first and then roll strategy and is nearing the end of his sorting phase. Brian, on the other hand, has chosen to jump right in on the rolling directly. He's passed his 50 roll mark and is still going strong."

"That's right. But the more exciting part is what we see with our lady contestants today."

"I agree. Sue set the stage for presorting and started doing so, but when others, and by that I mean Rochelle and Brian, approached 15 completed rolls, she switched over to rolling. At first, it looked like she was changing tactics but we soon learned the truth, didn't we, Marv?"

"Indeed, we did, Gary, indeed, we did. She rolled 50 rolls, depleting her supply of sorted silverware, and then started sorting again!"

"A brilliant change-up!"

"Indeed it is! She's dividing the work of sorting and rolling the same way Mark does, but she's doing it in stages instead of all at once!"

"Marv, it's a new world here with this change, but that's not even the big news."

"You're right, Gary, the big news is Rochelle."

"Do you want to tell our listeners why, Marv? Or shall I?"

"Well, Gary, it started out looking like Rochelle was wasting her time by setting up sort bins because she just dove in and started rolling ... but, then ..."

"Then she started putting extra pieces in the sort tubs! Sorry, Marv, I got so excited I had blurt it out."

"That's ok, Gary, I'm right there with you. It's exciting that she developed a new strategy to get ahead on rolling and not waste the handling of pieces she doesn't need."

"It's a brilliant innovation in strategy!"

"It sure is."

"So, what's the score at Marv?"

"Well, Gary, it looks like Brian has a slight lead, at 75 ... 1,2,3: 78 completed rolls and, as I said that Rochelle hit 75. Sue is not far behind, hitting 60 units, and ..."

"And Mark has his first roll on the table!"

"That's right, Gary, Mark has finished his sorting and is hitting the rolling hard."

"So now we're in a straight-up speed challenge between Brian and Mark against the new strategies brought in by Sue and Rochelle. I can't even begin to speculate who will hit 300 rolls first."

"Neither can I, Gary. Neither can I."

"Marv, we're approaching the regulation bathroom break so you know what that means: another word from our sponsors and a rundown of the other events today. For the Rollers watching, we will have a brief coverage of the other events, and we'll give a quick summary of the big Dishwashing match today as well as the leaders in the Hole Digging events around the country."

"Gary, I'm on the edge of my seat to see what everyone else is doing."

"Me, too, Marv. Me, too. Rollers, we'll be back in about 15 minutes!"

[15-minutes lapse, playing updates of various other events and commericals]

"Aaaannnnnnddddd we're back! It's an exciting day in Hole Digging but no surprises in the great Dishwashing match."

"That's right, Marv. It's an even match, so the only real surprise will be which one is the final winner. We will have a rebroadcast of that on this channel tonight at 11 for anyone who wants to follow it."

"Good to know, Gary. Where do we stand?"

"Well, Marv, Brian and Rochelle are pretty much even, at 173 and 168. Sue is not far behind them at 150. The real news here is that neither Sue nor Rochelle are losing ground using their new strategies, and it looks like Rochelle will be well-positioned for the last stretch."

"All true, Gary, and Mark's fans will be glad to know he's making up for lost time. He's passed the 100 mark and is, quickly, closing in on 125 completed rolls."

"At this pace, if he can keep it up, he is still in the game."

"I hadn't ruled him out."

"Neither had I, Marv. We know this is his strategy, and he trains for it."

"Yup, but I wanted to make sure the fans don't think he's out of the game just because he's behind at the moment."

"That's a good call."

"Oh! Gary, did you see that?"

"I sure did, Marv. We have a game-changer here. Mark got careless and a second fork came out of the tub and flew onto the floor. That's a foul, right there."

"It sure is, Gary. He's going to have to deal with that to finish."

"Absolutely, Marv. Either now or at the end, he's going to have to spend clock time to take that fork to the kitchen and get a replacement. There's no way around it."

"It looks like it rattled his cage a bit."

"It sure does."

"Oh, no! Gary, he's done it again! A second fork down!"

"It's a good thing he didn't run the other one to the kitchen. If he had, he'd lose the clock time twice. This way he can take them both in one trip. I'm sure his fans hope he lets them lie until he needs them to finish."

"I'm sure they do. I'm also sure that those who think he's a cheater feel he deserves it."

"I bet they do."

"What's our score at the moment?"

"It looks, as I'm saying this, that Rochelle is switching to the sorted silverware. She's pushed the initial tub off the table in a show of bravado to show everyone it's empty. The clatter appears to have rattled Brian and Mark a bit."

"That's a part of the game, Marv. "

"It sure is."

"I bet it doesn't help that she and Brian are still 'neck and neck' and closing in on 225 completed rolls. They're in the home stretch now."

"Gary, that can't make Mark feel secure in his decision."

"I'm sure it can't. Even Sue, with her alternating pattern, is well ahead of his 175 rolls."

"That's right, she's behind the lead at 200, but still ahead of Mark."

"Marv, looks like Sue has switched back to sorting again. She must be almost done with sorting."

"Obviously, she is. She's finished a third of her overall goal, meaning that she has 100 of each left."

"And look at her go. She is, obviously, feeling the pressure of Mark's progress."

"Gary, I don't think she can stay ahead of him. He will be well past her by the time she finishes the sorting, and then it's all but over for her. I'm going to make my call now."

"Really?"

"Yes, Gary, really. At the pace they're going, I see Rochelle finishing first and Sue last. The real question is will Brian or Mark take second? I think

Brian will because Mark still has that foul to resolve."

"Marv, I totally forgot about the foul! That's still underfoot for him."

"It is. It's going to cost him about 45 seconds to resolve, and those seconds will really count at the end."

"I think now is a good time to go to our final break so we can be back for the tense final moments. What do you think?"

"Gary, I agree. Let's hear these last sponsor messages!"

[3 minutes of commercials]

"We're back for the final stretch. Everyone is slowing down. Brian's struggling to keep up as he sorts and rolls at the same time. Rochelle has rocketed ahead as she works from her pre-sorted tubs. Sue is now all sorted and is about 7 completed rolls behind Mark, who is still rolling steady."

"That special training really appears to have helped him out."

"It sure does, Gary, to the chagrin of his detractors, I'm sure."

"Would you look at that?!"

"I see it, though, I'm not sure I believe it."

"Rochelle has stopped. On her last roll, she has stopped."

"No, she's not stopped. She's just going slow."

"She's raising the completed roll and she dropped it on the stack!"

"Now she's flipping the empty tubs in a show of victory!"

"She's done it, her new strategy is the winner of the day!"

"Look at that! Her show of victory rattled both Brian and Mark and they jerked ..."

"It's too late for them! That was a critical mistake. Brian is trying, desperately, to stop the tub of silverware from falling off his table but the leverage isn't in his favor!"

"It's not, and it's not for Mark either. He bumped the tub, and his spoons are all over the floor."

"This is a major upset. This type of mistake isn't even normally seen in amateur rolling competitions, let alone at this level."

"Well, at least Sue is in a better spot. She's, now, closing in on second place for today."

"Mark's scrambling to recover. He's scooping up the spoons and putting them back in the tub. And he's off to the kitchen!"

"That will take a while. They need to replace the exact number of spoons he lost, and he'll be back with them to finish."

"Marv, do you see what I see?"

"I do, Gary, I do. Mark forgot the forks from earlier. He is going to need to go back to the kitchen a second time."

"Brian is grabbing his silverware, and he, too, is on his way to the kitchen."

"And here comes Mark back from the kitchen."

"Marv, do you think he's realized he forgot the forks yet?"

"I don't know Gary."

"Ooooohhhhhhh!"

"Whoaaaaa!"

"He does now."

"He sure does."

"Marv, is there a rule against stepping on dropped silverware?"

"I don't think there is, Gary. I don't think it's ever come up before."

"Brian's back from the kitchen, and he's jumping right back in!"

"Mark is realizing his mistake. You can see it on his face."

"Marv, you totally can."

"He's picking up the forks from the floor and, wow, is his face red!"

"You're not kidding. That's the reddest I've seen a face since the outdoor Rolling competition in Florida a few years ago."

"That was quite the day. No one avoided a sunburn that day."

"Wow!"

"That was unexpected!"

"This competition is over."

"Brian is completing his last completed roll for third place and Mark just got himself disqualified."

"He sure did. Throwing those forks in anger would have been enough but throwing the tub of spoons sealed his fate in this. He'll probably…"

"Holy cow!"

"… Definitely be banned for all of next season."

"Marv, he sure will be."

"Toppling your own tower in anger is another disqualification event. That's three in a row in a matter of less than a minute. He's definitely out for next season."

"That was an exciting end of the match."

"It sure was. I'm sure we'll be talking about it for weeks."

"I'm sure we will."

"To recap, Rochelle debuted a new strategy and took the match. Sue's new strategy and consistent performance allowed her to take second, with Brian's foul costing him the second-place spot. The real upset is that

Mark's fouls put him so far behind that he couldn't recover and he lost his temper, incurring what will, surely, be league penalties to keep him out of next season."

"It was an exciting match, though."

"It sure was."

"Well, Rollers, thanks for turning in. As always, we're Marv and Gary, and we look forward to giving you the play-by-play of the next round of the finals in three days."

"Have a great night and stay out of trouble."

"And don't forget to tip your servers."

Syrup Harvest

Lecture

The unseasonably warm and dry weather is having no effect on the new students of the university. They're milling about the campus with the same level of excitement that comes every year. The Professor's keen observation skills, honed by years of teaching, note the jubilation present on their visages; it will be another great year.

The culinary arts building sports a neutral red exterior, a fact that the Professor has always enjoyed as it generates a calming sensation on the approach to class each day. Today is no different. The Professor notes the continued effectiveness of the hue on the countenances of the students, watching the relaxation ripple through them as they breach the threshold. Each of these semblances represents a mind and a future chef who will partake of the syrup-making course at some point. Each one is a unique being to be remembered for the future just as each will recognize the Professor's markings passing them by.

Sometimes the grappleway is full of eager students on the first day and, other times, completely empty. There is no pattern to this phenomenon, and over the years it has become apparent that it has no impact on the way the courses will run. Today, the grappleway is clear, allowing for quick and easy ascent to the third level, where the Professor's educational work takes place.

The Professor's routine is the same for every class. Arrive two hours early to check on the preparedness of the Learning Lab and all of the necessary ingredients for the day and then quietly and patiently wait in the empty lecture hall for the first students to arrive. The quiet time is relaxing and generates peace of mind.

The first students filter in, and the Professor notes the individual visages and the coloring of their skin. It's important, after all, to know one's students. The light green coloring of the interior walls of the lecture hall is specifically designed to have an immediate impact on the students. Their social centers are brought to a state of calm, and their attentive centers are maximized for optimal learning. The transition of the students from social creatures to learning machines is always fascinating for those, like the Professor, who have a calling to teach. When the last of the students alights in a learning spot, the Professor activates the presenter and begins the lecture.

The first day of class is always the most exciting. Watching the students discover the origin of their favorite garnish is invigorating; the excitement they bring as they learn to discover the secrets of how to make it is an indescribable reward. The lecture always starts the same, when the last of the students settle in for their lessons.

"The expansion into and exploration of the galaxy has brought us many wondrous new things. New cultural ideas and philosophies, new art, new technologies and science concepts, and as you've all come to learn about, new food products." The Professor spends another two hours outlining the most basic history of the galactic expansion and what it has brought to the food industry before coming to a terminus of the lecture. "You will learn a great deal more of these wonders and the overall history of our civilization throughout your schooling, but for now, we will focus on food and, in particular for this class, the syrup."

The Professor turns to address the full lecture hall directly and, rather than disgorging the words into the air lecture style, speaks to the accumulated group, "How many of you enjoy syrup with some of your favorite dishes?"

The Professor quickly scans the class to note unanimous approval of syrup among the students. "Excellent, you'll all enjoy the next several weeks as we learn how to take the raw ingredient and process it into syrup; there will be plenty of opportunities to taste-test along the way!" The last comment incites an excited murmur among the students, rippling from the front of the lecture hall to the back, and then around in a cascading wave of poorly hushed voices.

Pausing mid-turn, momentarily, to idly look out the high window at the gray sky littering everything below it with giant, slow-moving raindrops and rivulets of water that weave across the glass pane, the Professor returns to the broken thought, "We will also cover how to use the final product in a variety of dishes to enhance the natural flavors of the foods, and, of course, there will be sampling of that process, too."

Gesturing toward the large display hanging in the air at the front of the hall, the Professor indicates the course syllabus to the class, "As you can see, we will start by discussing the different properties of the source specimens and how those properties can be refined and blended together to make a variety of different nutrient mixtures and flavoring combinations."

As the indicator slid along the display to the next part of the outline, "Then we will cover how to select specimens for their probable flavoring subtleties and which attributes pair well with which types of other foods. For example, a specimen likely to have a higher sugar level makes a much better dessert variant, whereas a different mixture of sources, including higher protein or fat counts, might be a good sauce for a high protein meal."

Stopping to face the class, the Professor continues, "You will learn that when specimens are carefully monitored and harvested at the right time, they can have additional properties. In some situations, a specimen can even also have considerable volumes of aphrodisiacs and general sex hormones, or performance boosters that help with overall physical exertion flowing through them. These, like the other properties, become more potent as the solution is reduced under the low heat."

"As this is our first class on the subject, I won't expect you to know much, but I will test what you do know as we move into the Learning Lab for your first direct experience." The Professor glided across the front of the hall toward the portal to the lab, "As we move into the Learning Lab for this lesson, you will

need to be aware of the core anatomy of the specimens. Their core trunks can be tapped as a source, but we find that it is often easier to manage collection if the tap is placed into one of the smaller of the branches that springs from it. The larger branches, while effective, carry several different risks associated with them including the potential to hit a core supply channel that creates a nearly unmanageable flow of material and can often result in waste of the core ingredient and premature expiration of the specimen itself."

Syrup

The Professor takes up residence on a podium to maintain mindful observance over the entire class at their lab stations. "It is best for beginners, therefore, to work with the target areas on the smaller branches. The ideal location for the taps will be marked on your specimen for you. If you choose to go into the profession of syrup making, you will gain the experience needed to be precise in tapping the other regions to manage the flow of material at a rate and volume that meets your needs without permanently damaging your supply."

As the last of the students slides into their lab stations the Professor continues with the instructions, "You will find the tools you need available on either side of the portal, and you will find a variety of stations prepped for your direct lesson. Among your tools, you will notice rough diagrams of different shapes and sizes of specimens with the likelihood of what specific properties their product will yield. We will focus on this more intently later in the course, but it is important to examine it with your first tapping." The Professor holds a copy of the quick reference guide aloft so the students know what they should be looking for.

"Accompanying these diagrams, you will find a pamphlet that outlines the best tapping locations and processing methods to make syrup from these various specimen types. It is important you take care of this pamphlet as it will be a great guide for the remainder of the course." The Professor holds up a copy of the pamphlet to illustrate the item described.

Opening the pamphlet and displaying the center pages to the class, the Professor continues, "It is interesting to note that, while they look very different, these specimens are all of the same species. They can be cultivated and cross bred in farms to yield future specimens that have differing traits or combinations of traits that yield desired flavorings. These cultivated specimens are often sold at a market premium due to the effort it takes to specifically balance out the traits desired and enhance them for the preferred flavors. Unlike those expensive breeds, the specimens you will be working with were harvested from their natural habitat and have been maintained specifically for training purposes. The syrup made from them will be as delicious as any general grade, non-specialized genuine syrup on the market."

"We use feral specimens because it is very common for beginners to have trouble tapping specimens in an effective and efficient manner. The feral specimens cost the least, so we use them to avoid wasting resources, including your tuition because school is expensive enough already." The Professor emits the sounds of mirth at the joke, and a few students follow suit.

The Professor taps a plate on the wall and an overhead conveyor begins to move. The students chitter excitedly as the specimens, hanging from the tracks above, start to be conveyed into the lab. Some of them squirm from their suspensions and others simply hang limply. The smaller branches of the specimens vary in position from specimen to specimen, waving and flailing about in different patterns.

From beside one of the students in the middle of the group, the Professor continues to the next portion of the lesson.

"I am often asked if the specimens are aware of what is happening to them, and I assure you, we have no indication that they are. Our best scientists have concluded that they respond to stimuli much like your reflexes do. Your reflexes are not aware of what is happening, they just respond. Repeated studies have shown their inability to communicate or, it seems,

even sense communication directed at them. So, when the time comes for you to tap your training specimen, have no worries that you are harming a being; they are not aware in any way. They WILL, however, jerk and react. They may even emit a low-frequency noise that is at the lower end of our hearing spectrum, so low that only some of you will be able to hear it at all. This is normal and will pass after a few moments, and with each successive tap, the specimens seem to become accustomed to the stimuli of the tap. You will see that each tap will produce a smaller and smaller response from the specimen until they are completely passive and wholly unresponsive." The Professor continues the lecture as the specimens float toward the corrals, silently swinging from the overhead conveyor while working around the room to examine each student's readiness.

"As you can see, all of the specimens are different, but they all carry the same general shape." Stopping in a specific corral, the Professor indicates the specimen prepared, "This one here, for instance, is smaller and has a tighter casing than the one on the far end," a quick indication of a particularly saggy specimen hanging in the farthest corral causes the entire class to momentarily redirect their attention from being split between their own specimen and the Professor to the

end corral. "Those are both very different from the gigantic specimen three spaces down," another indication and the attention of the class shifts.

With a quick upward motion to indicate the longer and thicker parts of the specimen where they anchor into the rack, the Professor continues, "Note that the larger branches are what we use to anchor the specimens to the conveyor; this is because those branches are what the specimens rest upon when not being processed. They can handle the weight of suspension easily. Suspending them in this fashion also helps the collection process as it inverts the gravity feed of the syrup base, allowing for an easier flow into your collection bin." The Professor brushes the wavy strands hanging in the air so a ripple cascades in a dark wave below the specimen, "It also allows their odd, feathery substance that dangles below them to fall out of your way." The Professor flicks through the dark strands, absently caressing the smooth fibers before withdrawing to continue the instruction. The Professor's voice is slightly distant and wistful as though the feeling of the fibers sliding over the outer dermal layer generated a soothing sensation in his appendage. With a hint of regret, the Professor continues, "Some processors cut it off before processing to ensure it does not get caught in any equipment or soak up any product but doing so is not necessary." Turning away from the specimen and snapping back into the moment of instruction, the Professor continues, "We have yet to determine a reason why the feathery substance varies so wildly in length, color, and coverage on the specimens; it must just be part of their naturally selective biology and does not appear to serve any functional purpose that we can determine. "Now, I would like you to prepare your taps and tap your very first specimen."

The student adjacent to the Professor positions the tap with one tentacle and grasps one of the smaller branches of the specimen just inside where it splits into five tiny branches. The student notices that the bulbous appendage where the feathery material drapes toward the floor from is a pinkish hue while the terminations of the large trunks are much whiter. Protruding from the core trunk are three bulbous areas: two symmetrical ones that are adjacent to each other and a third that does not jiggle and which has multiple orifices in it. The student examines the various orifices in the bulbous appendage and ponders what their purposes might be before driving the tap into the branch between the selected joint and the next joint above it.

Three of the orifices open wide. Two of them reveal emerald circles ringing black pits, all on top of a white field. As the student watches, the white becomes laced with intricate lines of bright red, a red the same color as the syrup base being harvested. The third orifice reveals a nasty-looking array of porcelain processors, meaning it must be the orifice used to process nutrients. The student hears the slightest tremor of a scream at the lowest end of its hearing, so low and so quiet that the student is not entirely sure if the sound is imagined or real.

The specimen spasms, jerking its trunk in a variety of contortions that are completely unexpected and flailing its lower, smaller branches in completely unpredictable circles and at shocking angles. The larger, bulbous appendage snaps back and forth, and the two smaller blobs bounce and jiggle around in response to the motion. The tap, during the flailing, tears a large gash in the branch, leading to a fountain of syrup base spraying out onto the student and coating the walls of the processing pen with the ruby-colored liquid.

The Professor hurriedly approaches the student's corral to assess the situation. "Oh, my, it looks like you've managed to tap a particularly energetic one. Sadly, I think the damage it did to itself when it jerked and flailed cannot be repaired. We shall catch what syrup base we can from it and then I will call you a second specimen to try." The Professor pauses to change the audience from the individual student to the entire class, "This is an important lesson to experience. Every class will experience it at some point, at least once, but it is not every class that we experience it in the first learning lab. Everyone please come and take note of what happens when a specimen's reaction to tapping causes it to jerk and twist underneath your tools. Note that the mess can be significant and the loss of product is a terrible waste. This is exactly why we use feral specimens to teach."

Within minutes the specimen hangs limply, syrup base dripping in a slowing pitter-pat to the floor. Several pints of base were collected from the spraying specimen and will be processed into syrup. The teacher touches a release plate and the specimen is released from the hanging conveyor and hits the floor with a subtle, and silent, concussive wave that passes through the floor. The floor then splits and swings downward, allowing the spent specimen to fall into the dark disposal shaft below.

A new specimen is shuttled out from the storage area. This one is much larger, with less feathery substance dangling from it and a massively wide trunk. It, too, has a jiggly nature but it is more all-encompassing instead of sequestered to specific areas.

The Professor asks, "Does anyone care to guess, based on your pamphlet and quick reference guide, what the likely attributes of the syrup base to be harvested from this one?"

The student responds, "Low female hormones. High cholesterol. High fat content. Average protein content."

The teacher replies concisely, "Correct. Well done. Tap it."

The specimen's symmetrical orifices slide slowly open and then shoot open fully at the site of the student and the tap. The food orifice opens as wide as with the previous specimen, but no audible sound emits. The student taps the specimen and begins to collect the syrup base for processing.

Harvest

The pleasant afternoon was shattered by the distant sounds of harvesters.

Long ago, so long that no one knew how long it had been, humanity's perception of dominance in the universe was crushed, utterly obliterated, by the arrival of an alien species. Since that day, when the cities were destroyed and humanity was smashed back into the medieval era of subsistence living, the fear of a harvest was constant. No one alive knew of any other way of life. So, now, when the sound of harvesters buzzes through the air, everyone scrambles to hide.

Aljeena remembered the last harvest her tribe experienced. It was many years earlier when she was still a child. She had been too slow to hide, and her mother had, foolishly, tried to protect her from the harvesters. Her mother was taken. The monsters had pried her mother, weeping and screaming, off of her and hauled her into the harvester before moving along to catch the other adults who were too slow, or too stupid, to hide effectively. They always, ALWAYS, left the small children. No one knew why, perhaps they felt some sort of compassion for the young, perhaps it was for some other reason.

In the years that had passed, Aljeena's village had known an unusual level of quiet; it was rare for a single month to pass without a harvester, let alone several years. Despite the time, they had not allowed themselves to forget the meaning of the crackling buzz in the air. The younger adults in the village, those around Aljeena's age, began to believe it meant that they were safe, that the monsters had moved away and were not coming back. Many, Aljeena included, laughed at their foolishness. She knew that it was only a matter of time before they came back, a matter of time before they stopped terrorizing some other village and returned here. She knew they would be back, and she intended to be taken by them. Since her mother was stolen from her, she had been plagued with nightmares and a driving obsession to know what happened to those taken. She knew the only way to find out was to be taken herself.

After years of waiting, her day had finally arrived.

She pretended to run for cover to prevent someone from rescuing her from her own decision. The other villagers were occupied rescuing the young adults who had doubted the existence of the harvesters or doubted that they would return. The children ran amok, screaming and causing chaos because they could not understand what was happening nor could they understand why the adults were so terrified. They, though, were safe, meaning the adults did not have to concern themselves with protecting the children from a harvester.

The low-frequency buzz grew in intensity and enveloped the entire village. The children covered their ears, and many of the adults winced from the pain that the terrible noise induced on their ears. Some survivors of the harvest would lose their hearing completely, having their eardrums shredded by the intensity of the sound waves. The elders knew that the threshold of pain from the harvesters meant that they had come into view, and one needed only search the sky for the reflective dot that rapidly grew as it approached them. The sound itself refused to betray its source direction, but sometimes, the fleeing wildlife that ran from the intensity of the sound would give notice as to where it was coming from. Today was not one of those days. It was a wonder that the monsters could ignore the sound so readily; it was as if they simply could not hear it at all.

The dot, once spotted, became the focus of attention for all eyes in the village. Even the children, amidst their crying and screaming, watched the anomaly grow in intensity as their hearing was destroyed by the loud sound.

The harvester slid into place over the village square, and Aljeena watched, helplessly, as one child fainted, blood running from his tiny, little ears, his fallen body directly under where the harvester would land. The boy was already dead; no one could save him from the horrible fate of being crushed by the landing harvester. If she tried, she, too, would be crushed under the ship. The monsters consider such losses to be of no more consequence than the villagers apply to the accidental deaths of rodents in their homes. Aljeena watched other children run, some with bleeding ears and others simply covering theirs, from the center of the square. She watched and waited as the harvester completed its landing, the sound of the child being crushed into pulp was lost in the intensity of the buzz.

The harvester came to rest with a physical thud that reverberated through the ground. Quite suddenly, the world was plunged into silence. The buzzing was gone, for the moment, and the wake of artificial silence that descended upon all who were around was disorienting and confusing. The lack of physical pressure of the sound waves brought relief and shock to those who were close enough to the ship to have felt the sound with their entire bodies. Aljeena was one of these. The sensation rekindled her buried memories of the moment tentacles wrapped around her mother and pulled her away. She stared at the ship, focusing her rage and hatred at it, when a door slid aside. Several monsters emerged, each sliding along the ground using four of their tentacles as legs.

Much like the hunters of her village hunting for food, each monster had a different way of catching its prey. It has always been that way and probably always will be. The arsenal of black and silvery equipment they deployed varied from monster to monster with some items resembling tools Aljeena was aware of. One monster pointed a device at an older man, and a net appeared from the end of it to entrap the man; another pointed a smaller device at a woman Aljeena disliked and saw her fall to the ground as a crumpled, silent body. One monster had a pole with a loop on the end firmly grasped by two tentacles, while a third carried a shiny, metal rod of some sort which elicited a shrill cry from whomever it touched.

With a deep breath in to master her fear, Aljeena stood up and stepped forward. She yelled at them without result. Again, it was as if they could not hear her yells. She walked toward the center of the square and toward the nearest of the monsters. It was not looking her way, she thought, as she progressed toward it, still yelling at it. Her speculation was confirmed when it turned toward her and reacted, in obvious alarm, at the human standing so close to itself. It dropped one of its tools as it fumbled with several of them, and had she been trying to harm it, she would have had enough time to get close enough to do so. Instead, she stopped a few feet from it and simply stared directly, and intently, at it, allowing her hatred and loathing to pour out of her eyes. Her venomous intent remained unnoticed by the monster as it raised a tool whose purpose she could not guess and pointed it at her.

She felt a tiny prick in her skin, like a harsh insect bite, and then the world melted away into a colorful blend of fading reality.

Transport and Holding

Aljeena woke in the darkness. She was bound. She could not move. She could not see. She tried to sit up and hit her head, hard, against something flat and metal above her. She tried to wiggle to one side and was met with a wall; she tried the other side and was met with a mesh net. Scooting up yielded another hard surface and inching toward her feet the same. She was trapped. She could, however, talk. She spoke into the darkness, inquiring if anyone was there and received several replies. The replies came from near and far; she could tell by the loudness of them. Some of the voices sounded familiar, while others did not.

A brief discussion among those around her told her that they were from at least six villages. She was one of seven taken from her village. Everyone had the same story of what had happened and the same ages-old tale of the harvesters. The only thing that differed was the name of the village and who was taken.

No one really felt like a sustained conversation, so the talk slowly faded. One person, somewhere deep in the darkness beyond her feet, sang quietly while a few others cried. Mostly, though, everyone suffered their fears in quiet.

There was no food, no water, no facilities. Some people were unable to hold their needs back, and the hold began to smell of various human functions. Aljeena was hungry and thirsty, and she definitely had to pee. Aside from this, the passage of time was impossible to determine.

Eventually, the sensation of movement began, making them all feel like they were falling, ever so slowly, toward their heads. This sensation, too, stopped after a short while only to be replaced by a variety of jerking motions in a variety of directions. After a time of complete passivity, they were all crushed under an enhanced weight for several minutes before floating in their individual berths. Aljeena heard the sounds of several people vomiting throughout the hold. She was glad she was not one of them.

The floating only lasted a few minutes before their weight slowly scaled up for them. They experienced a slight push toward their feet and then an odd sensation that could not be adequately explained. It was as if they were being stretched into oblivion while being crushed into a tiny speck. The sensation passed, almost instantaneously, and was followed by a reverse of the sensations they had previously experienced that stopped after the period of mismatched jostling.

A light appeared at one end of the hold, photons streaming into the hold and inducing sharp pains on the retinas of everyone inside. Some gasped, some cursed, some groaned, and one captive screamed. Aljeena squinted quietly and tried to position herself to see where the light came from. It was a futile maneuver.

She could hear, and feel, the machinery remove berth block after berth block; she could hear the helpless individuals screaming in each one as they were moved to some unknown, new fate. Her block's turn came, and she felt the ungentle movement as she was bounced around her berth with a complete disregard for the discomfort that the jolting would cause her. She was moved out into the light, inducing more pain in her eyes than before, and she could see a vast building, much like the community store house in her village, only larger than any building she had ever imagined. It was filled with berth blocks, each having a person inside each berth. She watched in horror as a large machine with a monster inside reached an arm into each berth and pulled out people who appeared to have died during transport and tossed them like garbage into an open compartment at the back. Within moments an arm like the one she saw intruded on her space and grabbed her arm; it held for a moment and then retreated, moving down to the berth below her. Her amazement at the scene she was seeing was shattered, momentarily, as the man who had been below her was tossed through her field of view into the compartment of the machine that had checked her. She wiggled to the edge of the berth and looked down. The machine, which was moving to the next row, was filled with bodies flopped at odd angles within a large bin. Bodies just lying there. Bodies of the dead. Bodies being treated with no more respect than she would treat an insect that she killed.

For the first time she, quite suddenly, regretted her decision to try and find her mother. Aljeena knew, without a doubt, that her mother was no more and that she, too, would soon be ended. She wept. She wept from the realization and the hunger and the thirst. She wept and gave in to the situation. The cold and lonely darkness of sleep crept into Aljeena's green eyes and closed her eyelids, despite her best efforts to stay awake. Sleep was no reprieve from the horror of her situation.

She did not know how long she was out, but when she woke, she was in a new situation. She had been

cleaned from the filth of transport. Her new enclosure was a pen that she shared with several others. There was food, and there was water, and there was a hole in the floor to deposit waste. There was a means to rinse off.

She was stuck in this pen for a long time. She was not sure how long, but it was several months. Months of boredom with nothing to break the passage of time but to tell each other stories of their homes. Occasionally, one of them would be taken out and never return.

Syrup

Her day came along with the day for many others. The arrival of a new monster, one she had not seen before who wore different coloring, brought a level of activity to the keepers of the pens. Normally, small groups are taken from the pens, but this time, the largest extrication any of them had experienced since waking in the pen appeared to be happening. Aljeena tried to gain a better vantage point on what was happening and failed. She couldn't get a clean count on how many were being taken this time, but her guess was at least half the remaining people. Being herded out of the pens and into a line like livestock was disconcerting to Aljeena, and it made her think of how cattle and pigs were treated back home. Aljeena was encouraged to follow the line of her cohort with sharp and harsh pushes from the monsters. She complied while trying to see what the new monster was doing. Eventually, the new monster slipped into a passageway and used the bars within it to climb out of sight. As Aljeena approached the only door, she could see that it had a sharp turn ahead which masked the front of the line from her view, but the repeated sounds echoed back, ricocheting off the cold metal. Passing through the door confirmed the purpose of the sharp corner; it was to hide the terrible fate of those at the head of the line from the view of those behind to prevent panic. The man preceding her winced from a quick jab of a needle that darted out of the wall before retreating again. He grimaced at the opening where the needle retracted before starting to slump and collapse to the floor. Halfway to the floor, metal pincers grabbed his ankles and hoisted him into the air, allowing his head to crack against the clean, expressionless metal walls. Before Aljeena could take any action, she, too, felt the sting of the needle and started to lose consciousness.

After waking from the drug, Aljeena still couldn't observe what was happening to her companion as it was happening to her, too. A variety of metal tentacles held and manipulated her in midair. The pincers that had grabbed her feet became clamps that docked into a conveyor overhead. When those clamps locked into the conveyor, still uncomfortably tight around her ankles, she was released from the tentacles to swing. The gentle swaying of her weight encouraged the metal of her anklets to bite into the tops of her feet, each sway changing the force enough that she couldn't become accustomed to the pain and ignore it. Blood rushed to her head, and she bloated with the extra pressure behind her face, reinforcing the distorted perception of reality that came along with such an inversion. After a few moments, what felt like an eternity but probably wasn't, the combination of fear, pain, exhaustion, malnutrition, and being upside down conquered her consciousness and blackness claimed victory over her.

Swinging abruptly rescued Aljeena from the horrible nightmares that her subconscious had created for her and returned her to the nightmare that her waking world presented. Consciousness evaded her, but she struggled to catch it, each moment an eternity of time that came to a sharp end by the smooth, warm, and very disconcerting touch of a monster's tentacle on her skin. She was in the process of willing her green eyes to open when the pain lanced through her arm. Her eyes stopped fighting for more sleep and snapped open, along with her mouth, so all three could scream in unison. There, staring at her face, were two monsters. One was holding an instrument that had been mercilessly jabbed into her arm while the second, a slightly larger monster, stood calmly and watched. She writhed in her anklets and jerked away from the pain, inducing a much worse pain that spanned much of her arm. She felt the warmth of her own blood pouring out of her arm and down toward the floor, so she raised it to look. Blood was pulsating out of a long gash in her arm, a gash that she knew would kill her. A gash worse than many animal bites or other wounds she had seen take the lives of others back home. With the realization that this was her death, she let her arm fall and relaxed her head. She saw the larger monster wrap her arm in some material that kept the blood from squirting everywhere and channel it into the bucket below her. She watched, her strength fading as the bucket filled. She didn't have the strength to say any words or scream again as the darkness and cold enveloped her being. She relaxed as the light of life faded from her bloodshot eyes, the emerald coloring staring blankly at rivulets of her blood making their way to the floor and into the seams below her. As the last remnants of her consciousness faded, the pincers released her ankles. A vague sense of impact echoed through the last remaining active synapses in her mind as the floor opened beneath her. The very last image that reached her mind was the light disappearing overhead as the trap door reset above her. There was nothing of Aljeena left in her body when it hit the bottom of the disposal shaft, only the depleted corpse, empty of all syrup base.

Accompanying Artwork

For this edition of this book the artwork has been consolidated into this section rather than placed throughout the interior.

This is for formatting purposes to ensure the best artwork experience for you, the reader.

SlipNSlide

Savantia

QUARANTINE
EVERYONE IS SPECIAL

Quarantine

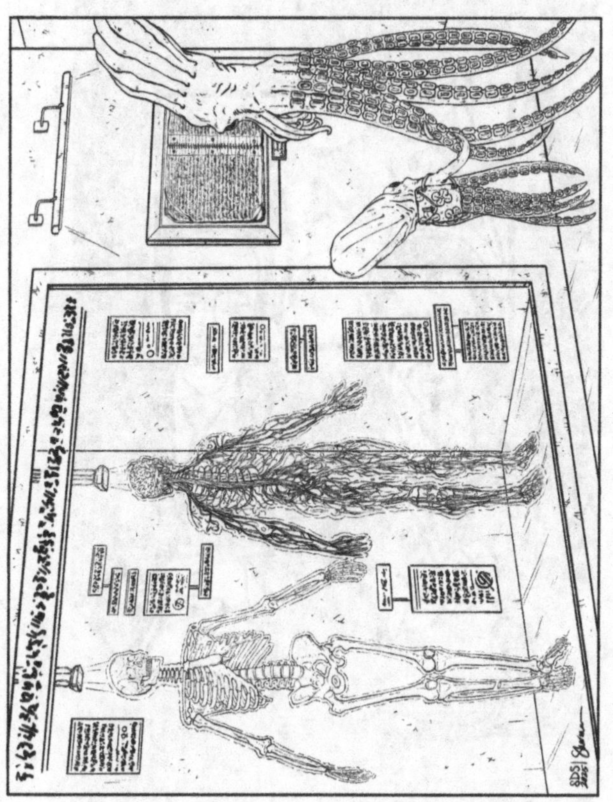

Championship Match

Syrup Harvest

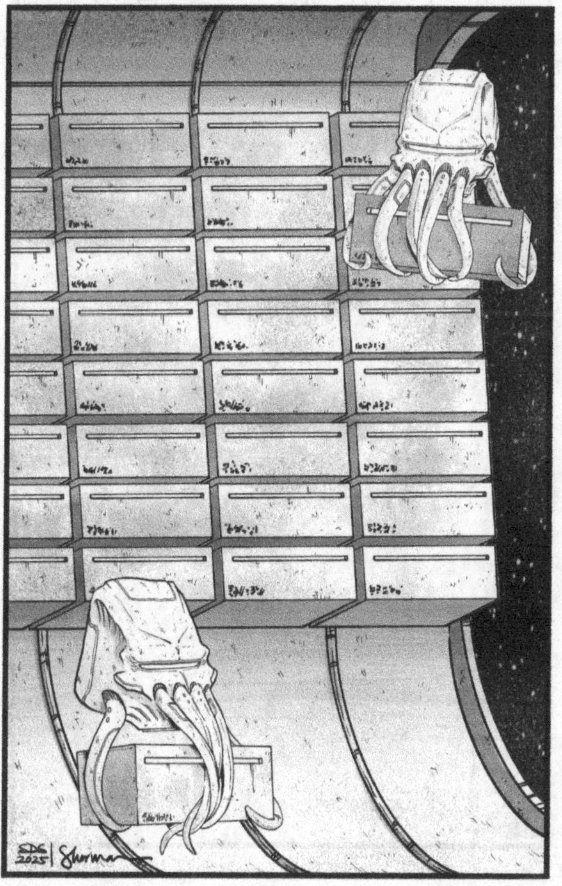

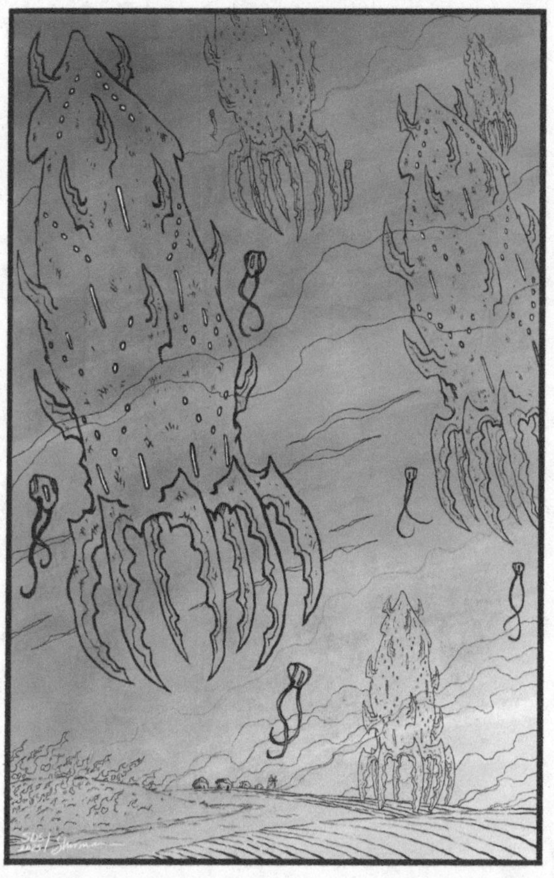

Artwork Appendix

Artists in Alphabetical Order

Alyssa Avery
    alysaavery.com
    Pages: 215, & 216

Bonniejean Boettcher
    bonniejeanb.com
    Narrator (anticipated)

Laura Cassellius
    artwanted.com/lehorning
    Pages: 205

Matt Haynes
> narratormatt.com
> Narrator (anticipated)

Sheldon Hussierre
> Pages: 201

Pavlo Kandyba
> www.masterogon.art
> Cover Artwork: Astral Travel

Michelle Kapschull
> Cover Design

Malakai Rodier
> cara.app/goatpaws/portfolio
> Page: 210

jorolero - creative
> jorolero.com

Pages: 207, 208 & 209

Scott Sherman
WitchRender.com
Pages: 202, 203, ,204, 206, 211, 212, 213, & 214

Story Notes

SlipNSlide - written for [HFY]

Savantia - circa 2011. Not previously published.

Quarantine - published to FutureAbandonedBlog in 2016.

Championship Match - circa 2015 as a response to the fervor that happens around a certain sporting event. Not previously published.

Syrup Harvest - written in spring of 2016 as a response to tapping trees to make my own maple syrup. Not previously published.

About the Author

Justin T. Cole spends far too much time sitting in front of a computer, whether it is performing his regular vocational duties, writing something, watching some video program, or fiddling with a half-dozen other projects. When he is not busy on his computer, he spends time supporting his wife and kids' artistic efforts in a variety of ways or telling one of his dogs to "move your butt" because it has chosen to lay in the exact wrong spot ... again.

THE THREE INVESTIGATORS

IN

THE MYSTERY OF THE JANUSIAN JACKPOT

BY

ELIZABETH ARTHUR
& STEVEN BAUER

BASED ON CHARACTERS
CREATED BY ROBERT ARTHUR

Hollow Tree Press 2025

CONTENTS

1. Freya Asks A Favor
2. Meeting Jimmy Littlewolf
3. A Trip To Hector Sebastian's
4. A Revealing Chess Game
5. Worthington Comes Through
6. Mallory Goes Undercover
7. A Very Lucky Break
8. A Hypothesis Needing Proof
9. An Indecisive Morning
10. A Jumping Off Place For Further Questions
11. Freya Gets The Goods
12. Pete Sees What Really Matters
13. A Dial Canyon Triumph
14. Dr. Paxton and Billy Redsmoke
15. A Janusian Jackpot

Freya Asks A Favor

As Bob Andrews coiled his bright red climbing rope at the base of the rock face at Palisade Point, he was thinking about a call he'd gotten on his cellphone just minutes before. He and his friend Mallory MacLeod − as of this summer, a full-time Special Consultant to The Three Investigators − had been resting at the top of a tricky pitch when all of a sudden the phone in his pocket had buzzed.

Normally Bob would have ignored his phone when he was on a climb, but he'd checked to see who was calling − and when he'd seen it was Hector Sebastian, he'd taken the call.

Bob and his fellow Three Investigators Jupiter Jones and Pete Crenshaw had known Mr. Sebastian for a long time now. He'd not only been an early supporter, he'd written up their early cases, and although he'd stopped that the summer before − when he'd moved from California to Wyoming − he'd said Bob had the talent to write up the cases himself.

Nine cases later, Bob was starting to believe that Hector Sebastian had been right. At the very least, he'd gotten a lot more confident than he'd been when he'd just started out. The day before, he'd finished polishing the report for their last case.

Now Hector was back in California for the summer. He owned a strange Tudor-style house south of Rocky Beach, in Dial Canyon, and although he'd been renting it while he was gone, he had the house back for July and August.

He'd moved to Wyoming because he wanted to write mysteries set in the Old West, but as he'd told Bob, in the writing business, you had to keep in contact with people – "remind them you were still alive and hungry," as he'd put it.

Bob and Mallory, together with Jupiter and Pete, had been invited to Mr. Sebastian's house tomorrow. Now, as Bob coiled the rope and slung it over his shoulder, he wondered what Hector had meant when he'd said he had something he wanted to talk with Bob about privately.

When Bob had asked what it was, Mr. Sebastian had said, playfully, "Think Janus, the Roman god of beginnings and endings. He's always depicted as having two faces and looking to the past and future simultaneously. He's a very ingenious guy. Creative, actually. Very, very creative."

"O.K." Bob had said. "But why do you want to talk to me about *that*?"

"Oh, I don't know," Hector had said, "I like to think that you and I have something in common with Janus. And we creative types have to stick together!"

Bob had been flattered that Hector Sebastian had linked his talents with Bob's, but when he asked him to explain, he'd just laughed. "You'll have to wait until tomorrow to find out."

Now, as he and Mallory stowed the rest of their climbing equipment in their backpacks, he asked her if she knew anything about the Roman god Janus.

"Not much," she said. "I think the adjective Janusian might have something to do with being able to think two things at once. Two things that contradict each other."

"Oh!" said Bob. "I guess that makes sense, if Janus can see both the past and the future at the same time. Though actually *every-one* can do that. I mean, I have no trouble re-membering that you and I just came down from a climbing pitch, and at the same time thinking that tomorrow we're going to see Hector."

He and Mallory started to hike down the dusty, rocky trail from the climbing cliffs to the parking lot. Leif Haldorsson – one of the Jones Salvage Yard's carpenters – would be waiting to take them back to Rocky Beach in a Salvage Yard truck.

"True enough," Mallory said. "But you don't think about the past and future at *exactly* the same time. And of course, you're not *really* seeing into the future. You're just imagining it."

Mallory reached over her shoulder to grab her water bottle from an outside pocket of her backpack. As she did, Bob gave in once again to feeling sorry that Mallory had never been interested in him as a boy – that all she'd ever wanted was to be his friend.

Among a lot of other things he liked about her, he liked how smart she was. He also liked the way she could be either very concise or very long-winded, depending on the circum-stances.

A lot of people who enjoyed tossing ideas around never shut up, while others couldn't put two sentences together to save their lives. Bob liked the fact that sometimes Mallory talked a lot and sometimes she didn't.

It was a bit of a hike to get back to the parking lot, and since the trail was single-file, Bob had his own thoughts for company during the walk.

For the last few days, he'd been reading a novel called *We* by a Russian writer named Yevgeny Zamyatin. The Three Investigators' last case had involved an elderly Russian émigré named Annika Vasiliev, who had told Bob that this novel has been the first book banned by the Soviet censorship board.

Since then, Bob had discovered that it was also considered the world's first dystopian science fiction novel. Reading *We* was really blowing Bob's mind. Weirdly enough, it was also making him wonder if he himself might have some talent writing fiction.

He loved writing up The Three Investigators' case notes – and he *did* think he was getting pretty good at it! – but as a reader he'd always been drawn to science fiction and fantasy.

The way writers like Yevgeny Zamyatin could extrapolate from the world around them to the world they *might* live in if things either went totally well or horrible badly wasn't just cool, it was truly mind-blowing.

Because, of course, it was true that normal people – which was to say, people who weren't Janus! – couldn't *really* see into the future but could only try their best to imagine it, as Mallory had said. And while everyone had *some* imagination, it was a rare human being who could see what might lie ahead for the human species if the wrong things happened in the present.

Bob deeply respected writers like that, but he was afraid his own talents didn't lend themselves to writing that relied on a kind of prescience. He was a good observer, and he could analyze the meaning of events, but to write a book like *Fahrenheit 451* or *Brave New World* or *Nineteen Eighty-Four* – well, *that* would take a kind of talent Bob already knew he didn't have.

Still, there was a lot of good fiction in the world, and maybe Bob could try his hand at a short story sometime. In the meanwhile, he had his hands full with both The Three Investigators' cases and his case notes. Now, walking side by side, he and Mallory rounded the last bend in the trail between the climbing area and the parking lot.

To Bob's surprise – and confirming that he certainly couldn't read the future! – not only was Leif Haldorsson standing next to the Salvage Yard truck, but so was his younger sister Freya. Leif and his brother Magnus lived with their parents and sister in Palisade Point, and sometimes Jupiter's Aunt Mathilda let one or the other brother drive The Three Investigators somewhere they needed to go.

It would still be a year-and-a-half before they could apply for their learner's permits, so getting from one place to another was always a problem. The summer before, the boys had bought their own car — a black and gray Ford Flex they all thought was perfect for detectives — and they frequently hired their friend Worthington to drive them wherever they had to go.

This afternoon, Leif had taken some time off from work to run some errands for his parents, so it had been easy to get permission to ask him to drive Bob and Mallory to their climb.

But Bob hadn't expected to see Freya. She and Leif were both waving. Leif was tall and broad-shouldered and Freya was shorter and slender, but anyone could see at a glance that they must be brother and sister.

The summer before, some letters their Norwegian father had inherited from *his* father had wound up being important in a case involving the Second World War and a painting of a medieval falconer, and Bob had become uncomfortably aware that Freya had what could only be called a crush on him.

"Hi," Leif said. "You're both still alive! When it comes to climbing up a rock like a spider, I always think what goes up must come down. Hard."

"Not today," Mallory said, smiling.

"You remember Freya, don't you?" Leif asked. "When she heard I was picking you up, she said she really wanted to see the two of you." He grinned mischievously. "But maybe especially Bob."

Freya rolled her eyes and punched her brother on the arm. Bob sympathized. Though he still sometimes wished he'd had a brother or sister, siblings seemed to spend a lot of time trying to embarrass one other.

"Hi, Freya," Bob said. "Great to see you." He unslung the backpack he'd been carrying on one shoulder and the coiled rope he'd had over the other.

Freya looked taller than the last time he'd seen her. Her face, which last summer had seemed a bit vague, now had real definition. Her cheekbones were highlighted by a reddish blush and her blue eyes seemed sharper, even icier.

Her hair, which was the same white-blond as her brother's, was now parted in the middle and came just to her shoulders. The long Scandinavian braid was gone. She seemed older and more serious.

"You cut your hair!" Mallory said.

"It was too much trouble," Freya said. "I'd been growing it since I was a girl. It was time for a change." She shook her head, and her hair flew around her. Smiling, she brushed it off her face.

"Are you coming back to Rocky Beach with us?" Bob asked.

"No," Freya said. "Leif will drop me at the house; it's on the way but I wanted to see you. I have something to ask you. All four of you. I mean The Three Investigators."

Leif walked around the truck and climbed behind the wheel.

"Why don't you sit up front?" he said to Mallory. "Bob and Freya can talk in the back."

The truck had two seats in the cab, though the back one was a little tight. Bob's knees were pressed against the front, while Freya sat sideways, turned toward him.

"You guys have been busy," she said admiringly. "I've kept up with all your case reports. They're as good as ever."

"Thanks," he said. When he'd first met Freya he'd learned that it was his writing that had made her get interested in who he was, and he was happy to hear she was still reading his case notes.

"That blue geranium you gave me last summer?" Freya said. "It's doing really well. Maybe when we stop at my house, you can see it."

Bob had forgotten about the geranium until Freya mentioned it. His father had gotten it from a colleague at the Los Angeles *Sun,* where he worked as a journalist, and since he hadn't wanted to keep it, he'd suggested that Bob take it to the Jones Salvage Yard to give it to Jupiter's Aunt Mathilda.

Instead, Bob had wound up giving it impulsively to Freya. She seemed to think it meant a lot more than it *did* mean, and now she was smiling rather broadly, her eyes focused intensely on him.

"I'd like that," Bob said somewhat awkwardly. He couldn't help noticing that Freya was really very pretty. Embarrassed, he quickly looked to his right out the window at a rocky outcrop they were passing. It seemed she hadn't lost the crush. Bob was surprised to find he was glad of that.

"Are you working on a new case?" Freya asked.

"Not at the moment," Bob said. "We just finished our third case of the summer, so we've been taking a little break. Are you still playing Odin's Hammer?"

This was an online role-playing game that Freya had been obsessed with the summer before. Her avatar had been the Norse goddess whose name she shared.

Freya frowned. "No, no, no," she said, swiping at the air with her hand as though something that had once been so important to her was now of no interest whatsoever. "I gave that up months ago. It wasn't very challenging once you did it for a while. I've taken up chess now."

"Chess?" Bob said. "Really?" He was impressed.

Freya nodded firmly. "I was a little intimidated at first," she said. "I thought you had to be a super genius or something, but I found an application that actually teaches you how to play the game. It's fascinating."

"I've only played a few times," Bob said. "I wasn't very good. It seemed the main thing that mattered in chess was not making any bad mistakes."

"That's a great way to put it," Freya said. "Anyway, when I looked for real people to play with, I found an online group, and one of the members turned out to go to high school with me. He's a year ahead of me and a member of the chess club. My parents encouraged me to join, so I did."

Bob could sense that Freya's topic really wasn't chess and that she was taking a winding road to get to her point. Mallory hadn't been watching Freya's face, but she'd been listening. Now she turned around. "Did you know that the earliest form of chess was invented in India more than fifteen hundred years ago?" she asked.

Bob couldn't tell if she was speaking to Freya or to him, but it really didn't matter since they both said, "No."

"The game spread from India to Persia," Mallory said, "and after the Arabs conquered Persia, it spread throughout the Muslim world and into southern Europe. Indians still play chess much more than people in any other country."

Freya opened her mouth to talk, but then shut it as Mallory rattled on.

"I bet you didn't know," Mallory said to

Freya, "that Scotland and Norway are also connected by chess. A very famous set of chess pieces was discovered in Scotland, on the isle of Lewis, in 1831."

"What does that have to do with Norway?" Freya asked politely.

"The British Museum thinks they were made there, in the 12th century," Mallory said. "They were carved from walrus tusks and they think a Norse trader must have brought them with him at a time when part of Scotland was owned by Norway. They're called the Lewis chessmen. There were four complete sets with something like five pieces missing. One of the missing pieces was just discovered in a drawer in Edinburgh. It sold for close to a million dollars."

"For a single chess piece?" Leif said incredulously.

"Yes," said Mallory.

Once again, Bob was impressed by how much Mallory knew. In fact, he thought, she might know as much as Jupiter, and the two of them together were like a walking encyclopedia. But in this case, he wished she either hadn't known so much or hadn't decided to switch from her quiet self to her talkative one. He could tell that Freya was bursting to get to her point – which, Bob assumed, had something to do with the boy in her high school who played chess.

He knew that Mallory had probably just been trying to connect to Freya, but because of where she was sitting, she hadn't seen that Freya – who was really very shy – had been working up the courage to get to her main point.

"Do you like being in the chess club?" Bob asked Freya, trying to encourage her.

"Very much," Freya said. Bob could see how grateful she was that he had helped her get back on track. "Of course almost everyone in the club is better than I am, but Jimmy – the guy I met online – is way better. He's my mentor."

"Your mentor?" Bob asked. Although, in a way, he thought of Hector Sebastian as *his* mentor, he was surprised to hear Freya use the term in relation to someone playing chess.

"Yes," Freya said. "All the younger play-ers are paired with one of the older and better players. I was lucky to get assigned to Jimmy Littlewolf. He's really great, and a terrific teacher. He's an Indian. At first I thought I wasn't supposed to call him that, but he told me that although some Native Americans prefer that term, most don't mind the word 'Indian' at all. I mean, it was never an insult, when you think about it – just a misunderstanding."

"That's right," Bob said. "Christopher Columbus was looking for the country of India when he sailed west. He never intended to land in the New World; he didn't even know it was there. So the native inhabitants were called Indians by mistake."

Freya looked at Bob as though he, too, knew everything.

"That's exactly right," she said. "Anyway, Jimmy's Shoshone. He grew up in northern Nevada, but he moved to California with his parents two years ago."

Mallory had turned and was now looking at Freya keenly – which seemed to make her nervous. For a moment, Bob thought she might stop talking altogether.

"Go on," he coaxed.

"He's the reason I wanted to see you today," Freya said. She took a deep breath. "I was talking to him one day about The Three Investigators and how great the four of you are at solving mysteries. He said he'd like to meet you. He and two other members of the chess club are coming to my house this afternoon to play a couple of games. In fact, they should be there by now. So when Leif said the two of you were here in Palisade Point, I thought maybe I could convince you to come by the house and meet Jimmy."

Bob wondered what Freya had told Jimmy Littlewolf, and why he wanted to meet them.

"He didn't exactly ask me if I'd introduce him to you, but one day when we were talking, he told me about his father," Freya said. "His father's name was Thomas Littlewolf."

"Was?" Bob asked. "I thought you said Jimmy and his parents moved to California two years ago."

"That's right," Freya said. "But Jimmy's father died six months later."

"Gosh, that's terrible," Bob said. He glanced at Mallory whose face had clouded over. Her own father had died suddenly and unexpectedly about a year-and-a-half ago, too, and he knew how much it had affected her – though she didn't talk about it much.

"Jimmy's father grew up on a reservation in Wyoming," Freya said. "He went back there to visit his sick sister, and while he was there he was killed. Jimmy said something about how he wished that real investigators would look into his father's death. I guess the authorities weren't able to solve the murder."

Murder! Bob thought. The Three Investigators had never really investigated something like that before. But there was no reason why he and Mallory couldn't talk to Jimmy Littlewolf, if that was what Freya wanted.

"I can stay and talk to him for a while," Bob said, "if Mallory can."

Freya looked at Mallory hopefully.

"Sure," Mallory said. "That'd be great."

"That's wonderful," Freya said. "I'm sure you'll like him."

Bob was sure they would, but he couldn't help wondering, for just a moment, whether Freya had the same kind of crush on Jimmy Littlewolf that she had on him.

He was surprised to realize that he hoped she didn't.

They were quiet for a few minutes until Freya sat forward in her seat. "Here we are," she said. Bob recognized the distinctive house with its second story balcony and its steeply pitched roof. The Three Investigators had been here a year ago, to see a painting and to have Freya translate the letters inherited from her grandfather.

Leif pulled into the driveway and parked. As Freya jumped out of the truck, Bob saw that two card tables had been set up in a shaded section of the yard, with two folding metal chairs at each. A boy and a girl were seated at one of the tables. They looked up briefly at the sound of the truck, but then turned their attention back to their chess game.

An older boy was seated at the other table, and when he saw Freya waving, he stood up and started walking toward the driveway.

That had to be Jimmy Littlewolf, Bob thought.

He was tall and lean − taller even than Pete, Bob thought − with long arms and legs. He wore blue jeans and a black tee shirt with a stylized eagle on it in turquoise and silver. Around his neck was a leather choker decorated with silver beads.

He had a wide and open bronze face, a small scar above his left eyebrow, and a broad forehead, visible because his fine black hair had been pulled back into a ponytail. He would have seemed friendly but for his eyes, which were dark brown and peered out at the world warily, giving him a haunted look.

He had to be sixteen, Bob thought, if he was in the grade ahead of Freya, but he looked older − as though he'd seen a lot of life and wasn't sure that he'd liked what he'd seen.

Clearly, he carried a heavy weight.

He smiled briefly at Freya, squinting his eyes, which then darted from Bob to Mallory. Already Bob felt great sympathy for the boy. What would it be like to know your father had been murdered and the killer never caught?

Bob stepped forward and stuck out his hand. "Hi," he said. "I'm Bob Andrews and this is Mallory MacLeod. You must be Jimmy Littlewolf."

"That's right," Jimmy said. Mallory smiled at him and shook his hand, too.

"I'm going inside now," Leif suddenly interjected. "But I promised Mrs. Jones I'd have the truck back in the Salvage Yard about an hour from now. We should leave in half an hour. Forty minutes at the latest. O.K.?"

"O.K.," Bob said. "Come and get us when you're ready."

"Thanks, Leif," said Freya. Then she turned to Jimmy. "Bob is a member of that Three Investigators firm I told you about, and Mallory works with them. They wanted to meet you."

Bob glanced at Freya. What she'd said wasn't strictly the truth, but it was close enough if it would make Jimmy more comfortable.

A look crossed Jimmy's face that was a

little hard to read, but he certainly seemed interested − even excited − to learn who they were.

"Let's go over here," Freya said. She led the way to the card table where she introduced her fellow chess club members. They looked up briefly, too engrossed in the game they were playing to be more than momentarily polite, and then Freya ushered Jimmy, Mallory, and Bob to a shady corner of the yard, bordered by a low stone wall where they sat on the grass in a ragged circle.

For a moment, the four of them just looked at one another and Bob began to gauge the depths of Jimmy's shyness.

He would catch Bob's eyes and then quickly look away, though the rest of his face was immobile. Freya − who clearly felt the need to get things going − tried to encourage him to talk about chess by complimenting him on his ability, but he just frowned and shook his head once, abruptly.

Bob finally took out his wallet and in a very formal manner presented Jimmy with a Three Investigators business card. He watched as Jimmy studied it. Although it might be hard to get Jimmy talking, Bob had the feeling he really wanted to − and when Jimmy glanced from Bob to Mallory and then back to The Three Investigators' card, he had a feeling he wanted to even more.

2

Jimmy Littlewolf

As Mallory, too, saw Jimmy do this, she watched him with quiet compassion. She'd liked him immediately. He had an intelligent soulful face and was clearly quite unhappy. After shaking her hand, he'd appeared not to know what to do with his own hands, so he'd put both of them on his hips – a stance that might have seemed intimidating in someone else. But Mallory could tell that Jimmy Littlewolf didn't have an aggressive bone in his body.

She resolved to listen to his story carefully. Not only did she feel a kinship with him as someone who had also unexpectedly lost a father, but she was embarrassed for not realizing earlier where Freya's story about chess had been headed. She should have seen that Freya was taking a roundabout way of arriving at what she wanted to say – whereas Mallory would have been much more likely to get straight to the point. As she had when she'd blurted out all that stuff about the Lewis chessmen.

She could kick herself now for having

done so. It had derailed Freya, and besides, Mallory felt like a bit of a know-it-all for interjecting details that had nothing whatever to do with Freya's story. But maybe she was being a little hard on herself. After all, she really *was* interested in the Lewis chessmen and she'd had reason to think about them recently.

Uncle Titus, at some time in the distant past, had, in his wanderings, bought a reproduction set and brought it back to the Salvage Yard − where he'd promptly forgotten all about it. Mallory had recently unearthed it in her work of sorting and classifying, and she'd taken it back with her to the shed where she worked. She'd been so enamored of it that at first she'd wondered if, by some miracle, hidden among the pieces was one of the missing originals. But that had been a fantasy, of course. The set she'd uncovered was a fine reproduction, in red and yellow soapstone. Not a piece of it was made of anything like a walrus tusk.

She'd set the chessmen aside rather than photographing them immediately for the Salvage Yard's website and prospective sale. They were beautifully made, and in the place of rooks were a pair of dunce-capped wild-eyed Viking berserkers, their mouths full of teeth, their swords held tightly against their cheeks.

For a day she'd carried one around in her pocket and rubbed her thumb against it from time to time, as if for good luck. It wasn't that the set was particularly valuable − she'd done some research on pricing − but the pieces were very cool, and she'd grown fond of them.

Still, she felt like an insensitive jerk when it turned out that what Freya had really been leading up to was the fact that Jimmy's father had been murdered, and that maybe The Three Investigators could help figure out what had happened to him. Now as she looked at Jimmy sitting there, trying to look impudent while radiating vulnerability, she felt a wave of sadness.

It was horrible enough to lose your father when he died unexpectedly, of natural causes, right there close to you, but how much more horrible must it have been for Jimmy to have his father vanish when he was a thousand miles away − because someone had killed him − and not to know who that someone was, or why he'd done what he'd done.

Jimmy stopped studying the card and looked up.

"This symbol at the bottom of your card?" he asked. "With the eagle and the bob-cat and the bighorn sheep? It looks Native

American.”

“Does it?” Bob asked with interest. “It actually came about because of a decal we found on the back window of a car we bought last summer. It's an artist’s rendering of a chimera – a creature from Greek mythology. The three animals stand for me and my friends Jupiter Jones and Pete Crenshaw.”

“Are they your spirit animals?” Jimmy asked.

“Not exactly,” Bob said. “I mean, they didn't come to us in a vision quest, or anything like that. But we each resemble our animal in some way.”

“And what about you?” Jimmy asked Mallory.

Of all the things Mallory might have imagined Jimmy saying just then, that would never have been on the list. It seemed the comment of an unusually sensitive person. Although Mallory had grown up in Scotland, where she’d never run into a Native American, she’d gotten the impression from American movies and television shows that they were frequently impassive. Of course, she knew that was a stereotype, but even so, she was somehow truly touched by Jimmy’s question.

“I've only been a part of The Three Investigators for a short time," Mallory explained. "I'm a Special Consultant. I wasn't around yet when Pete designed the chimera."

"Pete?" asked Jimmy. "Which one is he?"

For a moment Mallory wasn't sure what he was asking, and then she said, "Oh! I see! The bobcat is Bob, Pete's the bighorn sheep, and Jupiter's the golden eagle."

Jimmy nodded. "The Shoshone have always had a special reverence for the golden eagle, and my father told me that the Wind River Reservation in Wyoming has bighorn sheep again. So it's got all three of The Three Investigators' spirit animals now."

Again, Mallory was amazed at how sensitive this comment was. Jimmy slipped the business card into his jeans pocket. "Thanks for this," he said. "Freya's told me some about The Three Investigators, but you can tell me more."

"Well," Bob said. "Jupiter, Pete, and I have been friends forever. We're all young for our grade in school, and we just naturally started hanging around together. We've been best friends since first grade. Maybe kindergarten."

Jimmy nodded at that and looked wistful,

clearly wishing he had such friends.

"Jupiter is the real brains," Bob said, "and it was his idea to start a detective firm. Our first case involved a haunted house – or a house we thought might be haunted. We found out it wasn't."

"This summer we've solved three cases so far," Mallory said. "And since we've only *had* three cases, that's a pretty good record. But what about you? Freya told us just a little about you. Not very much. But we got the impression that there was a bit of a mystery about your father's death."

Jimmy looked at Freya and smiled very faintly.

"Well, yes," he said. "My father was eastern Shoshone. He grew up on the Wind River Res. He was a rodeo rider – he was a wizard with horses – and he met my mother, who is western Shoshone, while he was out performing on the circuit. She was working in the medical clinic on the Shoshone-Paiute reservation in northern Nevada."

He paused and uncrossed his legs. "That's where my parents settled," he said. "On the Duck Valley Res. It stretches into southern Idaho, but it's sort of small compared to the Wind River Res, which is huge, and has tons more people living on it. The government told the Shoshone to share it with their mortal enemies, the northern Arapaho. Go figure." He grimaced, as if to say that was about what you could expect from the government.

"But your father didn't die in Nevada, did he?" Bob asked.

Jimmy shook his head. "No," he said. "He went back to Wyoming to visit his sister, and I never saw him again. They found his body at the bottom of a cliff on a piece of land just outside the border of the Wind River Reservation."

"So who investigated the death?" Bob asked.

"Because it happened off the res, BIA couldn't touch it," Jimmy said.

"BIA?" Bob asked.

"The Bureau of Indian Affairs," Jimmy said. "They run the police department on the reservation. But they can't arrest non-Native people, so it might have been for the best. The Lander County sheriff's office did the investigation. At first they thought it was an accident and that my father fell off the cliff and broke his neck. But the medical examiner found that he'd been hit on the head with something before he fell. He had a big gash on his forehead.

She called it a 'blunt force trauma.' It knocked him out, but it didn't kill him. It was the fall from the cliff that did."

"I'm so sorry," Mallory said.

Jimmy had been speaking in a matter-of-fact tone as though the story he was telling didn't involve him, but she could see from his face how painful the details still were.

"Did they find what he'd been hit with?" Bob asked.

Jimmy shook his head. "I'm not even sure they looked real hard. A rock? I don't know. It didn't really seem to matter to them. All they said was that he'd been hit on the head and then fallen off the cliff."

Mallory could tell that there was more to the story — some detail Jimmy didn't want to think about or talk about, something that really bothered him. She wondered if she and Bob should encourage him to talk some more, but he started again on his own.

"He had booze all over his clothes," Jimmy said. "But that's just wrong. My father didn't drink. He stopped when he was twenty — almost ten years before I was born. He never touched a drop after that. He used to talk about the way he grew up hearing about Indians and "fire water" and how we couldn't handle alcohol. When he was growing up, he thought it was a myth. But after he started drinking, he began to believe it. He said it didn't take much at all to make him drunk."

"So he quit," Bob said.

"Yeah," Jimmy said. "He'd only been drinking for a few years, anyway, and he knew it was a total dead end. Then he married my mom, who's a nurse, and she told him there was scientific evidence that alcoholism can be genetic. It runs in families, and in some Native American tribes."

"Why did he have alcohol on his clothes?" Mallory asked.

"The only explanation is that someone threw it at him or poured it on him," Jimmy said, clearly upset by this. "Either after his death or just before. The coroner did blood tests that proved he had no alcohol in his system."

"It's an awful story," Bob said. "I'm really sorry."

Jimmy shrugged. "Yeah, well," he said.

"Why did you and your parents move to southern California?" Mallory asked.

"My mom worked at a clinic on the Duck Valley Reservation when I was growing up," Jimmy said. "She'd had only the simplest kind of training but she was very good at what she did. The tribe decided to pay for further nursing education so she could be even more helpful. We came here so she could get a more advanced degree and also work in a larger hospital."

"Do you like it here?" Bob said.

"It's all right," Jimmy said. "We were planning to go back to Nevada after I finished high school – my mom thinks the schools are better here – but now that my dad's dead, I wish we could go back right away."

The more Jimmy talked, the more Mallory got the impression that his father's death wasn't the only thing that was bothering him. He seemed unhappy, or discontented, in a general way that went beyond the specific tragedy. Though he was obviously finding it hard to ask for anything at all, Mallory felt that, in some obscure way, he was looking for help from The Three Investigators that went beyond solving the mystery of his father's death.

She felt more and more sympathy for Jimmy, not just because she thought she understood how he felt about his father, but because she shared his general experience – at least to some degree. When she'd first come to Rocky Beach, she'd felt like a complete outsider, with her red hair and her Scottish accent and her familiarity with a culture very different from that of southern California.

In fact, she thought she might still feel like a complete outsider if it hadn't been for finding Jupiter, Pete, and Bob. How much worse must it have been for Jimmy Littlewolf?

"Do you have any brothers or sisters?" she asked him.

"A half-brother," Jimmy said. "He's eight years older. Same mother, different father. My mom had him before she met my dad. His name's Jake Blackhorse. He's staying with me and my mom here in Palisade Point – at least most of the time. He grew up on the res in Nevada, too, but he moved out when I was eight and went to live with his dad for a while.

"Now he works part-time at a Mission Indian casino near Highland and part-time at a small ranch outside Redlands, near the San Bernardino National Forest," Jimmy continued. "He worked for years at a casino in Jackpot, Nevada, not far from the Duck Valley res, but he moved back in with us about eighteen months ago, after we moved to Palisade Point, a couple of months before my dad died."

"There's really a town called Jackpot?" Mallory asked in surprise.

Jimmy nodded, slightly amused. "It was founded by a guy who ran a casino in Idaho, but when they were banned, he moved south, right on the border, and started up again where it was legal."

"Are the two of you close at all?" Bob asked.

"Not really," Jimmy said. "We're very different. And eight years is a lot. We don't have much in common. And besides, with his two jobs, he's gone a lot." He looked at Bob and Mallory appraisingly, then decided to take the plunge. "He's a bit of a bully and not the swiftest thing on two legs. And he's always been jealous of me because I had a great dad and his was a loser and a deadbeat. In and out of jail. He deserted Jake and my mom when Jake was very young."

"Gosh," said Bob. "That's really too bad."

"And now Jake just sits in a cage all day and sells casino tokens. Except when he's riding horses. He's good at that, I guess. He got the job at the ranch through my father. My dad was amazing with horses – a sort of horse whisperer, if you know what that means. It was in his blood. The Shoshone are a horse people. They were the first northern tribe to get horses from the Spaniards."

"Do you ride, too?" Mallory asked.

"Me?" Jimmy said. "I missed that gene. My dad tried to teach me, but I could never get the hang of it. It was weird. He could read horses' minds, but I couldn't make them understand me at all."

Mallory sensed that talking about this subject made Jimmy both unhappy and uncomfortable. She could almost see his defenses go back up. "Anyway, if the Lander sheriff couldn't figure out who killed my father when he was right there, I don't see how you could discover what happened over a year ago and a thousand miles away."

Jimmy sounded cynical, but Mallory knew that he had warmed to them over the course of the conversation. Though he'd tensed a bit, he no longer seemed so cautious or reserved, and in his quiet way, he was clearly eager for their understanding. She identified with him more and more − they both were shy and wanted to make friends but were wary and even a little doubtful that such a thing could happen. Jimmy was hopeful The Three Investigators could help him, but at the same time he'd given up hope that *anyone* could.

Mallory looked at Freya, who was staring at Jimmy with a concerned expression. The summer before, Mallory had thought Freya was very young for her age, but it was more and more evident that she'd been too fast with her conclusion. Freya had said she'd been lucky in having Jimmy assigned to her as a mentor, but Mallory could see it ran the other way as well – Jimmy had been lucky to be assigned to someone as kind and generous as Freya.

"I don't know if we can help," Bob said, "but I'd sure like to give it a try."

He smiled at Jimmy, who smiled back – this time a more relaxed smile, as if he were almost as happy for the offer as he would have been for the solution to his problem.

Mallory caught sight of Leif walking toward them across the grass.

"O.K., you two," he said, waving his hand toward Mallory and Bob. "You told me to come and get you."

Bob hopped to his feet. "Just one more second," he said. He turned to Jimmy. "Are you free tomorrow afternoon?" he asked. "We have an appointment in the morning, but we're open after lunch."

"Yes," Jimmy said. "I think so."

"You could come to Rocky Beach and meet Pete and Jupiter," Bob said. "After the four of us talk, we can decide what to do next."

"Do you have a way to get there?" Mallory asked.

"If my mom will let me take the car, I can drive myself," Jimmy said. "I've been driving ever since I turned sixteen."

"That's another year and a bit away for us," Bob said. "But that's great. So we'll see you after lunch tomorrow afternoon."

"I'll make sure he has directions to the Salvage Yard," Freya said. She looked earnestly at Bob. "But before you go, you said you'd take a look at the geranium you gave me last summer."

Bob looked questioningly at Leif, who grimaced slightly but nodded. Freya led Bob away from the group and across the backyard to the small perennial border.

Mallory found this interesting. On the drive from the climbing area to the Haldorsson's house, she'd thought that maybe Freya had exchanged her crush on Bob for one on Jimmy Littlewolf, but it was pretty clear from her expression as she and Bob walked over to the geranium that she hadn't.

In fact, it suddenly seemed likely that her desire to involve The Three Investigators in this case had come about only partly out of a desire to help Jimmy. The rest of it seemed to be because she knew she'd get credit from them — and particularly from Bob — for bringing a case to their attention.

"How's the geranium?" Mallory said when Bob and Freya returned.

Bob looked at her as if he'd understood what she was really asking. "It's doing really well," he said. "It's over twice as big as it was."

Freya nodded eagerly. "It was happy to be out of its pot and have room to grow," she said. "I water it every other day."

"And sometimes she waters the rest of the flowers too!" Leif said. "Come on, let's go."

By now, Jimmy had gone back to the card table where a chessboard had been set up, ready for the match with Freya to begin. He stared down at the pieces as if planning the game he would soon play.

"Thanks so much," Freya said to Bob and Mallory, "for coming to talk to Jimmy. I don't know if you could tell, but he really appreciated it. He can be hard to read."

"You can say that again," Bob said. "He wasn't giving much away."

Mallory was surprised by this, but didn't say anything. She had thought that Jimmy had been fairly easy to read.

Freya walked them to the truck. "If I can help with the case," she said, and then her voice faltered as she seemed to understand how unlikely that would be.

"If you can, we'll let you know," Mallory said. "And we'll be sure to keep you informed about what's going on. If anything does."

They said goodbye, and then Mallory offered the front seat to Bob. "Go ahead," she said. "You were a bit cramped on the way over." Gratefully Bob accepted.

As he climbed in next to Leif, Mallory got in the back. She locked the door on the passenger side, leaned against it, and threw her legs up on the seat.

"I really liked Jimmy," Mallory said.

"Me, too," Bob said, "and I'm glad he's coming to the Salvage Yard tomorrow. But he got it right, I'm afraid."

"What do you mean?" Mallory asked.

"Remember when he said 'over a year ago and a thousand miles away'?"

"In Wyoming," Mallory agreed. "I wonder how we'll even start."

"Wyoming?" Bob said. "Of course! What was I thinking?" He hit himself lightly in the forehead with the palm of his hand. "That's where Hector Sebastian's been living! I know it's a big state, but I wonder if he's ever heard of the Wind River Reservation. When we see him tomorrow, we can ask."

They were quiet for most of the rest of the way back to the Salvage Yard. In fact, Mallory was feeling a bit drowsy. Her eyelids kept closing. The adrenaline from the climb had faded, and she'd been on high alert the entire time she was listening to Jimmy.

She thought briefly about the things he'd said. Had someone tried to make the murder look like an accident, or had Jimmy's father's fall been a mishap? Why had someone doused his body with alcohol? She imagined the place where it had happened − a hot sun, a hot wind blowing across a desert landscape, small shrubby things, a hawk circling, looking to swoop down on a lizard or a snake.

Leif pulled into the Salvage Yard and parked next to the shed where he and Magnus had their woodworking shop. Mallory and Bob thanked him for the ride, then carried their climbing gear to the shed where Mallory spent most of her time when she was working for Jupiter's aunt and uncle. She and Bob were keeping their gear there for the summer.

As they came back outside, Jupiter came walking toward them from the direction of

Headquarters.

"Hector Sebastian called while you were climbing," Jupiter said. "To make sure we were coming tomorrow. He sounded just like he always has. It's good to know a year in Wyoming hasn't changed him. When he asked for you, Bob, I told him to call you on your cellphone. Did he get you?"

"Yes," Bob said. "But he wouldn't really come out and tell me why he was calling. All he said was that us creative types had to stick together and a bunch of stuff about Janus."

"Janus?" Jupiter asked. "The Roman god?"

"Exactly," Bob said

"Hmm," said Jupiter.

"But that's really not the most important thing that happened," Bob said. Before he could tell Jupiter about Freya and Jimmy Littlewolf and the commitment he and Mallory had made to both of them, Pete came whizzing into the Salvage Yard on his bicycle, fresh from a couple of hours' work at the Rocky Beach Animal Rescue Center.

As always, Mallory was glad to see him, but she was particularly glad he'd gotten here in time to hear the Jimmy Littlewolf story.

Since it was a hot day and they didn't

want to crowd together in Headquarters, the four of them went to their outdoor workshop and settled down on their green metal chairs. Bob went to get some cold drinks from the refrigerator in Mallory's shed, and when he got back, he and Mallory told Pete and Jupiter everything they could remember about what Jimmy had told them.

Pete was particularly interested in what he'd said about the Shoshone.

"I know about those guys!" he said excitedly. "I'm not that great with history, but my dad and I saw a movie called *Dances With Wolves* a couple of years ago, and it was all about this Anglo who basically *became* one. A Shoshone! Kevin Costner played him, and there was a buffalo hunt where the Indians had just bows and arrows and were riding their horses bareback!

"The Shoshone had a chief named Chief Washakie whose name means 'Shoots the Buffalo Running.' And I found out afterwards that all those Plains Indian tribes – the Cheyenne and the Comanche and the Blackfoot, and the Crow and stuff – were nomads who followed the bison and hunted them on horseback. I don't think the Shoshone were Plains Indians though. And they lived in a bunch of different places."

"That must be right," Bob said. "Because Jimmy Littlewolf told us that his father was an Eastern Shoshone from Wyoming and his mother was a Western Shoshone from Nevada. His mother's a nurse and his father met her while he was on the rodeo circuit."

"And his half-brother Jake had a different father?" asked Pete.

"Yes," Bob said. "Jake's working at a ranch near Redlands, and at a Mission Indian casino near Highland. I've always thought it was really depressing that so many Indian tribes needed to make their money off gambling."

"I agree," Jupiter said. "Native Americans *did* sort of gamble – with dice games mostly – though they preferred games of skill that tested their dexterity and coordination. But since Indian reservations are really sovereign nations within the United States, with their own governments and laws, the Supreme Court ruled that states had no jurisdiction over the gambling. After that, Indian tribes were allowed to build casinos on reservations, even in states that didn't allow gambling, like California. That makes Indian casinos the only game in town in a lot of places."

Mallory was interested to learn this. She hadn't known it — though she *had* discovered something about Mission Indians that had disturbed her greatly when she'd first moved to California. It seemed that "Mission Indians" was a collective name given to a number of tribes and bands in southern California who had been taken out of their villages and off their ancestral lands, jumbled together, and made to live and work on the Spanish Franciscan missions.

They'd been forced to abandon their languages, religions, and culture and had been baptized as Catholics. Due to overwork, starvation, and disease, over ninety per cent of them had died in just fifty years.

And although what had happened to the Shoshone seemed a good deal better than *that,* as Mallory looked at Jupiter, Pete, and Bob, she hoped against hope that The Three Investigators could somehow solve the mystery of what had happened to Thomas Littlewolf.

She'd really been drawn to Thomas's son, and she had the feeling that if Jimmy got the right kind of help, at the right moment, from people almost the same age as he was, his whole life might end up different — and a whole lot better.

3

A Trip To Hector Sebastian's

It was just before ten the next morning, and as Jupiter sat in the back seat of the The Three Investigators' Ford Flex heading for Hector Sebastian's house in Dial Canyon, he was thinking about what Mallory and Bob had told him and Pete about Jimmy Littlewolf.

He was looking forward to meeting Jimmy that afternoon and filling in the gaps in his story. He and his friends had never investigated a murder before, and Jupiter already sensed that it might be one of the toughest cases he'd ever encountered. The trail was cold, the murderer either long gone or hiding in plain sight, and the clues had undoubtedly been obscured by time.

If The Three Investigators were to succeed in getting to the bottom of what had happened in Wyoming that day, they would need some inside help. Not just a list of suspects, Jupiter thought − people who had a reason to harm Thomas Littlewolf as well as the means and opportunity to do so. They also needed to see the report the sheriff of Fremont County and his investigators had submitted when the investigation was complete.

As Worthington turned off the highway and onto the road that led into Dial Canyon, Jupiter wondered whether Chief Reynolds, Rocky Beach's chief of police and an old friend of The Three Investigators, could help out. Maybe he knew somebody. Anyway, Jupiter would have a much better sense of the case after he'd talked to Jimmy.

Just then – as Worthington came around a bend in the road – Jupiter looked up and caught a glimpse of Mr. Sebastian's mock-Tudor mansion. As always, he was taken aback. What was an architectural style from 15th-and-16th-century England doing in southern California? He glanced at Mallory, who had never seen the house before. With her love of the genuine, not the ersatz – particularly when it came to buildings – he could almost imagine what she was thinking.

The house's façade was creamy white stucco crossed with dark brown half-timbers, and its windows were made of leaded glass divided into diamonds. A red and white striped awning stretched over a patio that faced west, toward the Pacific, and the very large fenced yard contained a swimming pool, a gazebo, and a small guest cottage.

Mr. Sebastian hadn't built the house, but he liked it, and, in spite of its fakeness, Jupiter could understand why. It had breathtaking views, an open floor plan, large rooms, and a place outside the main house for guests to stay. Next to some of the ostentatious and completely bizarre homes on the slopes of Dial Canyon, it was downright tasteful.

Worthington turned right onto the long gravel drive that led to the house. As they approached, Jupiter wondered what it would be like to see Mr. Sebastian again and what it was he thought Bob might be especially interested in.

"Would you like to join us, Worthington?" Jupiter asked.

Worthington smiled. "No, thank you," he said. "I'd just be in the way. Plus, I haven't read the morning paper yet." He brandished a copy of the Los Angeles *Sun*. "I'll be under that tree." He pointed to a Ponderosa pine not far from where he'd parked.

Jupiter led the way to Mr. Sebastian's front door. He noticed that the cement walk had been replaced with cobblestones. But everything else looked the same.

"Everyone ready?" he asked. He looked

around at three expectant faces. "Here we go."
He knocked three times, hard.

It took no time at all for Mr. Sebastian
to open the door. Though Jupiter knew it was
him, he was flabbergasted by the transforma-
tion. A man who had dressed quite formally,
usually with an ascot, now wore blue jeans, a
pair of cowboy boots, and a long-sleeved ging-
ham shirt. He'd lost weight and his face, which
had rarely been outdoors when he lived in California, was tan and even a bit weathered. He
looked healthy, vibrant, and happy. Where was
his pipe? Jupiter couldn't remember ever seeing
him without it.

He was going to ask, but Pete beat him
to it. "Mr. Sebastian!" Pete said. "Where's
your pipe?"

Hector Sebastian looked down at his
hands as if they would hold the answer to Pete's
question. "Why, I gave it up!" he said. "And
you and the others are commanded to finally
start calling me 'Hector,' not 'Mr. Sebastian.'
I think I've earned it."

He paused. "Now, before we really get
started, I know who Mallory is, of course, but
I'd still like someone to introduce us formally!"

Jupiter felt momentarily embarrassed.

"This is Mallory MacLeod, Mr. Sebastian – I mean, Hector," he said. "I know Bob has already told you she's a Special Consultant to The Three Investigators, and that she works for my aunt and uncle at the Salvage Yard. Did he also tell you that she's designing a new Headquarters for the firm? We'll be building it next spring."

He found that he was strangely pleased and proud to be able to say all this about Mallory.

Bob nodded to Hector. "And you and Mallory talked to one another that day you told us about Vadim Fedorov's story," he added.

"Indeed we did," said Hector. He took Mallory's hand quite formally. "It's a pleasure to meet you at last, my dear. I feel like I already know you. I've read Bob's case reports, of course, and you've made yourself indispensable to these three boys."

Jupiter had never seen Mallory blush, and he wasn't sure that it was happening now, but it did seem as though the tip of her nose turned pink.

"And a Special Consultant! That's never happened before," Hector said.

"We always wanted to have a girl operative," Pete said.

That wasn't exactly true, Jupiter thought.

It was Pete who had always wanted to have a girl operative. But maybe he'd been right all along.

"I'm amazed to hear that you'll be building a new Headquarters for the firm. Right there in the Salvage Yard?" Hector asked Jupiter.

"Yes," he said. "My aunt and uncle have given us permission. The old Headquarters is a little small. We're going to keep it, of course, but, at Mallory's suggestion, we're going to call the old one HQ1 and the new one HQ2."

"I think it's an excellent idea," said Hector. "Did you notice that I've improved my house, too? I've put down a cobblestone walk. The old cement path was ugly. Cobblestones suit the place, and it was easier to have it done when I wasn't here." He looked from Jupiter to Bob to Pete, studying each of them for a brief moment. "Time waits for no man," he finally said. "You all look older and more mature."

"You don't look older," Pete said. "But you look different!"

Hector laughed. "I guess I do. Wyoming is so energetic and physical. It's been good for me. I'm almost certainly going to spend another year there. After a rough start, I'm well along on a new book that may be the best I've ever written. It's a cross between a Western and a mystery. I'm calling it a Westery."

Everyone laughed, and Hector added, "Come in, come in. The refreshments are in the kitchen."

He led them through the entry hall, which looked the same − the carpet on the floor with its rich maroon field was familiar, as was the dark wood furniture along the walls − and into the kitchen. The table had been moved, but otherwise it hadn't changed; as always it held a tray with glasses, a pitcher of lemonade, and a plate of cookies. The immaculate black and white tiled floor still shone, and the light from the southern-facing glass doors flooded the room.

"Pick up the tray, will you, Pete?" Hector asked. Pete didn't have to be asked twice.

"Sure, Mr. Sebastian − I mean Hector," he said.

Hector led them through the book-lined living room and out onto the awning-shaded patio where, a year before, he'd introduced them to his friend Isabella Chang and their first case of the summer.

Jupiter couldn't help but think of how much had changed in the fifty-six-or-seven weeks since he'd last been at Hector Sebastian's house. At the time, he hadn't even met Mallory – though Pete and Bob had. Since then, he'd finished a year of high school, had learned how to fence, and The Three Investigators had solved nine major cases. They'd bought a car, had set up a sizable bank account for the firm, and had put money into their college funds.

On top of all that, Jupiter really did feel more mature and aware than the last time he'd been here – though he didn't usually notice that when he went about his daily life. The changes were so incremental they were hard to see.

Just then, Pete finished his first pass at the lemonade and cookies. "Tell us about where you live now. Tell us everything!" he said.

"You'll have to come visit me at the Double Fork sometime before I move back to California," Hector said. "What do you want to know, Pete?"

"Have you seen any wolves?" Pete asked.

"Yes, I have," Hector said. "The winter was long and hard, and a pack of wolves came down out of the mountains to the ranch. But they kept their distance and didn't hang around long. They weren't after me. They were after the elk. But mostly they eat rodents. Of which there are a good number."

"Bob said you've taken up horseback riding?" Jupiter asked.

"That's right," Mr. Sebastian said. "I've become good friends with Reese Carson, the ranch's owner, and he's taught me how to shoot a rifle and use a fly rod. I'm getting to be a pretty good rider and a good fisherman. Do the four of you ride?"

"A little," said Bob. "Enough to sit on a friendly horse and follow its lead. I don't know if you remember, but when Pete and I were on that case in the Napa Valley wine country, a long time ago – the Green Ghost case, with the Ghost Pearls? – we went riding with this really cool kid from Hong Kong named Chang Green, and at the end of it, when Jupiter joined us, we all went riding together."

"That's right!" said Hector. "Of course! You were really impressed with Chang Green and he was really grateful to you for helping him and his aunt – "

"Aunt Lydia," Bob said.

"Yes, and his Aunt Lydia, the way you did. Which makes me think that the first thing I should have asked you is whether or not you guys have a case right now."

"We do," said Jupiter. "A murder mystery, of sorts."

"A murder mystery?" Hector asked, raising his eyebrows high.

"Well, maybe," Jupiter said. "Yesterday Bob and Mallory met a boy whose father died about a year ago, and he wants us to try to help figure out who killed him. The authorities, it seems, have given up."

"And guess what?" Pete interjected. "He died in Wyoming, when he was back there visiting a sick sister. He's Native American − a Shoshone − and he grew up on this big reservation called the Wind River Indian Reservation."

"The Wind River Reservation?" exclaimed Hector, raising his eyebrows even higher. "Why, the Double Fork, where I'm living, practically runs right into it. In fact, when we're out riding, we have to be careful not to cross the boundary onto the res! I actually gave a reading at the reservation high school in the spring. The Shoshone and Arapaho who live on the reservation these days have had a terrible time − unemployment is unbelievably high, young people drop out of high school at an alarming rate, and there's a lot of alcoholism, violence, and drug use. It's tragic, really. The land is beautiful, but so many of the people live in poverty and unhappiness."

"Wow," Pete said. "That sounds pretty bad."

Jupiter agreed. It certainly sounded like more than any kid should ever have to deal with. He hoped that the Duck Valley Reservation, where Jimmy Littlewolf had grown up, was better.

"So how did this man die?" asked Hector.

"He broke his neck falling off a cliff," Jupiter said. "But the reason he fell off it in the first place was that someone hit him in the head with a blunt object − presumably a rock. And although he had no alcohol in his system, his clothes were soaked with it. The authorities in the town of Lander never figured out why that had happened, and they seem to have given up trying."

"Do you have any contacts in the area who might be able to help?" Bob asked. "I was really excited when I thought that you might know something about the place where this happened."

"Actually, Reese Carson's brother Rory lives in Lander," Hector said. "I think he might even work for the police department. But just before I flew to California, Reese mentioned that his brother had gone to New Mexico for a month for some sort of Outward Bound course. I'm not sure he could have helped you much, anyway.

"The whole area has a fascinating history, though," Hector continued. "There was a famous Shoshone chief named Chief Washakie who learned some French and English and became friends with trappers and traders. He was a diplomat and a shrewd negotiator and a visionary in his approach to dealing with the government. He made sure his people were granted their ancestral homeland."

"I already told them about Chief Washakie!" Pete said. "From *Dances With Wolves*, I knew what his name meant.'"

"That was a great movie," Hector said. "Of course the government later took away some of the land they'd granted, but as I told you, the part that remained was still huge. Chief Washakie was very well respected by the Army. They named a military outpost after him, and when he died in 1900, he was given a full military funeral."

"If you think of any way you could help, please let us know," Jupiter said. "I've already called Chief Reynolds to see if he can meet with us. He may be able to help us get the basic information about Jimmy's father's death, but I wish we had a contact who really knew about the Wind River Reservation, from the inside."

"I agree with your approach," Hector said. "It's almost always insiders with their inside information who manage to solve these difficult cases."

"I wonder if Phillipa Paxton could help," Pete said suddenly. "Didn't she grow up in Wyoming?"

"I was wondering the same thing," Mallory said.

"What a good idea," Jupiter said. "Now that you've brought it up, I thought the name 'Lander' was familiar. I'm pretty sure I recognized it because I think that's where Phillipa Paxton grew up."

"How great is this!" Pete said. "Maybe she'll know something we can use!" He looked at Hector Sebastian with a big smile. "Besides, ever since we heard you were coming back for a visit, I've been hoping we could introduce you to Dr. Paxton. I think you'd really like one another."

Jupiter looked at Mallory and Bob who were peering skeptically at Pete. He seemed intent on pairing up all the unpaired adults they knew. Jupiter had to admit he might have a knack for it — he'd introduced Connor O'Malley and Dr. Paxton's niece Charlotte Mitchell and they'd hit it off at once.

"That's kind of you, Pete," Hector said, looking amused. "Do you think I'm in need of some female companionship?"

"No!" Pete said. "I mean, yes! I just have a hunch the two of you would get along. Besides, she grew up in a town that's not that far from where you're living now, and you're both writers. She's a historian and writes about the west — she wrote a book about John Frémont, the first U.S. senator from California — and you're writing mysteries set in the old west. Why shouldn't you like each other?"

"John Frémont, eh?" Hector said. "Both Dubois and Lander are in Fremont County. What's the name of this Dr. Paxton's book?"

"It's called *Bear Valley*," Bob said.

"*A Prodigious Destiny*," Pete added. "That's the subtitle."

"It's mainly about Frémont and his wife Jessie," Mallory said.

But Hector had taken out his smart phone and had looked up Phillipa Paxton. "Hmm," he said. "Interesting-looking woman. By all means, introduce us!"

Pete beamed. He was getting good at this, Jupiter thought.

"In fact," Hector said, "maybe you could invite her to come here sometime this week, and all six of us could put our heads together about this case." He placed his phone on a table and stroked his chin. "Phillipa, eh? Did you know her name means 'lover of horses'? I bet she's an excellent rider. Maybe she'd even know of some stables where we could rent horses and go on a trail ride within a few hours of Los Angeles. One must keep one's hand in!"

"I'll call her this afternoon," Mallory said. "We became friends earlier this summer on a case up in the Napa Valley."

"The one at Castello Serreno!" Hector said. "I really enjoyed that one!"

Everyone sat looking happily at one another until Bob suddenly spoke.

"You said you wanted to talk to me privately about something involving the Roman god Janus? And creativity?" he asked.

"No need for privacy," Hector said. "At the time I had no idea that the four of you were about to launch into a new case − and one that sounds particularly challenging! I doubt you'll have time for this other thing now

– though it wouldn't actually take all *that* much time!"

"Well, what is it?" asked Pete.

"Hmm," said Hector. "Officially, it's called the Janusian creativity study."

"The what?" Pete said.

"A geneticist at U.C.L.A. is interested in finding out whether there are any specific genetic markers for creativity," Hector explained. "She's asked me and fifteen other writers to give her DNA samples and then take a bunch of tests. Her hypothesis is that creative types who regularly engage in something known as the Janusian process may have similarities in their genetic codes."

"Wow," Pete said.

"She's looking for a gene for creativity?" Mallory asked.

"Something like that," Hector said. "Not a gene, but a sequence of genes. Something that might incline certain people to a specific habit of mind. She's getting her volunteers mainly through California's colleges and universities, and the alumni office at Pomona College gave her my name."

"Yesterday, Mallory said she thought that 'Janusian' might have something to do with being able to think two things at once.

Two things that contradict each other," Bob said.

"That's right!" Hector said, looking very impressed. "The term 'Janusian process' was coined by a psychiatrist who believed that creativity involves putting together opposing thoughts at the same instant and then making use of the clash between them. It's like hitting steel with flint, and sparking a brand new fire."

"Like your idea of putting together Westerns and mysteries and coming up with Westerys," Jupiter suggested.

"Well, maybe!" Hector said. "Too many people think being creative means making decorative-looking things, when what it really means is thinking differently. What particularly interests me about Dr. Yang's study is that she's throwing a wide net and involving people we don't normally think of as creative. In addition to writers, she's studying scientists and businessmen. Even investigators!"

When he heard this, Jupiter nodded. He himself was constantly seeing someone as both a potential ally and a potential adversary and trying to imagine that something was both true and not true at the same time. Really, all four of them did this. When it came to investigations, it was crucial to keep an open mind about whether someone was guilty or not, and whether someone was telling the truth or lying. You needed to consider both possibilities and see where that led you.

"But I'm still not sure why you wanted to talk to me about this," Bob said.

"Because every adult who's been invited to participate in the study has been asked to recommend a younger person in his or her field to participate as well. A number of the older writers are recommending their own children, but since I don't have any children, I immediately thought of you."

Hector looked at Bob intently. "Would you be interested? It would involve giving a DNA sample and then taking the same battery of tests I'm taking. I'm pretty sure that when you write up your case notes you utilize the Janusian process even if you don't think of it that way."

Jupiter could see that Bob was flattered by Hector's suggestion but also a bit uncertain about whether he wanted to participate.

"If I decided I wanted to take part in the study," Bob said, "how would I go about it?"

"Dr. Yang will be working all this week in one of the science labs on the Pomona campus," Hector said. "All you'd need to do is go there and tell her I recommended you." He gestured to Jupiter, Pete, and Mallory. "You should all go," he said. "It's a beautiful campus, one hundred and forty acres of it, nestled right next to the San Gabriel Mountains. I'm sure you'd all like it."

He turned back to Bob. "Didn't your father go to one of those small eastern colleges?" he asked.

"Yes, he did," Bob said.

"Well, Pomona was founded by members of the Congregational Church who wanted a New England-type college in southern California. Go see it! It's one of the best small colleges in the country. I loved it."

"Thanks, Hector," Bob said. "I'll think about it."

"Well," Jupiter said, standing up. "It's been a pleasure seeing you again, and we have a lot more to tell one another. But we'd better be going for now. We're meeting Jimmy Littlewolf back at the Salvage Yard in about an hour."

"Then you should be on your way!" Hector said. "It's been great seeing you all, and meeting you, Mallory. Let me walk you to the door."

At least that was something that hadn't

changed, Jupiter thought as they all said good-bye and started down the new cobblestone path, headed for the car.

"Are you going to do it, Bob?" Pete asked.

"I wouldn't be too quick if I were you," Mallory said. "I'm not sure I'd want my creativity messed with. If it works, there's no reason to look at it too closely."

"I don't know," Bob said. "I sort of agree with you and sort of don't."

"See?" Pete said. "You're doing it already!"

On the way back to the Salvage Yard, while Mallory and Bob talked about the visit with Hector Sebastian and Pete sat mostly silent – apparently thinking about something he didn't share – Jupiter turned his mind again to Jimmy Littlewolf and their upcoming meeting.

He trusted Mallory's assessment of Jimmy and wondered how he might get him to relax when he got to the Salvage Yard. After all, he'd be on unfamiliar territory and he'd be meeting two new people and two others he'd just met yesterday. Perhaps, Jupiter thought, they could play a game of chess. Would that be a good ice breaker?

It had been a while since Jupiter had played chess. He had used to play with his uncle in the evenings – at least until he became reliably better than Uncle Titus and they both lost interest. It was a fascinating, multilevel, and challenging game, and if Jimmy Littlewolf was good at it, he would have to be smart, adept at strategy and at thinking ahead, and – Jupiter was sure – also quite creative.

4

A Revealing Chess Game

All the way back to the Salvage Yard, Pete was thinking about what had happened at Hector Sebastian's. It had been great to see him again after a year, but Pete was surprised by how different the man seemed — less fussy and formal, more genial and happy. Pete wouldn't have been surprised if he'd changed his name from Hector to Heck!

Boy, Pete thought. Wyoming must be quite a place. When he'd looked at it on a map it had seemed unreal — almost perfectly square, as though someone had sat down with a ruler and a pencil and made a state.

Actually, on a map, it looked boring, and yet it was home to bison and wolves and grizzlies, wild clear rivers and gigantic mountain ranges. It sure had done Mr. Sebastian — no, Hector! — good. Pete hoped that he'd been serious when he'd said The Three Investigators should come visit him at the Double Fork sometime before he moved back to California. Pete wondered why it was called the Double Fork. The double fork of what? A river, he guessed.

Pete also thought about his suggestion that Hector should meet Phillipa Paxton. Aside from the fact that Hector had clearly liked the way Phillipa looked, Pete had a hunch they'd really like each other – and he'd been right when he'd thought the same thing about Connor O'Malley and Charlotte Mitchell.

He'd introduced them at The Three Investigators' birthday party at the end of the previous summer, and the last time Pete had seen Charlotte, she'd told him that she was going to be spending the summer with Connor up in Auburn. He was batting a thousand so far, he thought.

The only thing was, ever since their second case of the summer, he'd been wishing he could do the same thing for himself. What he'd said at Hector's about The Three Investigators having always wanted to have a girl operative – well, while it was undoubtedly terrific that Mallory had joined them and was working out so well, the fact was that Pete felt ready for a girl-friend of his own.

In fact, two cases ago, he and the others had been waiting for a ride from Rocky Beach to Santa Barbara, and Mallory had acciden-tally left the messenger bag with her phone in it on the steps of the Salvage Yard's office. When it had rung, Pete had answered it, thinking it might be Mallory's mother. He'd been surprised and pleased when it turned out to be Mallory's friend, Califia García-Williams.

He'd first met Califia the summer before, when she was playing Juliet in a local production of *Romeo and Juliet,* and this summer she was in a play in which she'd been cast as the Greek goddess Aphrodite, the goddess of love and sex and beauty. She was really very talented – and also very nice, and pretty. Pete wished he could think of some way in which the two of them could get to know one another better, away from Rocky Beach.

It wasn't that Rocky Beach wasn't great; it was just that Pete felt that being somewhere else with Califia might give them a chance to really be themselves. He frowned. That wasn't the business of the day, he thought. The business of the day was Jimmy Littlewolf.

Pete was really looking forward to meeting him – and not just because of *Dances With Wolves.* Bob and Mallory had mentioned what Jimmy had said about the three animals that made up the chimera being a bit like Native American spirit animals.

When Pete had come up with the idea of

the chimera in the first place, that was what he had thought, too. But since then, someone had told him that you could only have a spirit animal if you were actually a Native American, and Pete had thought that was really too bad. And maybe not even true.

Back at the Salvage Yard, he saw that the sometimes sleepy place was alive with activity. Uncle Titus was helping Leif and Magnus carry some lumber into their workshop. Uncle Titus was an expert at getting bystanders to help with whatever he was doing, so Pete was glad to see they were almost finished.

As the four of them climbed out of the Flex, Uncle Titus spied them and beckoned them over. Uh oh, Pete thought.

"Come on, come on," Uncle Titus said. "No need for suspicion. I don't have any work for the four of you to do — aside from the work that Mallory knows she's responsible for. But if you give me a minute, I'll come up with something." His eyes gleamed.

"No, no," he said. "Only kidding. I just came across this riddle — "

Pete looked at Jupiter. For years now, Uncle Titus had "just been coming across" riddles that he tried to stump his nephew with. So far *he* was batting zero. Jupiter had solved every single riddle or puzzle, usually in record time, and though at first he'd quite enjoyed the little game, as it went on he'd gotten somewhat tired of the whole thing.

In fact, Pete had thought that Jupiter and his uncle had come to an understanding — no more riddles, especially ones that made Jupiter feel like a performing pony in front of his friends. But now, at the announcement of a new riddle, Jupiter just looked resigned, not annoyed, and there was even a hint in his eye that he was beginning to enjoy them again.

"Now this one is so easy I don't even know why I'm bothering," Uncle Titus said. "Listen closely. A young boy leaves home, running as fast as he can. He runs for a while and then he makes a sharp left. He runs some more, the exact same distance, and then turns left again. He runs the same distance again and turns left one final time."

Home! Pete thought. He was getting back home. At least that was what Pete thought the answer would be.

But he was wrong. "When the boy got home, he saw two masked men. Who were they?" Uncle Titus asked.

Two masked men! Pete thought. Whoa! The Lone Ranger and Zorro?

Jupiter smiled. "That's clever," he said. "I like misdirection. It's important to recognize it in the course of investigations."

"That may be so," Uncle Titus said. "But quit stalling. Who are the masked men?"

"The umpire and the catcher," Jupiter said. "The boy is playing baseball."

"That's my boy!" Uncle Titus chortled, doing a little jig in the gravel. "I can always count on you."

Pete smacked himself on the forehead. He'd been visualizing it all wrong. He'd settled immediately on thinking of "home" and "masks" and got misdirected.

"How did you do that, Jupe?" Pete asked.

"The boy ran in a square," Jupiter said, "starting and ending at a place called 'home.' Logically there was only one solution."

Pete smirked. Logically shmogically, he thought.

"O.K.," Jupiter said, as his uncle picked up one of the last pieces of lumber, "let's go over to the outside workshop and get ready for Jimmy Littlewolf."

Their four green metal chairs were in their customary positions. Pete went to the Salvage Yard's fence where they'd stored a couple more and grabbed one to bring back for Jimmy.

"I'll go get us some drinks," Bob said. "We should probably offer Jimmy something."

"Good idea," Jupiter said. Pete watched as Bob hurried across to Mallory's work shed, where they had a small secondhand refrigerator, and quickly returned with a carrier with five cans of soda.

"It's great that we can meet out here," Pete said. "But it'll be even better next year when HQ2 is ready."

As Jupiter and Bob agreed, Bob turned to Mallory. It had been a number of weeks since Jupiter had finally approved the idea and had given Mallory the assignment to plan the new building. She really hadn't brought it up in a while.

"How's it going?" Bob asked her. "Have you started putting anything down on paper?"

Mallory looked startled and then a bit guarded. "I've been thinking about it a lot and I've been working on and off. But I don't want to show anyone anything yet, or really even talk about it. I'm still in the very beginning stages, and it's all pretty tentative. I'm not far enough along in the process to risk it."

"I know just what you mean," Bob said.

"At the beginning of any creative project, you don't want to say too much in case something someone says throws you off or makes you lose faith."

"Is that really true?" Pete asked.

"I think it is," Mallory said. "You've got to find your feet and start building your confidence. Criticism, even helpful positive criticism, can stop you dead if it happens too early. At the beginning, you have to be open to every idea that comes your way, no matter how silly it might seem at first. But that also means that if anything negative comes your way, you'll be open to that, too."

For some reason, Pete thought about his work at the Animal Rescue Center, and how, when he'd just started volunteering, someone had said he was being too cuddly with the animals. It had made him self-conscious and embarrassed and tentative, as though he were doing something wrong. It had taken him several weeks to feel self-assured again.

"Criticism is useful," Mallory said. "In fact, it's crucial. You can't always see everything you're doing, and other people can have good ideas. But at first you need to play things close to the chest. There's a danger in too much sharing."

"This is all very interesting, I'm sure," Jupiter said, "but Jimmy will be here any minute. Mallory and Bob, is there anything you haven't told us about him?"

"Talk about playing things close to the chest," Mallory said. "Jimmy doesn't give too much away. My guess is that he wants our help and doesn't want it at the same time."

Bob nodded. "He's torn. There are things he likes about being as alone as he is, but he's also tempted to break out of that. And I think he's pretty sad."

"Not just about his father," Mallory said. "There's something else he's not talking about."

"Hmm," Jupiter said. "I've been thinking that it might be a good idea to invite him to play a game of chess with me. It would give him a chance to get used to the Salvage Yard and let his guard down. What do you think?"

"I think that's a great idea," Bob said. "As we were leaving the Haldorsson's yesterday, Jimmy was sitting in front of a chess set getting ready to play with Freya. He was a mass of tension earlier when he talked to us, but he looked much more relaxed in front of the board."

Jupiter nodded, as though he were

pleased to have his intuition confirmed, and then he got up and went through Easy Three and into Headquarters. He returned with a battered old chess set that Pete recognized as the one that Uncle Titus had given to Jupiter when no one wanted to buy it.

"I remember that set," Pete said. "I always thought the horses' heads were so cool. Didn't you play with your uncle? You were good."

"I did," Jupiter said. "But we haven't played in a while. I'm quite rusty. Jimmy will beat me easily."

"Don't worry," Pete said. "I'm sure it's like riding a bicycle. Or a horse."

"It isn't," Jupiter said.

Just as Jupiter had finished setting up the pieces on the board, a car drove into the Salvage Yard – a red Buick sedan with thick black racing stripes on the hood, quite old and a bit beaten up. There was a ding in the passenger-side door and the red was faded in places.

A tall teenage boy got out and stood for a minute in the hot sun, staring over at the four of them. He wore sneakers, blue jeans, and a cream-colored tee shirt. He had a choker around his neck, and his tanned skin gleamed. He looked a little nervous and a bit glum. He took off his sunglasses and put them on the crown of his head. Pete liked him right away.

He walked over to the boy and stuck out his hand. "Hi," he said. "I'm Pete. You must be Jimmy. I'm so jealous that you can drive already! Depending on how the investigation goes, maybe you can drive us somewhere."

"I can't," Jimmy said. "Not until I'm 18. I only have a provisional license."

"A provisional license?" Pete said. "What's that?"

"You get it after your driving permit," Jimmy said, "when you've completed Driver's Ed. But it's not like a real license, which you can't get until you're 18. It's got all these loopholes. They don't want teenagers driving around together, so I can't drive anyone who's under 20 unless there's an adult in the car who's 25 or older. And I can't drive late at night, like after eleven."

"Really?" Pete said. "I thought that when we turned 16, Jupiter, Bob, and I could drive together anywhere we wanted."

"Sorry to be the bearer of bad news," Jimmy said.

"That *is* bad news," Pete said. "So how do you get a provisional license anyway?"

"My mom took me to the DMV with a

form you have to fill out and a state-certified copy of my birth certificate." He frowned unexpectedly when he mentioned the birth certificate, as though thinking about it bothered him.

"Is something the matter?" Pete asked. He was afraid he'd asked too many questions or the wrong questions.

Jimmy looked at him blankly and then shook his head as if to clear it. "No," he said. "It's nothing."

"Come on over," Pete said, leading him toward the outdoor workshop. "You've already met Bob and Mallory. This is Jupiter, the head of our firm."

"Hi, Jimmy," Mallory said. "It's good to see you again."

"Yes," Bob said. "Thanks for coming."

Jimmy was looking at the chess set, which Jupiter had arranged on a small table with chairs on either side of it. His face was alive with interest. "Who plays chess?" he asked.

"Jupiter does," Pete said. "We think he's pretty good."

Jimmy gave Jupiter an interested look.

"Would you like to play a game?" Jupiter asked.

Jimmy smiled shyly. "Yeah," he said.

"That would be cool."

Bob gave everyone a soda as Jimmy and Jupiter sat down in the two chairs facing one another. Jupiter's side had the white pieces. "White first," Jimmy said, and Jupiter moved one of his pawns out two spaces.

Jimmy countered and the game started. No one said anything, certainly not the two players, and Pete, together with Mallory and Bob, watched, absorbed in the play. Pete tried to figure out what strategies the two were using, but since he'd only played chess a few times, he knew he was no expert.

Nevertheless, it didn't take an expert to see that Jimmy was way better than Jupiter. Before long Jupe started losing pieces, and it was no surprise when Jimmy said "Check," and then, not long afterwards, "Checkmate." Jimmy seemed embarrassed at how easily he'd won.

But Jupiter seemed quietly pleased – a bit of a surprise to Pete because Jupiter didn't usually like to lose. But maybe, Pete thought, he was winning at another game.

"You're very good," Jupiter said. "You whipped me."

"I was lucky," Jimmy said. "By the way, I understand that you're the golden eagle in the logo. The Shoshone have a special reverence for the golden eagle. And I told Bob that the Wind River Reservation has bighorn sheep again. So it's got all three of your spirit animals now."

"Are they really our spirit animals?" Pete asked, excited. "I thought you couldn't have one if you weren't Native American."

Jimmy frowned, as he had earlier about the birth certificate. "I don't know," he said. "I don't see why anyone couldn't have a spirit animal. Even Indians from India!"

"Let's play again," Jupiter said, turning the board around so that Jimmy would start. "Maybe this time we could talk a little as we play."

"O.K.," Jimmy said. "About what?"

"About why you came today," Jupiter said. "About your father and the police investigation and so forth."

Jimmy moved one of his pawns forward two ranks.

Jupiter countered, moving a pawn forward that opened up one of his bishops. He sat back, looking at Jimmy and not the board.

"Mallory and Bob told me that you and your parents moved to California so that your mother could get more training as a nurse,"

Jupiter said.

Jimmy moved another pawn forward. "That's right," he said. "It was great for my mom, but my dad didn't like it so much. He missed the horses. The Shoshone were the first northern tribe to get horses from the Spaniards. They have a whole herd of wild mustangs on the reservation."

Pete noticed a cloud pass over Jimmy's face. Why, he wondered, did Jimmy say "they" when he should have said "we"?

Jupiter took his bishop out one rank – into the space his pawn had vacated – threatening Jimmy's open rook. Jimmy countered by blocking him with a pawn.

"The res had a working ranch when my dad was growing up," Jimmy said. "My father was just a natural – really good with all kinds of horses. For a while he even rode the rodeo circuit, which is how he met my mom. She was a nurse at a rodeo in Nevada.

"It happened real quick," Jimmy went on. "They fell in love. He was twenty-one, I think, and he moved to the Duck Valley res, which was where my mom lived. He carved their names on one of the only trees around – Thomas + Jacinta."

Jupiter moved one of his knights out onto

the field.

"My dad worked with horses on the res in Nevada, and also out here after they moved. But he missed Nevada and Wyoming."

"Your mom must be a great nurse," Pete said, "to have the tribe pay for her to study out here."

"She's all right," Jimmy said. He stared at the board, his voice steady. Pete could tell from his tone that Jimmy and his mother didn't get along that well. "I think she'd stay out here if she could, but I miss my friends and want to go back. Not that she pays much attention to what I want."

"Your father still has family on the Wind River Reservation?" Jupiter asked matter-of-factly.

Jimmy nodded. "A lot of family. I've got relatives I've never even met. Some of my cousins have gone bad, though. They're into drugs, and there's a lot of guns and violence on the res. The sheriff even suspected that someone in the Littlewolf clan might have killed my father, but they could never find any evidence."

By this time, Jimmy had mobilized his forces and was mounting a full attack on Jupiter, whose pieces had gotten stuck in a corner of the board.

Jupiter moved a rook out as he asked about Jimmy's half-brother Jake.

"Bob and Mallory told me and Pete that he works in a casino, and also on a ranch near the San Bernardino National Forest."

"That right," Jimmy said. "Sometimes he stays down there. He got the job in the casino through a friend named Mackie something who's working there. He got the job at the ranch through my father, though."

"About Jake," Jupiter said, moving his queen out of danger, but enabling Jimmy to take one of his bishops. "I understand that he's been jealous of you because he thought your father was a better dad than his was. But your father must have tried to be his father, too, if he helped him get a job at that ranch."

"He *did* try," Jimmy said. "He taught Jake about horses – though Jake never got anywhere near as good as my dad was."

Jupiter captured one of Jimmy's pawns with a knight, but Jimmy swiftly took one of Jupiter's rooks. The game didn't look too good for Jupe, Pete thought.

"Can you tell us anything else about your father's death?" Jupiter asked. "Mallory and Bob told me that your father didn't drink but that his clothes were soaked with alcohol.

Did the police have a theory to account for that?"

"The police found broken glass at the top of the cliff," Jimmy said, "from a bottle of whiskey. Some moron in the sheriff's department concluded the bottle belonged to my father, but everyone on the res knew my father had stopped drinking a long time before. He was a hell-raiser as a kid, but he stopped drinking when he was twenty. He grew up thinking that Indians weren't any more likely to become drunks than anybody else, but after he'd been drinking for several years, he changed his mind about that. My mom thinks like a scientist, and she believes that Native Americans just don't have certain genetic protections that others have."

"All the cowboy movies I saw when I was young," Pete said, "showed Indians getting drunk a lot quicker than anyone else. Isn't that true?"

"Check," Jimmy said – but not to Pete. To Jupiter.

"Whoa!" Pete said. "Where did that come from?"

"Beware the subtle attack," Jupiter said admiringly. He moved his king out of danger.

"I think what Jimmy's trying to say is

that it *is* true," said Jupiter. "It seems that a lot of Native Americans *do* have a genetic propensity toward alcoholism."

As Jimmy listened to Jupiter, he looked more and more unhappy − even though all that Jupiter was saying was what Jimmy himself had already said. Finally, he moved his queen on the diagonal, held it in the air above a square on the board, and after looking carefully, put it down gently.

"Checkmate," he said quietly. But rather than looking happy, he looked even more depressed. Pete was mystified. Why would a possible genetic basis for Native American alcoholism depress Jimmy Littlewolf, if his father had managed to give up drinking when he found it wasn't good for him?

"Well," Jupiter said. "Thanks for the two games. You're very good."

"Thank you," Jimmy said − but he still didn't look happy.

"The Three Investigators will do everything we can to help you," Jupiter said. "I've already made an appointment with the Chief of Police here in Rocky Beach, and he's always been of great assistance. We also have a friend who's a history professor who grew up in Lander, and we're going to be consulting with her as well. We'll be in touch soon. Maybe we could meet Jake and your mother? It would be good to talk to them about the case – but without them knowing who we are or what we're doing."

Jimmy's expression changed. He suddenly looked hopeful and optimistic.

"That would be great!" he said. "Because I'm pretty sure that Jake knows something he's not telling. Like he's keeping it from me to torture me."

"If so, we'll try to find out what it is," Jupiter said. "Don't worry."

It seemed to Pete that Jimmy had been waiting the whole time he'd been there to say what he'd just said. Now that he'd said it, he felt a whole lot better.

"Maybe we could go undercover to that casino," Pete suggested. "The one over in Highland where Jake works. If he had no idea who we were, maybe we could get a better feeling for who he is and whether he really knows something. And maybe after that we could go and talk to your mom."

"That would work," Jimmy said. "My mother should be home tomorrow afternoon, and Jake's hours at the casino are in the morning. If you went there then, you'd be sure to catch him. Then you could come visit me and my mom in the afternoon. Do you have something to write on?"

Bob gave him a piece of paper and he quickly wrote something down and handed it to Jupiter. "The address of the casino near Highland," he said, "and our address in Palisade Point."

To Pete he looked almost like a different person, as though a real weight had been taken off his shoulders.

"Thanks a lot, you guys," he said. "I really appreciate this." He walked to the car with a lighter step. Everyone waved as Jimmy turned the Buick around and left the Salvage Yard.

"An interesting case," Jupiter said, "and a nice guy. I hope we can help him."

"I think we already have," Mallory said. "Between yesterday and today, we've made a difference."

Pete watched until he couldn't see the Buick any more. His mind had gone back to provisional driver's licenses and all the steps you needed to go through before California let you drive. He'd been so looking forward to tooling around in another year or so.

Oh, well, he thought. He really liked

Worthington and they could keep hiring him –
though he hoped Worthington would be happy
riding shotgun, while Pete and Bob and maybe
Mallory, actually drove the Flex when the time
came.

Even as he thought this, Pete realized
that thinking about his future driving at a time
like this wasn't very sensitive. He really *should*
be thinking about ways to help Jimmy Littlewolf. The only problem was that he had no
idea in the world how he and the other Three
Investigators were actually going to do that.
After all, none of them had ever even been to
Wyoming – and they weren't likely to get there
anytime soon!

5

Worthington Gets The Goods

The next morning Bob sat on the porch of his house, waiting for Worthington to arrive to pick him up. He looked at his watch. It was almost nine-thirty, and he expected Worthington and the others at any minute. Still, he thought, there was no need to simply sit. His laptop lay on his knees, his backpack at his feet.

They were headed to the Mission Indian casino near Highland where Jake Blackhorse worked, and Bob was doing a little quick research. Jupiter had been right, of course, when he'd said that Indian reservations throughout America were actually sovereign nations – like little foreign countries legally established and allowed within the United States.

They were distinct from the states in which they were located and they established their own governing bodies and made their own laws – though they were also subject to federal laws. The tribes themselves determined who was a member of the tribe and who wasn't, who could live on the reservation and who couldn't, and what businesses and other activities were allowed on their land.

When it came to the murder of Jimmy's father, it had taken place just outside the boundaries of the Wind River Reservation, but Bob saw right away that if it had happened inside the res, state and local law enforcement would have had no power – only federal and tribal authorities could have investigated. As it was, the local sheriff had been in charge.

It was odd, Bob suddenly thought, that when Leif had picked Bob and Mallory up from their climbing expedition to Palisade Point, he'd said something along the lines of You're both still alive! I always expect that when it comes to climbing, what goes up must come down. Hard."

At the time, neither Bob nor Mallory had known that soon they'd be listening to Jimmy Littlewolf tell the story of his father dying from a fall down a rock face. For all the confidence Bob had gained as a climber in the years since he'd hurt himself badly when climbing alone, there was something about this odd conjunction of events that seemed a bit unnerving.

Of course, odd conjunctions of events happened all the time, but they weren't always quite so personal – and as Bob thought about this, he closed his laptop and started thinking about how he might write a mystery story about a coincidence like that one.

Not case notes, but an actual story. A fiction, in which something strange and surprising was discovered to connect the death of a man who'd fallen off a cliff and the life of a boy who investigated his death. Maybe Bob *didn't* have the kind of talent that would let him peer into a dystopian future and warn humankind what might happen if they kept walking down a particular, dangerous path — but maybe this he could do. Write a mystery, of sorts.

By now, he knew a lot about them, and although at the moment he couldn't think of a single way to connect the cliff-related experiences of Thomas Littlewolf and himself, he had the feeling that if he thought about it long enough — and if he sat down at his keyboard with a brand new file opened up — he might come up with something.

Which, in turn, made him wonder whether he should actually take part in this creativity study Hector Sebastian had recommended him for.

The thing was, on the case during which he had called Hector on his cellphone when he was out riding on the Double Fork Ranch – a case involving a lost novel written by the Russian-American writer Vadim Fedorov – Bob and the others had been amazed when they'd learned that Vadim had been only one of four creative artists who'd been born in four generations of male Fedorovs.

Vadim's father, Fyodor, had been an actor who'd won an Academy Award; Vadim himself had been one of the most successful mystery writers of his generation; his son Yuri had been a composer who'd written soundtracks for the movies; and his grandson Ivan was a singer-songwriter.

Since Bob's mother was an evolutionary biologist and his father was a writer, even without the close-up and personal view of the Fedorov family, Bob might have been tempted to take part in Dr. Yang's Janusian Creativity Study.

Even so, he felt strangely reluctant to have anyone take his DNA and then cross-match it with his answers to questions on a standardized test.

In fact, he was afraid both he and Mallory might be right that there were dangers in having one's creativity messed with. At the beginning of any creative project, you really *didn't* want to say too much about it in case someone said something that made you lose faith in it. And if that were true with any specific project, how much *more* true would it be if the project you were just at the beginning of was your own life?

The sound of an approaching car interrupted Bob's thoughts, and he looked up to see Worthington glide to a stop at the curb. Mallory sat in the passenger seat of the Flex and waved to him.

"Come on!" she called.

Bob was secretly pleased that he'd been picked up last. Usually he had to ride in the middle of the back seat, wedged between Jupiter and Pete, but now Pete moved over into the middle and Bob got the window seat for once. Everyone was in good spirits as they took off for the casino, about an hour and a half away.

"I thought we were in trouble for a while," Jupiter said. "I called the casino and asked what the legal gambling age is at this particular place. Luckily it's 18 and not 21."

"Do you think we'll pass for 18?" Pete asked.

"I don't think passing will work," Mallory said. "They'll want I.D."

"So what will we do?" Pete asked.

"I asked if you had to be 18 to even get through the door," Jupiter said, "and they told me we can get in as long as we're accompanied by an adult, but only if we're there to eat at one of the restaurants."

"Worthington's an adult," Bob observed.

Worthington laughed. "Most of the time I pass for one," he said.

"So that will work," Pete said. "We'll eat at one of the restaurants!"

"But we need a plan," Jupiter said. "We can't just arrive there and walk in and hope for the best."

"I have an idea," Worthington said. "The real reason for this trip is to see if you can find out anything from this Jake Blackhorse. Is that right?"

"That's correct," Jupiter said. "He's a cage cashier. He sells tokens."

"Perhaps you could pretend to be my son if we're ever questioned – and Pete, Bob, and Mallory are your friends," Worthington said. "I'll buy some tokens from Mr. Blackhorse – maybe $50 worth – and try to engage him in conversation. The four of you can stand nearby and listen."

"What about the fact that you have an English accent and Jupiter doesn't?" Pete asked. "I mean, if you're father and son."

"Jupiter will just have to keep his mouth shut," Worthington said, "no matter how difficult that might be."

Everyone laughed at that, even Jupiter. "Besides," Worthington went on. "I don't even see how that would come up."

"Perhaps not," Jupiter said. "But Pete's right. We need to be prepared."

"I will be," said Worthington.

"I hope we have $50, Worthington," Pete said. "We sure don't want you to spend your own money."

"That's thoughtful, Pete," Worthington said. "But since I won't be gambling with the tokens, I can just cash them in before we leave and get my money back."

As they approached Highland, Bob started looking for the casino, but he didn't see it until Worthington started driving up the long approach. Compared to the huge electronic billboard, which was constantly changing, advertising the $3.99 all-you-can-eat buffet one instant and the number of slot machines the next in bursts of red, blue, and gold, the building itself was boring – squat and low and beige.

As they parked in the nearly empty lot, Bob had to remind himself that it was eleven o'clock in the morning, and that most people were at work, or living their lives. Anyone gambling at this hour was either on vacation or in trouble. He imagined that, at night, there were flashy spotlights and glitzy displays.

Before now, Bob had only seen casinos on television, and those had been in Las Vegas – gaudy and opulent extravaganzas, with fountains and exotic animals and limousines and re-creations of ancient Egypt and Rome. This was nothing like those. It seemed a little run-down.

They walked through the dark tinted glass of the entrance doors and Bob was instantly disoriented. It had been quiet outside, but, inside, the building pulsed with electronic music – a persistent beat that made Bob's heart pick up. It was dark, like endless night. There were no windows. He had entered an inside world of flashing lights, neon, loud noise, stale cigarette smoke, and the smell of spilled liquor.

The carpet underfoot was a riot of incoherent colors. Ranks of slot machines stood in front of them, blinking and throbbing. Bob saw you didn't need to walk far to start losing your money. His impulse was to run for the doors. How could people stand this? This was like every dystopian future Bob had ever read about rolled into one horrible place. He half expected to see killer robots emerge from the walls.

"Whoa!" Pete said.

"Yikes!" Mallory said. "Get me out of here."

"It's O.K.," Jupiter said, though he was clearly rattled as well. "We have a job to do. Lead on, Worthington. We'll follow."

Like the parking lot, the casino was largely empty, but among the ranks of slots, Bob saw bleary-eyed men and women, with plastic cups filled with tokens, walking like zombies up and down, feeding the machines, which whizzed and banged and sent off bugle calls when someone won. Some people sat on long-legged stools in front of video poker machines, staring at the display as if waiting for a message.

He and the others followed Worthington as he threaded his way through the slots, past a fancy coffee shop, to a more open area at the center of the casino. Overhead a dome opened up, decorated with a chandelier in the shape of a huge Native American war shield – a series of concentric gold circles and radiating lines at the ends of which large bulbs burned. This was where the gaming tables were found – black-jack and craps and roulette.

At one end was the cashier's cage, a circular kiosk with four counters, the whole thing encased in an elaborate gold enclosure. Only one of the counters had a cashier behind it. As they got close, Bob could see that he wore a plastic name tag that said JAKE BLACKHORSE.

"There he is," Jupiter said.

From what Bob could observe, Jake Blackhorse must have taken more after his mother than his father, since he didn't look very much like Jimmy at all. His black hair was cut in a fade, short on top and vanishing entirely on the sides and back. He had the same dark brown eyes, but while Jimmy's had looked haunted, Jake's looked hard. He was wearing a green plastic visor and stared vacantly out at the casino floor, searching for a potential customer.

The five of them stood to the side, out of Jake's range of sight, to firm up their plans.

"Any suggestions?" Worthington asked.

"I was thinking," Jupiter said. "We're trying to get Jake talking about Jimmy or things related to the case. What if you were to pretend to be a chess hustler who's never been in a casino before and is hoping that in some back room there's a chess match for money?"

"That's a good idea," Pete said. "If Jake

thinks about chess, he'll undoubtedly think about Jimmy."

"I can work with that," Worthington said. "Thanks, Jupiter."

"Whatever happens," Jupiter said, "we'll know more about Jake at the end than we do now. Good luck."

Worthington sauntered over to the open counter. Instantly Jake snapped to attention. Bob positioned himself as best he could to see and hear everything.

"Good morning, sir," Jake said. "How may I help?"

Worthington smiled broadly. When he spoke, his English accent was more pronounced than it had been in years. He put a $50 bill on the counter and pushed it at Jake. "I believe I need some – what are they called? – chips, if I am to play."

"Chips or tokens," Jake said. "You can call them anything you want, as long as you spend them."

"Ha, ha," Worthington said. "That's very good, young man."

"I like your accent," Jake said.

"Yes," Worthington said. "Right out of *Masterpiece Theater*."

Bob had never seen Worthington 'act'

before – though that was what he had done when he'd first come over from England. He was really very good.

"Are you here on vacation?" Jake asked, seemingly trying to be friendly.

"No," Worthington said. "I've been in America for years. I was wondering where the chess games were."

"Chess?" Jimmy asked. He looked puzzled.

"Yes," Worthington said. "I was hoping there was a room somewhere in this establishment where people played chess for money."

"Here?" Jake asked. "I'm afraid not. Poker, yes. Blackjack yes. But not chess."

"That's a shame," Worthington said.

"I didn't even know people played chess for money," Jake said.

"Yes, indeed," Worthington said. "When I first came to this country I lived in New York City. Often on the weekends I'd go down to Greenwich Village, to Washington Square Park, which is quite famous for its chess players, many of whom play for money. In fact, there are a number of built-in tables in the park's southwest corner. Usually, I'd go home with much more money than I'd come with."

"Sweet," Jake said. "A regular hustler."

Worthington smiled. "That's one word for it."

"I'll have to tell my brother," Jake said. "He's really good at chess. Maybe I should tell him he could earn a living like that."

"Part of a living," Worthington said. "The stakes are sometimes quite low. So you have a brother? I have a half-brother. He's eight years younger than I am. I know you're supposed to love your family, but I absolutely can't stand him."

Jake's mouth fell open. "How weird is that?" he said. "My brother's really my half-brother, too, and I'm eight years older than him. To tell you the truth, I can't stand mine either. He thinks he's so much better than me, and he's still wet behind the ears. But I get my own back."

"Really?" Worthington said, sounding interested. "How is that?"

"I mess with his head," Jake said proudly. "I tell him stuff that's only partly true, or not true at all, that he doesn't want to hear. Then I watch him squirm."

"And it works? Worthington said. "He believes you?"

"Absolutely," Jake said. "I've got him believing a bunch of stuff right now, and it's driving him crazy."

"Well, thanks for the tip," Worthington said. "I'll have to try that."

"Here are your tokens," Jake said, sweeping them into a plastic cup and pushing them across the counter at Worthington. "Good luck."

Worthington walked away from the cage, toward the gaming tables. Bob was watching him, so he didn't see the security guard until he was right on them. He was mid-fifties, overweight, his stomach bulging in his blue uniform. Bob was instantly alarmed.

"Excuse me," he said, in a tone both nasty and condescending. "I think the four of you are too young to be in here."

"No," Jupiter said. "It's all right. We're with my father."

"Where is he?" the guard asked.

By then Worthington had seen what was happening and had hurried over. "Is there a problem?" he asked.

Bob looked at Worthington in shock. All traces of an English accent were gone. He was an excellent actor, Bob thought.

"These youngsters with you?" the guard asked.

"Yes," Worthington said. "This is my

son, and these are his friends.”

“All right then,” the guard said. “Keep them close and away from the tables.”

“Thanks for the advice,” Worthington said. “Come on, you guys. Let's get something to eat.” Bob and the others followed him as he walked away.

“Worthington, you were great!” Pete said.

“Why thank you, Pete,” Worthington said. “I quite enjoyed that.”

“What should we do now?” Bob asked.

“We should do what Worthington said and hit the buffet,” Pete said. “I'm hungry.”

The all-you-can-eat buffet was in the back of the building, next to a large polished mahogany bar, and after they'd paid and loaded their plates, they took a seat at a round table. Bob glanced at Pete's tray. He'd managed a miracle − his plate held spare ribs, several egg rolls, a breast of fried chicken, four jumbo shrimp, crab legs, and a piece of broccoli.

“What are you looking at?” Pete said.

Between mouthfuls, they talked about what Worthington had learned from Jake Blackhorse.

“It might not seem like much information," Jupiter said, "but it's actually quite important to learn that he's made a game out of lying to Jimmy and that he does it intentionally to confuse him."

"It's a horrible thing to do," Mallory said. "But it will certainly give us a place to start when we talk to Jimmy and his mother."

"I bet he'll be relieved to hear his suspicions are correct," Bob said.

"We could ask him to tell us anything odd that Jake's said to him since his father's murder," Mallory said. "If there's a pattern to the lies, that could lead us somewhere important. After all, Jimmy must have been thinking of something specific when he told us that he thought Jake knew something he wasn't telling. Like the truth."

Bob looked at Pete, who was wiping his mouth and looking a bit pained. "Dessert?" Bob asked him.

"Are you kidding me?" Pete said. "That last egg roll did me in."

"Is there anything else we should do," Jupiter asked, "before we head back toward Palisade Point?"

"I've been thinking," Mallory said. "It would be great if we could find out more information from Jake. Who knows when we'll get a second chance?"

"What's your idea?" Jupiter asked.

"Maybe I could talk to him," Mallory said. "When he takes his next break, I could go up to him and do the same thing Worthington did and the same thing he's been doing to Jimmy — lie."

"Lie about what?" Pete asked.

"What if I pretend I'm a runaway with no money and nowhere to sleep and I've just been dumped by my Native American boyfriend, who's from the Wind River Reservation? I could act all flustered and like I need help. If I mention the reservation in a totally different context than the one he's used to, maybe I can surprise him into saying something about it."

"That's tricky," Jupiter said, "but an excellent idea."

"You'd have to be careful," Pete said. "You can't seem too helpless or maybe he'll try something."

"Don't worry," Mallory said. "I can take care of myself."

"I'm sure you can," Jupiter said.

Bob was totally amazed at Mallory's suggestion. He could see that she was excited by her idea. She'd pretended to be someone else in order to help them with a case a number of times before, and he knew she was a good actress. But she'd never tried anything like this before.

And that was another reason Bob liked her – because once she'd made up her mind to do something, she just plunged forward and did it. It might take her a while to make up her mind, but then – bam! Bob was a lot more tentative and cautious. Which was both a good thing and a bad thing, sometimes.

Right now, he was feeling slightly better than he had when they'd first come into the casino – sitting down and eating some food had helped a lot. Still, he found the place almost unbearable. When it came to gambling, he was mystified. The promise of turning a small amount of money into a fortune was a lure that most people just couldn't resist. Work was hard, which was why so many harbored the dream of instant wealth – the lottery, or the horses, or a slot machine that suddenly paid off.

And Native Americans and gambling were a weird match, Bob thought. When Bob, a few days before, had said to Jupiter that he'd always thought it was really depressing that so many Indian tribes needed to make their money off of casinos, Jupiter had said that although Native Americans *had* played games of chance, they had preferred games of skill.

Bob guessed you could argue that casinos were a way of taking back money from all the whites who had stolen their lands and livelihoods, but he was still shaken by the idea that Native Americans on reservations all over the country had become dependent on casino profits.

It seemed a final tragic indignity, really. Millions had died of diseases to which they had no immunity, brought by foreign invaders, millions more through the loss of their lands and livelihoods and through wars they were forced to fight against an army with rifles and muskets when all they had were bows and arrows. Bob was glad that Thomas Littlewolf, Jimmy's father, had been so good with horses and had found work through his own talents – although in a way, that actually made his death worse. It would be great if Mallory could find out something that would help.

But just as Mallory stood up and said, "I'm going back to the cashier's cage to keep an eye on Jake," a sudden loud and clangorous noise startled them all. It was the sound of a klaxon – loud, shocking, and very close. Bob's heart leapt. It almost sounded like an ambulance – a high-pitched bleat followed by a low growl, alternating every half-second, sending his pulse racing.

People were screaming "Oh, my God!" as spotlights began swirling, raking the walls and ceiling in sickening greens and pinks.

Jupiter had grown very still. Pete was on tiptoe, trying to see what was going on. Mallory put her hands over her ears, a pained expression on her face. People started rushing from the slot machines where they'd been seated, mindlessly pumping in tokens, to the middle aisle. Bob expected to see white-clad paramedics at any moment.

"Can we help?" Pete said anxiously.

"I doubt it," Jupiter said over the tumult. "It seems that someone finally hit the jackpot."

What? Bob thought. The five of them got up and peered around the bank of slots. Halfway down was a scene Bob could hardly have imagined. A man in his fifties, with a grizzled beard, was holding a cowboy hat under a spout that was shooting out tokens at an alarming clip. The hat was full and tokens were piling up on the carpet at his feet.

The man had an expression of fierce delight – even triumph – as if he had just finished wrestling a bull calf to the ground after roping it in a rodeo. Even stranger, from Bob's point of view, the people pressing around the jackpot winner were almost swooning – as if just by being near him they were upping their chances of a similar lucky win. Although no killer robots emerged from the walls of the casino to start wrecking havoc on the delirious and distracted human beings, Bob could tell that even if they had, the human beings would hardly have noticed.

In life, there was swift death and slow death, Bob thought. This was slow death. Anyone who thought it was a cause for celebration to have coins pile up at his feet – coins that probably couldn't make up for years of gambling losses – was to be pitied rather than congratulated. That should be left for real skill and real accomplishment, not this empty groveling in front of a flashing raucous machine.

6

Mallory Goes Undercover

Five minutes later, the tumult had finally died down, and Mallory repeated the comment she'd made just before the klaxon started blaring. "O.K. Now I'm really going back to the cashier's cage."

"Watch out for that security guard," Pete said.

"I will," Mallory said. "You stay here." As she walked back into the casino, headed for Jake Blackhorse, she gathered the thoughts that had been interrupted by the jackpot. She felt good about her idea – but also a bit surprised. To her consternation she'd realized she'd adapted the plot of a cheesy TV movie she'd found herself watching one night. There had been no Wind River Reservation in that story and no Indian boyfriend – the boyfriend had been quite generic. But otherwise it was the same sad story she was about to tell to Jake – at least if he gave her the chance to. Mallory hoped she wasn't becoming too American too fast.

The main point was that she had a lot of

114

sympathy for Jimmy Littlewolf – a *lot* of sympathy – and if she could help him by finding out something else from his older half-brother, she wanted to. Jupiter had told Jimmy they'd be at his house in Palisade Point by about two that afternoon, so she had about a half hour to discover whatever she could before they had to leave the casino.

The guard was patrolling the area between the blackjack tables and the roulette tables, and Mallory gave him a wide berth. She leaned against a mirrored pillar, which she kept between herself and him. Her position had a good view of the cashier's cage.

As it turned out, she'd gotten there just in time. Another young man, wearing the same uniform, came up to Jake and started talking. Jake nodded his head, opened a drawer, and gestured at it. Jake was about to take his break, and the other guy would be covering for him.

Mallory watched as Jake opened a hidden swinging door in the side of the cage and stepped through, no longer wearing his visor. He took off at a brisk clip, and Mallory had to rush to follow him. It turned out he was headed toward a Burger King franchise inside the casino where he stood in line, handed the cashier a chit of some sort, and then carried his tray to a booth along the perimeter.

Someone else was already sitting there; he wore the same uniform Jake wore − obviously another cashier − and it soon became clear to Mallory that they'd arranged to meet for lunch. Jake picked up the oversized cup from his tray and took a big gulp. Then he put it down and started laughing at something his friend had said.

The place was crowded; almost all of the tables were filled. Though Mallory wasn't in the least bit hungry, she ordered a small fries and a small coffee and then walked the room, pretending to have trouble finding a place to sit. With her red hair, she stood out in the semigloom of the burger place, and as she walked past Jake and then walked past him again, she caught him looking at her.

The third time, she stopped. "Excuse me," she said. "Do you mind if I join you? The other tables are mostly filled. I promise I won't bother you."

The guy opposite Jake looked a bit startled, but immediately smiled. He had a warm open face. His name tag read 'Mackie.' "Sure," he said. "We've got plenty of room."

Jake scooted over and Mallory sat next to him. "Thanks," she said. "I'm Mallory."

The two men were quiet, watching her. She picked up a fry and then put it back down on the tray and sighed. "I guess I'm not very hungry," she said. She hoped that if Jake thought she wanted help, not information, he'd be more inclined to open up and talk. "Do you two work here?" she asked, gesturing toward their uniforms.

"We sure do," Jake said. He looked at her closely. "You're not from around here, are you?"

"What do you mean?" Mallory asked.

"You have a strange accent. There was this guy, earlier, with an English accent. But you're not English, are you?"

"No," Mallory said, a bit alarmed at his mention of Worthington. "I'm from Scotland. But right now I'm from nowhere." She tried to make her voice sound as sad as possible.

"What's that mean?" Jake asked.

"I'm sort of homeless, I guess," Mallory said. "My mother and I moved to California a year ago, but we don't get along. So I ran away about six months ago with my boyfriend, and I've basically been living on the streets since he dumped me. I was hoping to find a job somewhere."

"How old are you?" Jake asked.

"Sixteen," Mallory said, "and a half." She didn't know if it would fly, but Jake didn't seem to think anything of it.

"How did you get in here? It's eighteen to gamble," Jake said.

"I walked," Mallory said. "No one stopped me."

"Well, you sure can't work in the casino," Jake said. "It's 21 to work in here. But you might find something at the hotel."

"There's a hotel connected to the casino?" Mallory asked.

"Yeah," Jake said. "It's nothing fancy, but they might be able to use you in housekeeping."

"Thanks," Mallory said. "I'll check it out."

Jake had finished his fries and was looking at Mallory's. "Are you going to eat those?" he asked.

Mallory shook her head.

"Do you mind?" he asked. As he reached to take them, Mackie slapped his hand away. "Don't be gross, man," he said. "The girl needs to keep up her strength."

Mallory looked at him with an expression she hoped conveyed gratitude. After that, she thought she ought to eat a fry or two, so she did.

"Your boyfriend dumped you, huh?" Jake said. "What's that about?"

"He's Native American," Mallory said. "I can't remember which tribe. He was originally from a reservation in Wyoming, but he came to California to check it out. He didn't like it much. He may have gone back there. I can't remember the name of the place."

Jake's face registered a good bit of surprise. "I'm Native American," he said. "Western Shoshone and Paiute. Did you know?"

"I sort of guessed," Mallory said.

"There's only one reservation in all of Wyoming," Jake told her. "And it's huge. It's called the Wind River Reservation. Was your boyfriend Eastern Shoshone or Arapaho?"

"Eastern Shoshone, I think," Mallory said. Jake nodded thoughtfully.

"Maybe I should hitchhike there," she continued. "Do you think I could find him?"

"Maybe," Jake said. "If he wants to be found. But I know someone who drives out to Wyoming from time to time − a guy I work with."

"Here at the casino?" Mallory asked.

"No," Jake said, moving a bit closer. "I

have a part-time job at a ranch in Redlands, just south of here. He drives horse trailers back and forth between Wyoming and California. He might be willing to take a passenger sometime." He grinned at her suggestively.

Mallory tried to move away without making it obvious. She took a sip of her coffee, which was now cold and bitter. "Really?" she said, trying to act as though that would be great. "What does he do in Wyoming? What's his name?"

"Travis Garrett," Jake said. "He was a friend of my stepfather's − which is how I got the job on the ranch. I bet if I asked him as a favor to take you on his next trip to Wyoming, he'd do it. Of course, you'd have to like horses, because that's what he does, bringing them back and forth. Some of the horses he handles can be pretty wild. So if you want to go, I might be able to arrange it."

"But whatever you do," Mackie said, leaning forward, "don't hitchhike. Do you know how dangerous that would be? You? Alone? You're crazy."

"I guess I wasn't thinking," Mallory said.

"You should take the bus," Mackie said. "It's a long way to Wyoming, but it's a nice ride, across Nevada and Utah and then up into

Idaho and over to Wyoming. Lots of great scenery. And the bus doesn't cost that much." He smiled encouragingly.

Mackie had light brown skin, dark curly hair, and mischievous eyes. Mallory liked him right away. He seemed completely different from Jake – more sincere and smarter. "Thanks for the advice," she said. "How do you know?"

"I lived in Nevada for a couple of summers," Mackie said. "I was staying with my parents. My dad's a doctor at the clinic on the Duck Valley res where Jake's mother worked. That's how I met this numbskull." He gestured with his chin toward Jake. "He helped me get a job at the casino where he was working in a town called Jackpot and I liked it a lot. Really open country, lots of space – not at all like California. I returned the favor and got Jake this job down here in this casino. I'm Mackie Gupta, by the way."

Good heavens, Mallory thought. When Jimmy Littlewolf had said his brother had a friend named Mackie, from the Duck Valley Reservation, she'd thought he was Native American.

"So you're an Indian from India," she said.

Mackie laughed. "Partly true," he said. "My dad was born in Mumbai, but my mom actually has some Native American blood, from a California tribe I can't pronounce. After my dad finished medical school, he got a job on a rancheria up north, which is where he met my mother. So I'm part American Indian and part Indian Indian. As a matter of fact, I know exactly which part is which. A while back, Jake and I took DNA tests together, as a kick."

Jake shifted in his seat and looked a bit uncomfortable. Mallory didn't know why and didn't know how to pursue the issue, so she pretended she was a good deal less knowledgeable than she was.

"I don't know anything about DNA," she said. "But I'd be pretty sure I'm Scottish even if I hadn't met my father's family. I mean, with my red hair and pale skin." She glanced at her watch and saw that it was time to leave.

"Where are you going?" Jake asked. "I thought I could take you to the hotel and introduce you."

"That's nice of you," Mallory said, "but I've got to meet someone. Could you tell me how to get in touch with Travis Garrett?"

"I don't have that info on me," he said. "But if you want to come by sometime to the

Mustang Ranch, outside of Redlands, I can introduce you."

"The Mustang Ranch," she said. "O.K. Maybe I'll do that." She stood. "Thanks for letting me sit with you two, and thanks for the help and advice. It was good to meet you."

She got rid of her tray and walked all the way out of the casino, past the buffet and the gaming tables and the slots, not looking toward Worthington, Jupiter, Pete, and Bob, but trusting they'd seen her.

Once she was outside in the blazing parking lot, she turned to see the four of them bursting through the tinted glass doors. They all hurried over to the Flex, climbed in, and headed back north to Palisade Point.

"How'd it go?" Pete asked almost immediately.

"Pretty well, I think," Mallory said. "But first, Worthington, you made quite an impression on our friend Jake Blackhorse."

"Did I?" Worthington said.

"Yes," Mallory said. "He mentioned the 'guy with the English accent.' And remember you telling us one of your grandfathers was from India?"

"Certainly," Worthington said.

"As it turns out I just met someone else

with ties to India," Mallory said. "Someone nice, I think."

"I thought you were going to talk to Jimmy's brother," Bob said.

"I did," Mallory said. "But he was having lunch with a friend of his — the guy Jimmy told us about yesterday. Remember 'Mackie something'?"

"Yes," Jupiter said.

"It turns out his name is Mackie Gupta, and he told me his father is Indian and his mother is part Native American. Anyway, I liked him and I was interested in his story. When I grew up in Scotland, just about everyone was just plain Scottish, but over here there's no such thing as plain American. One of the most amazing things about this country is that it's such a melting pot that just about any combination is not only possible but probable. Bob is half Chinese and half Scots/Viking, and Jupiter is part Welsh and part Serbian."

"And my dad's Mexican and my mom's got Spanish blood," Pete said.

"Even me," Mallory said. "I might like to think of myself as Scottish, but after all, my mother is American, and her family was originally from northern England."

"We're all mongrels," Bob said. "Or mutts, if you like that better. The best kind of dogs, I understand," he added.

"That's true," Jupiter said. "At least in the case of dogs. They're resilient and healthy and adaptive."

"So why *shouldn't* Mackie Gupta be part Native American and part Indian from India?" Mallory asked. "I said I might hitchhike to Wyoming to find my made-up boyfriend, and he was like an older brother, telling me to take the bus. He made northern Nevada and eastern Idaho sound so beautiful I almost wish I could!"

"I hope we can all go to Wyoming," Pete said. "Maybe Mr. Sebastian will stay there next summer, and he'll invite us!"

"That would be great," Mallory said. "Really." She was more than ready to see other parts of the country she'd already decided to call home, and after the crowdedness of California, the idea of open space was very appealing.

"But there's something I haven't told you yet," she said. "Remember Jimmy mentioning that Jake worked two jobs? When I said I might hitchhike to Wyoming, Jake said he also worked at a place called the Mustang Ranch outside of Redlands with a guy named Travis Garrett. He said Garrett was a friend of Thomas Littlewolf, Jimmy's father, and that he drove horses back and forth to Wyoming every now and then."

Jupiter pinched his bottom lip. "Hmm," he said. "That's very interesting. Maybe we should go to the Mustang Ranch and meet him. Though not today. We don't have time. Jimmy Littlewolf is expecting us."

Twenty minutes later, they arrived at his house. As it turned out, he lived in a small well-kept brick ranch house in a working class neighborhood in Palisade Point. When Worthington drove up, Jimmy was on the front lawn, pacing. He stopped and waved as soon as he saw the Flex.

Mallory and the others got out of the car, but Worthington said, "I'm going to drive around a bit. I'll be back in an hour to pick you up." The Flex drove away as the four of them shook hands with Jimmy.

"Did you meet Jake?" he asked with repressed excitement.

"*I* did," Mallory said. "And our friend Worthington did, too. These three just saw him from a distance. We've got stuff to tell you."

"That's great," Jimmy said, "but first

you'd better come meet my mom."

The living room had a worn-down shag carpet and a sofa and easy chair covered in a plaid fabric. All the windows were open to get whatever breeze there was. Jimmy's mother must have heard them, because she came into the living room from what Mallory assumed was the kitchen. She was a nice-looking woman, friendly and petite, with an inquisitive smile. She was wearing a white nurse's uniform.

"Hello," she said. "I'm Jacinta Littlewolf, Jimmy's mother. You'll have to pardon my uniform. I just got back from my shift at the hospital."

The four of them, one by one, introduced themselves.

"I'm delighted you could come," Mrs. Littlewolf said. "I'm always glad to meet Jimmy's friends." She smiled at her son. Mallory was a bit puzzled; she'd gotten the impression that Jimmy and his mother didn't get along.

"He hasn't told me anything about you, really. Are you all from the chess club?" Mrs. Littlewolf asked.

Mallory could see that Pete was about to correct her misimpression, but a swift glance from Jupiter kept him quiet.

"We do play chess," Jupiter said coolly. "We're not as good as Jimmy, though. We're all still learning. He's beaten me every time we've played."

Mallory smiled. That was true – even though they'd only played twice, and both games had been yesterday.

"What I like about chess," Jupiter went on, "is that it focuses the mind; you really need to concentrate. It encourages you to be careful about the choices you make, and to make good ones. Our advisor told us that, out of the incredible number of moves we could make in a game, we had to choose the right one and then to stand behind it. He said, in that way, it was a lot like life."

"That's so true," Mrs. Littlewolf said, smiling warmly. "I'm so glad to hear Jimmy is so good. I don't know where he gets it!"

Jimmy scowled at this, surprising Mallory. He was too hard on his mother, she thought. She'd just been trying to compliment him.

"How did you get into nursing?" Bob asked. Mallory knew that Bob was consistently interested in the reasons people chose the jobs they chose.

"It's an unusual story," Mrs. Littlewolf said. "When I was quite a young girl, living on the reservation, I was playing outside around the woodshop when I heard a scream. I ran to see that one of the older boys had been using a table saw and he'd cut his hand quite badly. Blood was everywhere. He was running around, yelling. He'd have bled to death if one of the adults who was supervising hadn't stopped him and calmed him and applied a tourniquet. I found out I wasn't afraid of blood and had a strong impulse to help."

"Wow!" Pete said. "What a story!"

"This was on the Duck Valley Reservation in Nevada," Mrs. Littlewolf said. "After they'd built a new medical facility. I thought I'd like to work there when I got my nursing license. And I did, for a while, until the tribe sent me here to learn more. My husband was with me when we came, but he died not long after that." She looked quite sad.

Jimmy scowled again. "Died?" he said. "That's an odd way to put it when he was murdered. Someone hit him on the head with a club or a rock or something and then pushed him off a cliff. You could at least tell the truth about it."

Jimmy's mother looked as though they'd

had this argument before, maybe many times, and she tried to smile soothingly at Jimmy.

"Why don't you take your friends out to the back yard?" she said. "I put some sodas in the fridge and they should be cold by now. You all have a good time."

She smiled weakly, walked down a hallway, and disappeared into another room. It was clear to Mallory that Jimmy really did resent his mother, though she couldn't see why.

They got their drinks and went into the small fenced backyard where they sat on the ground in a shady patch. "So," Jimmy said. "About Jake."

"Before we get into that, an update on our end," Jupiter said. "Our meeting with Police Chief Reynolds is still on for tomorrow morning in Rocky Beach, and it looks like he can help us in our inquiry."

"And I've left a message for Dr. Paxton, the historian we mentioned who grew up in Lander. I'm sure she'll call me back, and we'll meet with her, too," Mallory said.

"That's really great," Jimmy said. "Now, tell me."

"Yes," Jupiter said. "Our friend Worthington, who drove us, pretended to be a gambler, and he got Jake to admit that he – as he put it − messes with your head."

Jimmy looked bewildered. "What do you think he meant?"

"I think he meant he tells you things that aren't true to confuse and upset you," Jupiter said. "Can you think of anything that fits the bill? There's no need for you to decide if what he said was a lie or not. Just tell us anything he's told you that no one else has. That'll be a good place to start. But before you do, Mallory should tell you what she learned."

Jimmy turned his attention to Mallory, and she felt sorry for him all over again. He was trying to grapple with what Jupiter had just told him, and he looked quite distressed.

"When I talked to him," Mallory said, "I pretended to be someone else − someone he wouldn't be suspicious of. I managed to find him with another cage cashier having lunch. I told him a story that ended with me looking for a way to get to Wyoming, and he suggested that I could maybe get a ride with a guy named Travis Garrett who works at the Mustang Ranch, near Redlands. Jake said he was a friend of your father's. Do you know anything about him?"

Jimmy looked like he'd been struck by a thunderbolt. He jerked up, and his eyes widened. "Travis Garrett!" he said. "I'm almost positive my father mentioned him to me right before he left that last time for the res. He told me he knew the guy from the old days on the rodeo circuit, and he showed up at the ranch where my dad worked and asked for help getting a job.

"My dad was unsure, because Garrett had been trained to break horses in the cruel old-fashioned way – at least according to my father – but after they talked for a while, he decided that the guy had learned better. My dad said he'd seen Garrett do some pretty mean and stupid things with horses."

"Like what?" Pete asked.

"My dad didn't say," Jimmy told them. "But it's still weird that Jake's never mentioned the guy to me if he's been working with him for a year and a half."

Mallory could see that it upset Jimmy to hear Garrett's name.

"We're planning to go talk to him," Jupiter said. "Do you know whether this Mustang Ranch is a place where you can rent horses and go for rides?"

"Yes," Jimmy said. "My dad used to take people on trail rides up into the San Gabriel Mountains. I went once, and boy, was my butt sore!"

"Mallory, Pete, Bob, and I will get down there soon," Jupiter said. "We'll find out if by any chance this guy knows anything about what happened to your father."

"Would you really do that?" Jimmy asked. Clearly Jimmy wasn't used to people going out of their way to help him.

"Of course we will," Mallory said. "I also discovered something else. When you told us about your brother's friend Mackie, we thought he must be Native American, too. You told us his first name but not his last name. He was the one having lunch with Jake. His last name is Gupta. I was surprised to learn that he's Indian – from India – and that his father had been a doctor on the Duck Valley Reservation for a while."

"What?" Jimmy said. "He's from India?"

"Well, no," Mallory said. "But his father is. His mother is part Native American."

"I've never met him," Jimmy said. "I've just heard stories. Jake never told me his father was a doctor on the res, or that he was part Indian. Are you sure?"

"He seemed like a really nice guy," Mallory said, "and I can't think of any reason why he'd be lying. I mean, what for? He *looked* Indian, and his last name's Indian, and he even told me that he and Jake had taken DNA tests together when they both worked in Jackpot."

"He did?" Jimmy said. He looked perplexed and mystified. "But that was the summer I took a – "

"Who's that?" Pete said. "I just heard a car." He went to the side of the house and took a look. He came back quickly.

"It's Jake," he said. "The three of us are O.K. where we are, but it'll look a bit weird if he finds you here, Mallory. You better make yourself scarce."

"He didn't see the three of you?" Jimmy asked.

"No," Jupiter said. "Only Mallory."

She scrambled to her feet. "I've got my cellphone, Bob," she said. "Give me a call when the coast is clear." She darted to the side of the house away from the driveway and crept along until she could make a break for the sidewalk and then hurried down the street. She was about a block from the house when she saw Worthington driving on his way to pick them up. She waved her arms frantically and he stopped in surprise.

"What are you doing here?" Worthington asked. "Where are the others?"

"Back at the house," Mallory said. "I had to make a quick getaway because Jake just got home from work. He can't see you, either. We both have to stay out of sight."

"How will we rendezvous with Jupiter, Pete, and Bob?" Worthington asked.

"I'll call Bob," Mallory said, "and we'll choose a place to meet."

Just then her phone started ringing.

"This should be Bob now," she said. "I told him to call when the coast was clear." She snapped open her phone. "Hi," she said excitedly. "Where – "

But it wasn't Bob.

"Mallory?" the voice said. "It's Phillipa Paxton, returning your call."

7

A Very Lucky Break

The next morning, Jupiter sat with Mallory in the outdoor workshop, waiting for Pete and Bob, and then for Worthington. It was oddly satisfying to be alone with Mallory just then. It gave him a chance to appreciate just how great she'd been the day before in the casino. The previous afternoon, Jupiter, Pete, and Bob had all said goodbye to Jimmy Littlewolf soon after Jake had gotten home.

Though Jimmy had introduced the three of them, Jake had acted as though they were just little kids — friends of his half-brother. He'd shown no interest in them at all, and Jupiter had thought it was just as well that they didn't talk to him too much.

"So you actually talked to Phillipa?" Jupiter asked Mallory now.

"I did," said Mallory. "I called her back last night. I was too nervous to talk when she called as we were leaving Jimmy's. Anyway, she told me that not only had she grown up in Lander but that she'd gone to Lander Valley High School. The kids on the reservation have their

136

own separate high school, but the two schools actually met fairly often – playing sports and stuff like that. She knew a number of kids who grew up on the res, but she lost touch with all of them after she left Lander for college."

"That's too bad," Jupiter said. "If she had any old friends, they might have helped us."

"But Phillipa *does* have a younger sister who still lives in Lander," Mallory said. "She's a veterinarian. According to Phillipa she's mostly a horse doctor, but she takes care of all sorts of animals – dogs and cats, ferrets, rabbits, snakes. On top of that, she's sort of like the animal rescue center of Lander. People bring her wild, injured animals and she tries to save them if she can. Her practice is right on the edge of the reservation, and lots of her clients live there."

"This sounds very promising. Does she know the Littlewolf clan?" Jupiter asked.

"Phillipa had no idea," Mallory said. "But she promised to talk to her sister last night, and she said she'll tell us everything when we meet with her at Hector's later today."

"Pete will be thrilled," Jupiter said. "His plan to introduce Phillipa and Hector is working out. I hope his intuition was correct and that Phillipa and Hector get along."

"As far as I can see, the relationship between Connor O'Malley and Charlotte Mitchell
is proceeding nicely," Mallory said, smiling.

In fact, Charlotte Mitchell was spending
the summer with Connor at his house in
Auburn. Pete had many talents, but this was a
weird one, Jupiter thought.

"Anyway," Mallory added, "the main
thing Phillipa told me was that she was going
to try to set up a Skype call with her sister while
we're at Hector's later today."

"If she can do it, that would help a lot,
Jupiter said.

He remembered how Jimmy Littlewolf
had been waiting for them yesterday, and how
grateful he'd seemed when Jupiter had said they
would interview Travis Garrett down at the
Mustang Ranch. He'd really liked Jimmy —
when they'd played chess and yesterday at his
house — and he wanted to help him.

Even though he was a year older than
the four of them, he was still young, and it had
been a while — the previous summer with Daman Duwalia — since they'd had a youngish client. In their last case they'd helped a musician
in his 20s, and before that a professor in his
50s. Jupiter was always happy when The Three

Investigators could help someone closer to their age.

But Daman Duwalia was rich and famous, and Jimmy Littlewolf couldn't have been more different. Jimmy was hiding something, and Jupiter wished he knew what it was. Mallory thought so too; she'd told him that she thought Jimmy's unhappiness was about more than the murder of his father.

"After yesterday," Jupiter asked her, "do you have any better guess as to what's bothering Jimmy? I, at least, was struck by the way he reacted to your news about Mackie Gupta."

"About his father being Indian, you mean," Mallory said. "Yes. Right before Jake arrived, Jimmy said something like 'But that was the summer I took a – "

"Exactly," Jupiter said. "I've been puzzling over it, and I can't think of how that sentence could possibly end other than with the words 'a DNA test.'"

"I agree," said Mallory. "According to Mackie, he and Jake took DNA tests together as a lark. He didn't say whose idea it was or why they'd even thought of it."

"But why would Jimmy have taken a DNA test at about the same time?" Jupiter asked. "And where did he get the test? We need to follow up on that as soon as we possibly can."

"When I got to the Salvage Yard this morning," Mallory said, "I ran into Leif and he mentioned that Freya and Jimmy were going to a chess tournament together this afternoon. I could send her an e-mail, asking if she'd be willing to talk to Jimmy and maybe find out why he took the DNA test. When Bob and I met Jimmy at her house, she told us she wanted to help if she could. I'm sure she'd do it."

Jupiter nodded. As always, he found himself impressed with Mallory's thought process. This would get them the answer more quickly than if they waited to speak to Jimmy again themselves. "Could you do it now?"

"Sure," Mallory said. She opened her laptop, clicked on her desktop e-mail client, and starting typing. "This is better than calling," she said. "I can be clearer about what it is we're hoping that she can find out."

Jupiter sat and watched her, admiring her concentration and the speed with which she typed. Several times she backspaced and erased, trying to get it just right. She was a perfectionist, Jupiter knew.

Finally, she looked up at him. "Done!" she said. "Shall I read it to you?"

"I'm sure you did it perfectly," Jupiter said. "Just send it."

Mallory hit a button, and the e-mail was off. "I wonder where the others are?" she said. "Especially Worthington. This case has involved more back and forth than our cases usually do."

"That's true," said Jupiter. "And because of all the driving, we've been seeing a lot of Worthington!"

The day before yesterday, he'd driven them to Hector's house in Dial Canyon; yesterday he'd driven them to the casino where Jake Blackhorse worked and then on to Jimmy Littlewolf's house; and today he'd be taking them to both their appointment with Chief Reynolds and their appointment with Hector and Phillipa.

Although they could easily have ridden their bikes downtown, they'd decided to have Worthington take them so that after the meeting with the chief, they could head straight out to Dial Canyon.

Just then, Bob and Pete arrived on their bikes, and a minute later, Worthington drove in, too.

Bob had barely pulled through the Salvage Yard's gates when he started talking.

"I did what you asked me to, Jupe," he said. "I called the Mustang Ranch. Luckily Jake isn't working tomorrow, but Travis Garrett is. I made an appointment and reserved four or five horses. If Worthington can't take us, maybe Leif or Magnus can."

"I can take you," said Worthington. "My schedule this week is very light."

"Great," said Bob. "Do you want to join us?"

"On horseback?" Worthington said. "No, thank you. Make that four horses."

Pete laughed. "Don't you like horses, Worthington?" he asked.

"I like horses a great deal," Worthington said. "I like to bet on them occasionally, and I admire their strength and beauty. But I have long thought that admiration worked best when I had both my feet firmly on the ground."

"O.K., then," Bob said. "Four horses. A trail ride up into the mountains with Travis Garrett. That should give us time to get whatever information we want out of him. I thought that on the way back we might even be able to stop at Pomona College so that I can do whatever it is I have to do to participate in the experiment Hector told us about. I can meet this Dr. Yang and give her a DNA sample. Maybe

I can pick up the tests she wants me to take and bring them home with me."

"It's funny you should mention that," Jupiter said. "Mallory and I were just talking about Mackie Gupta and Jake Blackhorse taking DNA tests, and from what Jimmy said, we both guessed that he had also taken one — though for what reason we have no idea."

Worthington had reached the small downtown of Rocky Beach and in no time he had pulled up to the curb near the front of the Rocky Beach Police Station.

"Here we are," Jupiter said.

"I'll wait right here," Worthington said as Jupiter and the others got out of the Flex. In short order, the four of them were being ushered into Chief Reynolds's office.

"Hello!" the chief said, rising from behind his desk. "It's been a while."

That was true, Jupiter thought. They hadn't seen him in some months and hadn't needed his help since the summer before, when he'd been involved in two of their cases. Chief Reynolds had been an athlete when he was younger and might have had a career as a professional baseball player, but he'd been injured sliding into third base in college, and he still walked with a limp. He was a tall, energetic man, with friendly gray eyes and a strong square chin. He'd recently started to need glasses, which were perched on the top of his head. He was still in excellent shape, lean and fit, though his hair showed streaks of gray.

Jupiter admired his temperament. In spite of the work he did, he was cheerful, friendly, and always ready to help the citizens of Rocky Beach. He had a special regard for The Three Investigators and years before had even issued them cards for their wallets as Junior Deputies. It was only an honorific title, but Jupiter had still appreciated it.

"Hi, Chief!" Pete said, shaking his hand. Bob and Jupiter did likewise.

"And who's your friend?" Chief Reynolds said, smiling at Mallory.

"This is Mallory MacLeod," Jupiter said. "She moved to Rocky Beach last summer, and she was so helpful in a number of our cases that we made her a Special Consultant to The Three Investigators."

"I'm impressed, Miss MacLeod," Chief Reynolds said, shaking her hand. "I have the highest regard for Jupiter, Pete, and Bob, and if they have welcomed you into their firm, then you must be pretty special. I'm delighted to meet you. I'll have to think of the firm from now on as The Three Investigators 2.0!"

Mallory smiled – a little warily, Jupiter thought. "It's good to meet you too," she said. "I've heard a lot about you. According to these three, you're the reason I can sleep peacefully at night in Rocky Beach."

"I do my best," he said. "But Rocky Beach has always been a special place."

Though Jupiter knew that Mallory was generally skeptical about the police, he could see that Chief Reynolds had made a favorable impression on her. Now, he gestured to some chairs arranged in front of his desk.

"Why don't you all sit down? Pete, I heard you made quite a name for yourself on the baseball team this spring, but what have the rest of you been up to?"

"Bob and Mallory have taken up rock climbing," Jupiter said, "on the climbing wall at the high school, and on the cliffs down in Palisade Point."

"How's that going?" the chief asked. "The thought of it gives me the shivers."

"Pretty well," Bob said.

"And I've taken up fencing," Jupiter said. "I'm hoping to make it to the All-State fencing competition one of these years."

"That's great!" Chief Reynolds said. "I'd

have expected no less from the pack of you. And you're almost grown up! I must be getting to be an old man!"

"No," Pete said. "You look the same as ever."

Chief Reynolds grinned. "Except for the hair. Grayer every time I look in the mirror. Now tell me, what can I do for you. Jupiter? On the phone, you said you wanted to learn more about a murder that took place in Fremont County, Wyoming a couple of years ago. What's your interest in the case?"

"We're trying to help a boy named Jimmy Littlewolf," Jupiter said. "His father was killed just outside the Wind River reservation, near Lander, and, since the murder is still unsolved, Jimmy can't let it go. Right now he lives with his mother and half-brother in Palisade Point. He's a year older than we are."

"That's good of you," Chief Reynolds said. "This is a different kind of case for you."

"It sure is," Pete said. "We've never investigated a murder before."

"We feel it's safe for us to look into it because of the distance in time and space," Jupiter said, "but that's also the problem. Since it happened over a year ago in another state, we can't do much unless we can get some solid information about the original police investigation."

"I take it from his name and the proximity of the death to the Wind River Reservation that the boy and his father are Native American," Chief Reynolds said. "Is the BIA involved?"

"I don't think so," Jupiter said. "Just the Fremont County sheriff's office. We thought maybe you had a contact there. I know it's a long way from here, and you've probably never even been there, but don't police departments help one another?"

"Actually, I *have* been to Lander," Chief Reynolds said. "Years ago when I wasn't much older than the four of you. A bunch of my friends and I went on a tour of western rodeos and we hit the one in Lander. Quite a wild affair. Other than that, no, I don't have any personal connections. Still, I'm sure I could access whatever information has been made available to law enforcement by the sheriff's office."

"We'd appreciate that," Jupiter said.

Chief Reynolds turned to his computer – a large desktop model that Jupiter thought was almost as old as the one The Three Investigators had in Headquarters. Jupiter and the others sat quietly and attentively as the chief

147

logged into whatever database he had access to concerning criminal investigations.

"What was the victim's name?" the chief asked Jupiter.

"Thomas Littlewolf," he said.

When he asked for the date of the murder, Jupiter told him.

Jupiter watched as the chief entered the information that Jupiter had just given. The chief's face was lit by the glow from the screen, which illuminated his smile of satisfaction as he began to scan what he'd found. "It looks like I've hit the jackpot," he said.

After his recent visit to the casino, Jupiter couldn't help but envision the bells and whistles and cascading tokens when someone's slot machine paid off. *Hitting the jackpot* was an odd expression, he thought – and these days was frequently used to simply mean that someone was successful or lucky. Though "jack," Jupiter knew, meant money.

The chief's fingers flew, and suddenly his printer came to life and began to make copies of what he was seeing on his screen.

"From what I can gather," he explained, "there were no real suspects for the murder – or rather, there were far too many."

He read a little more and then sat back

in his chair.

"The sheriff's report states that the cause of death was originally listed as accidental. The investigators believed that Thomas had fallen off the cliff – presumably while drunk. His clothes were saturated with alcohol. But that was before the autopsy. The medical examiner found no alcohol in the victim's bloodstream and he ascertained that Thomas had been unconscious at the time of the fall, due to a blunt trauma injury to the head. Whatever he'd been hit with had a hard sharp edge. He had a wound on his forehead and his face was covered with blood when he was found. The cause of death was a broken neck – which had happened in the fall."

"So he was still alive after he was hit," Jupiter said.

"That's correct," the chief said. "But whether he was pushed or simply fell as a result of being knocked out is impossible to say. It seems that part of the reason the Fremont County Sheriff's Department didn't pursue the case as vigorously as maybe they should have is because they weren't really sure whether it was murder or simply manslaughter."

"What's the difference?" Pete asked.

"Intent," the chief told him. "If the perpetrator merely hit him, and he fell accidentally, it's manslaughter – and involuntary manslaughter at that. If the fall was part of the plan, it's murder."

He picked up another document that had just come off the printer and read it quickly.

"The Sheriff's Department conducted a thorough forensic examination and analysis, but they found no real clues. There were some scuffled footprints in the dirt at the top of the cliff and the blurred hoof prints of several horses. There were also a number of slices of apple – presumably for the horses – and a broken liquor bottle."

"Were the apple slices tested for DNA?" Jupiter asked.

"Yes, they were," the chief said. "Nothing conclusive on them, or on the broken glass. And unfortunately the weather had been dry for weeks when this happened, so there was no way of knowing for sure if the stuff they found and the foot and hoof prints even dated to the day of the murder."

"Did the sheriff have any theories?" Mallory asked.

"He believed that Thomas Littlewolf had been hit with a rock, but they couldn't find a rock that fit the pattern." He paused and looked at Jupiter carefully before moving on to look at each of them in turn.

"I don't want you to get your hopes up, guys," he said wryly. "Forty percent of all murders in America remain unsolved, and if something seems to have been a crime of sudden passion, that percentage can be even higher."

"You mean," Pete said, "that forty percent of murderers actually get away with murder?"

"That's right," the chief said, "which is where the expression comes from. Though usually it just means doing whatever you want and not getting punished, obviously!" he added.

"Did the Wyoming sheriff conclude that Thomas Littlewolf's murder *was* a crime of sudden passion?" Jupiter asked.

The chief shrugged. "The paperwork doesn't exactly say that," he told them, "but it does say that Mr. Littlewolf was very well-liked on the reservation, and that no one could be identified as an enemy, or as someone who would wish to do him harm. But if this had been my case – and based on my experience – I might have been led to conclude that someone simply lost his temper and acted without

151

thinking. That would be manslaughter."

Chief Reynolds stood and collected all the paperwork he'd printed, tapping it on his desk to make a tidy package.

"You're welcome to these reports if you want them. There's really nothing in them that I haven't told you already, just a lot of legal and medical language. There is, however, a list of the people who were interviewed in connection with the case – fourteen people from the reservation, friends and family and anyone else who might have had knowledge about what Mr. Littlewolf was doing out on the cliff that day. They also interviewed two residents of Lander who lived in the area where the death occurred, as well as a number of people who worked for one of them. Perhaps a place to start would be to follow up with some of these people and to interview them again."

"Thanks very much, Chief Reynolds," Jupiter said. He stood and took the papers that the chief handed him. "You've been a great help." He really had been, Jupiter thought, and, feeling unusually grateful, he shook the chief's hand again.

"You're very welcome, Jupiter. Good to see you all. And good to meet you, Mallory. If there's anything else I can do, just let me know.

I'm always ready to help The Three Investigators."

The chief walked them out of his office and all the way to the door. Jupiter noticed that he kept his eyes on the four of them as they got into the car with Worthington and waved as they took off.

"Well," Jupiter said to Mallory, "what did you think of the chief?"

"You were right," she said. "He's a good guy. I liked him a lot. If all the police in America were like Chief Reynolds, no one would ever have complaints. Still, after everything he said, and all the help he gave us, we're nowhere closer to being able to help Jimmy. We already knew that no one had been charged, but the details the chief gave us make me think that this looks pretty hopeless."

"Mallory!" Pete said. "You're usually so gung ho!"

"I know!" Mallory said. "But we're not there, and there were no clues, and – "

"I don't think it's hopeless," Jupiter said. "But we're definitely going to need a lucky break to have a chance of solving this case." He glanced down at the papers in his lap.

The chief was right; he'd told them everything – but not in detail. The details remained to be reviewed, and Jupiter was shuffling through the papers he'd been given when his eye fell on the list of people who'd been interviewed by the Lander sheriff's department.

On the list Jupiter saw a number of Littlewolfs − presumably all relatives of Thomas − as well as a number of other Native Americans with addresses on the reservation. Jupiter turned the page to a line in bold type that read "Residents of Lander." As he looked down it, his heart suddenly leapt.

"If we do need a lucky break," he said, "we may have found it."

"What do you mean?" Mallory asked.

Pete and Bob were looking at him. Mallory had turned around in the front seat to look back.

Jupiter smiled. "I think you're going to like this. One of the people the sheriff's department interviewed is named Georgina Paxton," he said with satisfaction.

"Georgina Paxton!" Pete exclaimed. "Is that the name of Phillipa Paxton's sister?"

"She didn't tell me, but I bet it is," Mallory said. "And Phillipa was going to try to set up a Skype call with her today, while we're at Hector's house. Her sister is a vet who lives right next to the Wind River Indian Reservation."

"Wow!" said Pete. "This sounds like more than just a lucky break! It sounds like that blaring horn is going off, and colored spotlights are shooting around on the ceiling!"

8

A Hypothesis Needing Proof

As he said this, Pete understood he might be exaggerating a little, but even so, he *did* think they'd had a very lucky break. For the rest of the ride to Dial Canyon, he wondered what Phillipa would tell them about her conversation with her sister and whether or not she'd been able to set up a Skype call for this afternoon.

Pete was also looking forward to seeing how Phillipa and Hector got along and thinking how great it had been to see Chief Reynolds. Pete had a special connection with him – perhaps because they both loved baseball so much – and as always, the chief had been very helpful to The Three Investigators.

Still, as the Flex sped down the highway toward Dial Canyon, Pete was feeling a bit cooped up. Although he almost always loved riding in the Flex with Worthington, there'd been an awful lot of driving in the last few days, and tomorrow they were going all the way to the ranch in Redlands, and after that, a stop at Pomona College. Maybe he could talk Bob out of wanting to add that to their itiner-

156

ary. Enough was enough, he thought.

He glanced over at Bob, who was looking at the firm's GPS device. When they'd bought the Flex, secondhand, it had lacked its own navigation system, so the GPS came in handy sometimes. They generally kept it in the glove compartment, but Bob had retrieved it after visiting the chief.

"I was right," he now said triumphantly. "On the way back from the ranch tomorrow, we'll practically be driving right through Claremont, where Pomona College is. It's not out of our way at all."

He passed the GPS around. Pete saw that Bob had programmed in the return drive from Redlands to Rocky Beach – and there was Claremont.

"That looks like it'll work," he reluctantly agreed. "Still, I'm tired of driving around in all this heat. Wouldn't it be great if after we get this case solved, we could go on a real vacation somewhere – somewhere cooler – like we did when we went to Yosemite last year?"

"With fresh water," Mallory said.

"Oh, oh! I forgot to tell you!" Bob said, as he took the GPS back. "This morning, I got an e-mail from Branko Petrovic up in Jackson. Mr. Petrovic won a raffle on the Fourth of

July, and he gave the prize to Branko. Guess what it is?"

A swimming pool? Pete wondered. He shook his head.

"It's a two-day rafting trip on the American River!" Bob said. "For six people! Branko gets to invite whoever he wants. So he invited the four of us and told us to invite someone else, too, if we wanted to."

"But that would be totally great!" Pete said. "We've never been on a rafting trip before."

"Neither have I," said Mallory.

"If we go, we can stay with Branko before the trip – and maybe after," Bob said. "We can see Jupiter's family. And the American River runs right through Auburn. We can see Connor and Charlotte, too!"

"*If* we go?" Pete said. "You mean *when* we go."

"But who should the extra person be?" Jupiter asked. "I think Branko should find someone."

"No," Pete said. "I think Mallory should ask another girl – maybe Califia García-Williams."

Mallory, Bob, and Jupiter all looked at Pete sardonically, but he didn't care This invitation from Branko was like an answer to a prayer. Just days ago, Pete had been wishing that he could think of some way he and Califia could get to know one another better, away from Rocky Beach, and now they would have the chance to – at least if she said yes to the invitation. And of course, if Mallory agreed to ask her, as a second girl.

"Just thinking about going on a rafting trip makes me feel cooler," Pete added as enthusiastically as he could. "Especially up in the mountains. And with Branko and Califia, too!"

At this, everyone just laughed – including Worthington. Pete blushed very hard, but when the laughter had died away, Mallory said kindly, "That's a really good idea. I bet Califia would love to come."

Pete knew they were all remembering having teased him about this subject just a few weeks before, when they were up in Santa Barbara on the trail of the Minoan Treasure, and Jupiter and Bob had seen a statue of Aphrodite in the museum in which the theft had taken place. Back then, he had just been embarrassed. Now he was also pleased. It was somehow reassuring to know that his friends knew how he felt.

Just then, Worthington turned into Dial

Canyon, and as the road rose in elevation, Pete tried to persuade himself that the air was getting cooler. But he wasn't convinced.

At the end of Hector Sebastian's driveway, Pete spied Phillipa Paxton's car – and the minute Worthington parked the Flex and the four of them got out, he heard voices. Phillipa and Hector were calling to them, poised in the doorway, urgently gesturing for them to come in. What was going on? Pete wondered. He and the others hurried up the walk, while Worthington pulled the car under the pine to get out of the sun. In spite of his curiosity, Pete couldn't help noticing that Phillipa and Hector looked relaxed and happy, as if they were already friends.

"Welcome, welcome," Hector said jovially as Pete and the others reached the pair. "Come in. Hurry up. No time to waste."

Amid greetings, as they walked through the house to Hector's study, Phillipa explained why they were in such a rush. The night before, she'd called her sister Georgina to ask whether she knew anything about The Three Investigators' current case, and her sister had told her that, yes, indeed, she'd been questioned by the sheriff about it. She'd set up a Skype call for today, so that Jupiter, Mallory, Pete, and Bob could actually talk to Georgina themselves.

As they walked, Pete noted happily the way that Phillipa and Hector looked at one another. He didn't know why he'd known they'd get along so well. But he'd been right. He had a knack for this. He hoped it would prove to be true in his own case as well as in other peoples'.

Phillipa's laptop was set up in Hector's study – a wood-paneled room with bookshelves on two sides and a wall of windows looking out at the world. On most days, Pete would have had a view of the pool, gazebo, and guest house, with the Pacific in the distance. But today Mr. Sebastian had pulled the drapes to keep out the glare and the heat and had set up chairs in front of the computer so everyone could participate. They were ready to go.

"This is great," Jupiter said. "We've just talked to Chief Reynolds, who gave us a report on the murder. We learned that a woman we thought must be Dr. Paxton's sister was on the sheriff's interview list, but we never thought we'd get the opportunity to talk to her so soon."

He'd barely stopped speaking when the call they were waiting for came through.

"Whoa!" Georgina Paxton said when she saw the group that had quickly taken their seats. "I didn't know I'd be addressing a convention. Hello, all."

Pete stared at Georgina Paxton. She was seated in a desk chair, wearing a wide-collared blue plaid shirt with pearl snaps. Her sandy blond hair was cut short and was pleasantly tousled. She had Phillipa's high cheekbones and thin lips. In fact, she looked a great deal like who she was – Phillipa's leaner and (in a good way) meaner younger sister. She gave the impression of being more active, more muscular – as though she might jump right through the screen.

But she didn't look like a Georgina to Pete; she looked more like a Frankie or a Hunter – something no frills and basic. In fact, a rifle and a shotgun rested on a gun rack on the wall behind her. The room she sat in was lined with unpainted pine boards – a sharp contrast to the dark wood paneling in Hector's study – and aside from the gun rack, Pete could see what looked like a lot of photographs mounted on the wall.

The combination of Georgina Paxton and her house made Pete begin to wonder once again what Wyoming was really like.

Georgina leaned forward, as though she didn't much trust the computer to carry her image all the way to California. "You'll have to excuse me," she said. "I don't do this all that often, but this time Phillipa talked me into it. Can you see me? Can you hear me?"

"Yes, Georgina," Phillipa said. "Loud and clear. I presume from your previous comment about the convention that you can see us." She laughed and quickly introduced everyone.

"I'm pleased to meet you all," Georgina said. There was a moment of awkward silence before she continued. "Ever since Thomas Littlewolf died practically on my doorstep, I've been hoping someone would figure out what really happened. Phillipa said you youngsters just might be the ones to do it," she said.

"We're not really youngsters," Jupiter said mildly. "We've been doing this a long time. May I ask what you mean by 'practically on your doorstep'?"

"Out here the distances are huge," Georgina said. "I walk a good distance just to pick up the mail. My neighbor discovered Thomas Littlewolf's body down the road from where I live and have my vet practice. He's a good friend of mine — a rancher — and he's convinced the Lander sheriff's department never tried hard enough to get to the bottom of what happened."

Pete saw Jupiter glance down at the papers that Chief Reynolds had given him.

"Is your friend's name Emmett Morgan?" he asked.

"Yes," Georgina said. "That's him."

"And his ranch is the Triple X?" he said.

"Yes," Georgina said.

"There's a bunch of other names here," Jupiter said. He read a few.

"Those men all work for Emmett," Georgina said.

"Is his ranch a tourist place?" Jupiter asked her.

"You mean, like a dude ranch?" Georgina asked. "No, no, no. It's a real western ranch, a working ranch. A lot of cattle and a lot of cowboys. Thomas Littlewolf worked there when he was younger. Emmett hired him because he was so good with horses. One of the cowboys Littlewolf had worked with when he lived in Wyoming ran into him in Lander when he was back visiting his sister. He invited him out to the ranch, but he never showed up. The afternoon he was expected, Emmett went for a ride by the river and saw something on the far side, at the base of the upthrust. At first he thought it was a dead antelope. It was quite

a shock to find that it was actually Thomas Littlewolf."

"Could you describe the area in a little
more detail?" Jupiter asked. "I'm having trouble visualizing the scene."

Pete was glad Jupiter had asked this
question. It was all a blur to him.

"Sure," Georgina said. "My house and
clinic are off a long dirt road that connects to a
paved road leading back to the highway. Further up the same dirt road is Emmett's ranch.
To the east of us is a small stretch of desert –
mostly sagebrush – until you come to a fork of
the Popo Agie River. On the other side, about
two hundred yards back, you hit the border of
the reservation. Sometimes people from the
reservation ride over, across the Popo Agie, to
get to Emmett's ranch."

"And the cliff?" Jupiter asked.

"On the edge of the reservation there's a
granite upthrust that falls off to either side.
Great views from the top, over the desert to the
mountains. It's not that high, but you wouldn't
want to fall off it," Georgina said.

Pete was getting a better sense of what
might have happened. Had Thomas Littlewolf
been on his way to visit the Triple X when he
ran into someone?

"This is very helpful, Dr. Paxton," Jupiter said. "But if you weren't there when the body was found, why did the sheriff's department want to talk to you?"

"They interviewed everyone within four miles," she said, "which tells you how many neighbors I have. Just Emmett, and the men who work for him. As it turned out, nobody saw or heard anything."

"So you really weren't able to help them," Jupiter said.

"I wish I could have," Georgina said. "I never knew Thomas Littlewolf but I know he was well-liked. Emmett certainly thought highly of him."

"Did the police have a theory?" Jupiter asked.

"At first they thought Littlewolf's death was an accident," she said, "but after the autopsy, they changed their mind and thought the killer might have escaped by following the river. Since I live so close to it, they wondered if I'd seen anyone that day.

"I told them no, but I did supply them with the digital files from my wildlife camera," she added. "I have it mounted to a tree near the watering hole to keep track of the animals who come by to drink. As you can see from my walls, I'm a photography nut. I take lots of pictures with a regular digital camera, too. Not just big game, but butterflies and humming-birds. Lots of birds."

She gestured to the wall behind her, dense with framed photographs. Pete could see more clearly now. Before he'd simply seen framed pictures. Now he could see the subjects.

"It's surprising I didn't see anything," Georgina went on, "because the day of the murder, and around the same time, I was out taking pictures of monarch butterflies. They're tricky to capture since they don't stay in one place for very long. I've been trying to help them out for a while now."

"How do you help a butterfly?" Pete asked.

"You help a monarch by planting milk-weed, mostly," Georgina said. "I've planted several big patches of Mexican whorled milk-weed between my house and the river. It's not pretty, but it does the trick. Monarchs are getting scarcer, even in Lander. People are now keeping track of how many there really are."

"It's too bad there weren't people out looking for killers that day you were taking pictures of the butterflies," Pete said. He was quite surprised when his comment made Jupiter sit up sharply.

"I wonder," Jupiter said. "How many pictures did you take that day, Dr. Paxton?"

"Oh, I don't know exactly," Georgina said. "Probably seventy-five to a hundred."

"I know you were focusing on the butterflies," Jupiter said, "but do you think it's possible you might have accidentally caught any cars that were moving by in the background?"

"Wow!" Pete said, excited by what his comment had made Jupiter think. "What a great idea! Maybe the killer escaped down the road by your clinic. Maybe you got a picture of the car or even a license plate!"

Georgina Paxton looked thoughtful. "That's an interesting possibility," she said. "I hadn't thought of that. When I'm taking close-ups of butterflies, I usually crop the picture afterwards so that it shows only what I'm interested in. But the computer keeps a digital copy of the original photo, so I still have access to the original pictures."

Pete saw Jupiter pinch his lower lip and get very quiet, the way he did when he was really intent on an aspect of an investigation.

"Do you think you could examine those photographs while we're on this call with you?" he asked.

"I don't see why not," Georgina said, "if you don't mind watching me work on my computer. I have another one I use for my photography."

She got up and disappeared from sight, but in a minute she was back with a silver laptop she opened and put to the side. She swiveled toward it. "Here we go," she said. "Here's the file. It looks like I took seventy pictures that day."

She swiveled back toward the camera, this time holding the laptop's screen in front of her. She held it up and Pete could see a dense cluster of thumbnail photos of butterfly pictures. Jupiter hunched forward intently.

Georgina swiveled again and put the computer down. "O.K.," she said. "Now I'm reverting each picture to the original uncropped version." She peered carefully at the first photograph she'd taken over a year before. "Nothing there," she said. "Moving on – No. No, Nothing."

Pete watched tensely as she worked her way from photograph to photograph, examining the background for evidence.

"Wait!" she said. "There's a car!" Pete's heart leapt. "No, sorry for that. It's just my mailman."

Georgina went on, methodically, shaking her head, no, no, nothing, no.

Pete was giving up hope and even beginning to feel a bit bored when Georgina Paxton said, "Here's something. But it's not a car. It's a horse. Two horses, actually. A cowboy riding one horse and leading another by the bridle. They're a little blurry, out of focus. I had the camera set for close-up so there's no real depth of field, but I can still make them out. Let me enlarge this a bit."

Her hands flew over the keyboard.

"There we go," she said. "Wow. That's a bit odd. I can't really make out the guy's face or anything, but the horse he's leading has very distinctive markings. It looks like a horse I used to treat. A piebald stallion with a white patch on his left rump that looked a bit like the Teton Mountains. He belonged to a guy who lived on the res. Anyway, the horse in the photo looks a lot like that horse. A *lot*. Here, take a look."

She swiveled again and presented the screen to the camera, holding it as close as she could.

Pete squinted and concentrated. In the foreground was a brilliant orange and black butterfly, its wings outstretched as it rested on what had to be a milkweed plant. In the background were two horses. The man on the lead horse was wearing a cowboy hat and blue jeans and a blue bandana around his neck. But it was impossible to see his face. The horse on the lead behind him had a startling white patch on his hindquarters.

"Wow," Pete said. "That does look like a bit like mountains."

"What can you tell us about the horse?" Jupiter asked. He was still hunched forward. Pete was intrigued by how carefully Jupiter was paying attention. Something was going on in that big brain of his.

Georgina Paxton shook her head. "Now, I'm wild about horses," she said. "Almost all of them. But this horse was a psychopath. He would rear up on his hind legs and strike out with his hooves. Any horse will do that if he's cornered or threatened; it's how they defend themselves. But this fellow did it to show he was the boss and to bully other horses as well as anyone trying to handle him."

Jupiter's eyebrows flew up and he sat back in his chair, pinching his bottom lip again.

"He sounds dangerous," Jupiter said.

"I'll say," Georgina said. "Really aggressive and hostile. My guess is that when he was born, the blood supply to his brain must have been shut off for a short time. That happens when the foal is turned around or the birth is difficult, and the lack of oxygen can leave the horse brain-damaged. Plus, he was male, and the guy who owned him wouldn't have him gelded, no matter how hard I argued."

"Is that unusual?" Jupiter asked.

"Unfortunately, no," Georgina said. "There are still plenty of horse people who think it's manly to ride a stallion. But it's just damn dangerous, and, as I said, this horse was more dangerous than most. The last time I saw Billy – the guy who owned him – I told him in no uncertain terms that the horse should be put down unless he could find someone who could train him properly. That horse was an accident waiting to happen. I heard Billy eventually did have the horse put down – though not by me. After that visit – when I said out loud what I thought of the way he dealt with horses – he never called on my services again."

"But you said that the horse in the photo looked like the one you treated," Jupiter said. "So maybe he wasn't put down after all."

Pete had seen that look before. Jupiter was developing a hypothesis, but what it could be was a mystery to Pete.

"That's a possibility," Georgina said.

"Out here people gossip about livestock more than about people, so what I heard about the horse being put down may not have been true. If it is the same horse, then what he was doing off the reservation is anyone's guess. I wish I could make out who the guy is who's leading him, but all I can tell you is I don't think it's Billy Redsmoke. He wears a cowboy hat with four eagle feathers and he's also pretty short, with narrow shoulders. The guy in the saddle is big and tall."

She went back and examined the remaining pictures, then turned again to the camera.

"That's all I have. I couldn't find any cars on the road in any of the photographs — except for my mailman. Still, it's amazing what you can photograph without even realizing it when you're focused on something entirely different!"

Jupiter cleared his throat. What was he thinking? Pete wondered. He was dying to know.

"I wonder," Jupiter said. "Thomas Littlewolf was hit on the forehead by a blunt object the sheriff never found. What if Jimmy's father wasn't killed by a man at all but by a horse? What if a horse's hoof was the blunt object that knocked him out and made him fall off the cliff?"

Pete felt as though he'd been hit in the solar plexus. What an idea! And Jupiter had put all the pieces together – the fact that the dangerous horse reared up and tried to strike out, the wound on Thomas's forehead, and the evidence from the photograph that the horse was very close to where the murder took place. Pete had been impressed with Jupiter's thought processes before, but this really topped them all.

"Jupe, you're a *genius!*" he said. And boy, did he mean it! But then he remembered how much Jupiter disliked anyone saying that, so he immediately took it back – though no one could stop him thinking it.

"I appreciate the compliment," Jupiter said. "Still, it's only a hypothesis."

But everyone had started talking at once, congratulating Jupiter excitedly. Hector Sebastian was particularly impressed.

"The minute you said that, Jupiter my boy," Hector told him, "I thought, 'Of course!' But even though I'm the mystery writer, it never occurred to me, and I really should have thought of it, since, God knows, I've read enough mysteries to have all the clues I could ever need. But even so, it was you who thought of it. Good work, Jupiter!"

Hector turned to Phillipa and to her sister on the screen. "The other day," he said, "when my four young friends were visiting, I was talking about how the hallmark of creativity is the ability to hold two opposing or contradictory ideas in your head at the same time. What I didn't explain was how hard that can be to do in practice. In this case, the two opposing ideas Jupiter put together were that Thomas Littlewolf was killed by another human being, and that he wasn't!"

"Yes," Jupiter said. "That's just how I would have put it – though of course Jimmy's father might have been killed, in a way, by another human being, depending on how you define the word 'killed.' The human being might not have been the actual agent of the murder, but he might still have been responsible. From what Dr. Paxton told us, anyone who allowed another human being to ride that crazy horse might be said to have been trying to get the person killed."

"That's true," Mallory said. "But we've been told that Thomas Littlewolf was a kind of magician with horses – a horse whisperer – just the kind of man Dr. Paxton was referring to when she said that the only way to deal with the horse other than putting him down would be to find someone who was capable of training him. Wouldn't Thomas Littlewolf have been able to ride and handle even the craziest horse?"

"Hmm," Jupiter said. "A very good point. And as I said earlier, it may be a good hypothesis to suggest that a horse killed Thomas Littlewolf, but it's just an idea — a good idea but one that will take a lot of proving before we can call it proved."

That might be so, Pete thought. But it sure sounded as if it was right — and for the very first time he was hopeful that they might indeed be able to solve a year-old murder and help Jimmy Littlewolf from a thousand miles away from where Thomas Littlewolf died. This case was a lot different from their normal ones, Pete thought, but with any luck, it would end like all the others — with the solution to a mystery.

And if it *did* end that way, then when The Three Investigators and Califia García-Williams went on the rafting trip Branko had invited them on, maybe Califia would want Pete to tell her all about it!

9

An Indecisive Morning

The next morning, as Mallory waited for Worthington to pick her up and take her and The Three Investigators to the Mustang Ranch in Redlands, she was sitting at the desk in her bedroom, trying to work on her plans for the new Three Investigators Headquarters. She was also thinking about Jimmy Littlewolf. It was funny how all of a sudden what had been a very solid foursome for over a year now had given way to a foursome plus three.

In the last few weeks, Pete had been serious about getting to know Califia García-Williams better; Freya Haldorsson had made it eminently clear that she still liked Bob a lot; and she and the other Three Investigators had all been touched and charmed by Jimmy Littlewolf.

Mallory had already checked her e-mail to see if Freya had written back about why Jimmy Littlewolf had taken a DNA test at the same time that his half-brother Jake had – and where he'd gotten the test in the first place – but there had been nothing from Freya in her

Inbox, and since she had some time before the gang left for Redlands, she'd gotten out her Headquarters plans.

She was suddenly aware of how swiftly the summer was flying by. It was already the second half of July. In a little more than four weeks she, Jupiter, Pete, and Bob would be back in school, and she'd more or less promised Jupiter that she'd finish the plans by the end of the summer. That way, the four of them could use the fall and winter to gather all the materials together and be ready to build the place in the spring, after the rainy season had ended.

Still, as she looked at her plans, she found her mind wandering to her mother. Earlier that morning, her mother had asked Mallory kindly, over breakfast, if she wasn't a lot happier in America than she'd ever expected to be. Mallory had just stared at her blankly as if she didn't know what her mother was talking about — though of course, she knew quite well.

When she and her mother had moved to Rocky Beach from Scotland after the death of Mallory's father, she'd been extremely unhappy, and had made her mother promise that if, after two years, things hadn't changed, they'd move back to Scotland.

Only a little over a year had passed, and already Mallory knew that she wanted to stay in Rocky Beach. Out of the corner of her eye, she could see the immigrant's trunk the boys had given her just five or six weeks after they met. On top of the chest sat Nessie, the rubber representation of the Loch Ness monster that she'd won at a Scottish music camp her mother had taken her to the previous summer.

Both Nessie and the chest were reminders of the very first Three Investigators' case she'd been involved with – and there had been many since. Her growing friendships with Bob, Pete, and Jupiter had given her a group to belong to and to contribute to, and her work with The Three Investigators had fired both her imagination and her intellect. In fact, working with The Three Investigators was the most satisfying thing she'd ever done; she couldn't imagine abandoning it to return to a dark cold climate where she hadn't had all that many friends to begin with.

Now, as she sat at her desk, alone, she wondered why she wanted to torture her mother by not telling her how she really felt. When she'd said nothing in response to her mother's observation that she seemed happier, her mother had desperately gone on to ask if she wouldn't be glad to stay on in America after the two years were up, and Mallory had said, quite firmly, and in a cool and steady voice, that she didn't know yet.

She hadn't meant to be cruel − not really. She didn't fully understand the impulse to keep how she felt to herself. But she knew she was at a point in her life when it felt good to pull away from her mother, to make her own life − and that included a life she lived inside her own head, with her own thoughts and feelings.

It was one thing to rebel by not making her bed or by coming home later than expected and not calling; it was another thing entirely to have an interior life that was distinct and apart from her mother. She was no longer defined by being her mother's daughter. She was Mallory MacLeod, her own self.

Even so, she promised herself she'd tell her mother sometime soon and take her out of her misery. As she studied her Headquarters plans, she remembered Pete asking her to tell them about her ideas, and how she'd refused to say anything specific. She'd said it was important not to talk about what you were doing at too early a stage in the creative process.

And then it occurred to her that that was

another reason why she'd refused to say anything to her mother. It was too early a stage in the process. She was worried that if she said it out loud − if she committed herself publicly − she might start having doubts about whether she was making the right decision.

Doubts gnawed away at you; they were terrible, could undermine your self-confidence, and keep you awake at night. She'd rather wait to announce a decision about something than to say it too soon and regret it afterwards. She felt a great sense of relief. She was glad to have figured that all out, and to think that even if it had seemed cruel to her mother not to tell her what she was thinking, at least her motive hadn't been cruelty.

As for the plans for the new Headquarters, it was also true that she was having a good deal of trouble making up her mind. Usually when she had a creative impulse, she charged ahead, trusting in her instincts. But this time was different. She'd found herself dithering − moving from one idea to another, seeing the pros and cons of many different approaches. Her indecision had made her understand how important it was that she do this job not just well but perfectly.

For the moment she was only partly

happy with what she'd arrived at. She'd had the idea that designing a perfectly square building – a building with four equal sides – might be fun. Although Mallory never expected to be made a fourth investigator, she still liked the idea of weaving a subtle joke into HQ2's design.

Also, on their last case, she'd been in a square house – an American Four Square kit house in the suburbs of Los Angeles – and at the end of the case the house's owners had given her a copy of the plans for the house as a gift. She'd put the plans on the wall of her bedroom.

Still, now that she was actually working on the plans, she wasn't as wild about making the new Headquarters square as she'd thought she'd be. She also wasn't entirely certain that building a new building from scratch was really even necessary. What she'd liked most about Ivan and Cassandra's house were the four long and narrow dormer windows on the second floor – and also the cupola in the middle of the hip roof – and now she was wondering if there was some way they could simply renovate the shed she mostly worked in at the Salvage Yard while giving it a brand-new roof.

Just then, there was a knock on her bedroom door, and she jumped. She was instantly irritated, and ashamed of being irritated, especially because of what she had earlier been thinking about her mother.

"Come in," she called, as warmly as she could manage.

"I'm leaving for work, Mallory," her mother said as she opened the door. "I'll see you for dinner, sweetie. Have a good day."

Mallory turned her chair so she could see her mother, who looked a little sad. "You, too, Mom," Mallory said. "And don't worry about anything."

Her mother smiled and closed the door. In another instant Mallory heard the front door of the apartment open and close. She looked at the clock on her bedside table and realized it was time for her to get ready, too. She put away her graph paper, ruler, and pencils in a drawer in her desk, then moved aside her curtains just in time to see Worthington pulling up to the curb.

As she grabbed her backpack and ran outside, Pete climbed out of the passenger seat and got into the back with Bob and Jupiter. Mallory thanked him and climbed in next to Worthington. Even before she had buckled her seatbelt, she noticed how hot it was. It was going to be a scorcher.

The four of them talked animatedly as the Flex sped east, and a little over an hour later, they were on the outskirts of Redlands. Bob had the GPS handy to give Worthington directions. The Mustang Ranch was to the northeast of Redlands, on the Santa Ana River, not far from the San Bernardino National Forest.

As they approached it, Mallory saw that the area was flat and dry – quite desert-like – although there were orange groves irrigated by the river, and the roads were lined with Russian olive trees and towering California fan palms. To the east the San Bernardino Mountains rose, arid and rocky, studded with twisted dwarf conifers.

Last year, Mallory would have been totally freaked out by the dryness, but now she was starting to get used to it, and even to see the beauty in plants that grew in such austere conditions. The dirt road leading to the ranch was washboarded and dusty, lined with wire fencing, but the sky was an intense blue and the day seemed bright with possibility.

"Now remember," Jupiter said, as they approached the entrance – a log archway with a cow skull nailed in the center. "This Travis

Garrett might be a good guy or a bad guy or something in between. We really don't know anything about him except that he knew Thomas Littlewolf and that he drives horses back and forth to Wyoming. We're going to try the same thing that worked with Jimmy's brother. We want Garrett to reveal things he doesn't know he's revealing. So we need to be careful. As far as Garrett's concerned, we know nothing about him."

Mallory thought this was excellent advice, but she had something else on her mind.

"I'm a little worried about riding," she said. "I've been on a horse before, but I didn't love it, and I have to say I agree with Jimmy. Horses are big and unpredictable. Do any of you guys feel the same way?"

"I sort of like horses," Bob said. "I've only been riding a few times, but I think it's probably like climbing. You just need to be aware of your body all the time, and if you are, the horse will appreciate it. Besides, at a place like this, I'm sure they use the most docile horses imaginable. They're not going to put you on a bucking bronco."

"I sure hope not," Mallory said.

"I've only been riding a few times, too," Pete said, "but I really loved it. I'm sure we'll all be in a line and the horses will be walking, so it won't be dangerous. At least I don't think so. What do you think, Jupe?"

"This is a commercial operation," Jupiter said, "which means they will do their best to give the customers what they want. If we make it clear we want gentle horses, then that's what we'll get. I've only been riding once, as far as I can remember − when we were involved in the case about the ghost pearls. I liked it all right. Obviously, I didn't like it enough to go out of my way to try it again."

"Hector Sebastian sure likes it," Bob said, "and Phillipa Paxton, too."

"But she grew up around horses," Mallory said. "Anyway, thanks for the reassurance."

Still, after this chat, she felt like the odd one out. None of the boys seemed to feel anxious at all about the riding they were going to do.

It was Worthington who came to the rescue. "If I were you, Mallory," Worthington said, "I wouldn't worry. After all, anyone who could fool Jimmy's brother as well as you did can certainly fool a horse. Just act confident − even if you don't feel confident − and the horse will act accordingly. I must say I think this is brave of you. I've already told you how *I* feel about horses."

Mallory laughed. "Thanks, Worthington. That helps a lot."

Worthington pulled the Flex into a parking space in front of what looked to be the main building − a low Western-style place made of logs stained a reddish-brown. The Mustang Ranch was large, with several horse barns and a number of corrals where men in chaps were exercising horses on long leads. But Mallory could see it wasn't a ranch as she usually thought of one − all horses and no cows, except for the skull on the entry gate.

"What's this place all about?" Mallory asked.

"All I know is what I found on the website," Bob said. "People board their horses here, and then come and ride them up into the mountains. The place raises horses, too, and trains them, and of course it offers trail rides. Come on. Let's go find Travis Garrett."

"You guys have fun now," Worthington said, "and be careful."

"You're sure you don't want to change your mind, Worthington?" Mallory asked.

Worthington smiled. "Not a chance," he said.

All of them got out of the car and started walking toward the main horse barn. Inside, it was dim and much cooler and smelled of hay and manure. They asked the first person they ran into where they might find Travis Garrett. He was chewing a piece of straw, and he didn't bother to dislodge it. Rather than talking, he pointed. At the far end of the barn, a man was stacking saddles.

He was tall, without an ounce of fat, and he had a weathered sunburnt face. He wore a red bandana around his neck, a pearl-buttoned shirt, a pair of scuffed leather chaps over his jeans, and well-worn boots. He'd taken off his cowboy hat, and his short sandy-blond hair was plastered to his skull with sweat. His legs were slightly bowed.

He looked to Mallory as though he were in his early fifties, and somewhat the worse for wear. His eyes squinted.

"Are you Mr. Garrett?" Jupiter asked.

"You found him," Garrett said. "You four must be my morning appointment." He looked at them appraisingly. Just for a moment she saw them the way he probably did – four fresh-faced youngsters from the city, without a lot of experience under their belts, out for a day's adventure.

"That's right," Bob said. "We asked especially for you. We heard you're the best." That seemed to work wonders with Garrett, who obviously was proud of the work he did with horses.

"I didn't pick out your mounts yet," he said. "I figured I ought to find out how much riding you've done first."

Travis Garrett seemed nice enough, Mallory thought, once he got talking, and she even developed some sympathy for him. Day after day he had to deal with another bunch of greenhorns, taking them out for a ride that by now must be painfully familiar. One by one they told him how much riding they'd done and what sort of horse they were looking for.

Though they all admitted that they were in no way experienced, Pete and Bob said they felt comfortable riding, and that just about any horse Garrett picked for them would probably do. Jupiter said he'd prefer to concentrate on the scenery, and on talking, rather than worrying about his horse.

"Me too," Mallory said, grateful to Jupiter that he'd said it first.

"O.K. then," Garrett said. "You guys stand over there while I get your horses and finish saddling them up."

It took a while, but Mallory was contented to stand with the others and breathe in the rich smells of leather and oil and hay, liniment and acrid sweat, and over it all the smell of horse – sweet and warm and faint, like clover.

Mallory's horse was named Lightning, which struck terror into her until Travis Garrett explained that she'd been given the name because of an irregular blaze on her muzzle and that there wasn't a gentler horse on the ranch. Soon all four of them had been fitted with cowboy hats – they had a choice between those and riding helmets, and they all chose hats – and were clambering up into the saddle and following Travis out of the barn and into the bright light of day.

Mallory found it a bit disorienting to have entered the horse barn on foot and to be leaving it on horseback. The ground was far away, and everything looked smaller from the saddle, which was about five feet off the ground. The sky looked wider. Travis Garrett had taken the lead, with Jupiter behind him. Mallory quickly understood that any attempt to talk to Travis Garrett as a group would be impossible, but she got directly behind Jupiter so that she would be able to hear them when he and Travis started talking.

Pete and Bob fell into line behind them as the horses walked under the log arch of the ranch's entrance and down the dirt road before cutting off on a well-trodden trail toward the mountains. It was desert, more or less, that they walked through – no irrigation here and just scrubby conifer shrubs and sagebrush. It was not particularly inspiring scenery, but Mallory was very glad to be on horseback and not on foot. Travis Garrett had given them each a bottle filled with clear cold water, and without letting go of the reins, Mallory managed to take a sip.

It was getting toward noon, and the sun was hot overhead. Mallory understood as never before why cowboys wore cowboy hats. Hers was a little small for her, and she looked with envy at Travis Garrett whose hat cast a broad shadow not only over his face and neck, but over some of his torso as well. Lightning was keeping a good steady pace behind Jupiter's horse. She seemed docile enough, a good reliable follower, and Mallory began to relax a little and let her guard down.

Jupiter was chatting amiably with Travis, and since they couldn't hear anything, after a while Pete and Bob fell back a bit to talk to one

another, while Mallory pushed forward –
enough so that she could hear the conversation. The horses were walking more quickly
now, though what they were doing couldn't be
called a trot. Lightning's head bobbed, and the
rhythm of the walk, the bounce Mallory felt in
the saddle, accelerated and made her tense
again. She tried to focus on Jupiter and Travis
Garrett.

"How long have you been working at the
ranch?" Jupiter asked Travis.

"Long enough," Travis said.

Uh oh, Mallory thought. Perhaps they
were in trouble. What if Garrett proved to be
so laconic that they'd get nothing out of him at
all?

"I heard you were really good with
horses," Jupiter said, and the compliment
seemed to unwind the man somewhat.

"Been around them long enough," he
said. "I've been riding horses since I was a
whippersnapper. Been taking care of them almost that long."

"Were you born in California?" Jupiter
asked.

"No, sir," Travis said proudly. "You
seen the Wyoming symbol of a bucking bronc
and rider? I was born and raised in Farson,

Wyoming, population around 300. Probably more horses than people. My daddy owned a gas station there, filling up the tank for tourists on the road from Rock Springs to Pinedale and Jackson."

"But you didn't want to work in a gas station?" Jupiter suggested in a questioning tone.

"I loved my daddy, but I loved riding more and I got on the rodeo circuit early. My father was fine with that. I did bareback riding mostly. I was pretty good – known across Idaho and Wyoming. But I stopped – got too old and saw how it was bad for the horses. You got to make them buck to put on a show, and they only do that if you make them unhappy."

"Are you part Indian?" Jupiter asked. "As well as a cowboy?"

Jupiter was putting on his dumb act, Mallory could see, but he'd skirted a bit close to the really dumb line, and Travis swiveled in the saddle to take a look at the rider behind him. Who knows what he might have said under normal circumstances, Mallory thought, but he calmly turned back around; Jupiter was a client after all.

"You think when they talk about cowboys and Indians they're talking about the same thing?" he asked, clearly amused.

"Not really," Jupiter said, sounding a little hurt.

"I ain't no Indian, that's for sure," Travis said, "though I've known plenty."

"Really?" Jupiter asked. "Is there a reservation in Farson?"

Travis laughed. "Farson's big enough for a post office, a gas station, and a general store, not much else. There's a reservation about two hours to the east, though. A big one. Arapaho and Shoshone."

"Did they have rodeos there?" Jupiter asked.

Travis Garrett took off his hat and wiped his forehead with his forearm. Casually he settled it back on his head and looked over his shoulder at Jupiter.

"You sure do ask a lot of questions, young feller," he said.

Jupiter gulped. "It's just that I never met a cowboy before," he said.

Mallory could hear Pete and Bob talking to one another, laughing as they lagged behind. She almost wished she were with them. Though Lightning had settled into a comfortable gait, Mallory was beginning to tense up again. It seemed Garrett was getting a little prickly.

The trail had reached the bottom of the foothills and Mallory was glad they'd begun to climb. The ground was chalky white, covered with hoof prints, and the shrub conifers the trail wound through were twisted and stunted. She sure didn't want to get thrown here. There were jagged rocks everywhere. She saw a jackrabbit, frightened by their approach, take long leaps into the distance. A fat snake sunned itself on a long flat rock. She was tempted to ask Travis what kind of snake it was, but she decided not to interrupt the conversation.

"Rodeos on the res?" Travis finally said. "Nope. But there's a good one every summer in Lander, which is just south of there. Fourth of July, during Pioneer Days. I used to go every year. I got to know a bunch of Shoshone riders – really good horsemen – who were on the circuit."

"Do you miss Wyoming?" Jupiter asked. Mallory was impressed with the way Jupiter was proceeding, though she thought he might give it a rest for a moment. She was sure Travis Garrett was not used to being peppered with questions by the people he took for trail rides. Still, everything Jupiter was asking seemed natural and spontaneous, as though

Jupiter was truly curious and not fishing for specific information.

Travis glanced back at him again. "Why would I miss it?" he asked. "It's not like I'm a stranger. I get back there, couple of times a year. I go back to the reservation to pick up horses and bring them to buyers in California. They've got some great horses there. As I said, the Shoshone are fine horse people."

Mallory felt a sudden thrill shoot up her spine. So Jake had been right. Travis Garrett traveled regularly between southern California and the Wind River Reservation in Wyoming. There'd been no reason to disbelieve Jake, but hearing Garrett say it himself electrified Mallory. She was amazed at the progress they were making on a case that, at the beginning, had seemed close to impossible. Suddenly she wasn't feeling nervous at all!

10

A Jumping Off Place For Further Questions

Jupiter's face flamed, and his neck and back were wet with sweat. It was hot out on the desert and in the foothills of the San Bernardino Mountains. He could only hope that Pete was right and that it would get cooler as they rode higher up.

His mind raced in light of the new information he'd just discovered. He'd been asking a series of more or less random questions, intended to push Travis Garrett only slightly, and he hadn't been at all sure he was getting anywhere useful. Then suddenly this: Not only did Garrett ferry horses between Wyoming and California, but he got them from the Wind River Reservation.

Jupiter's horse was a gentle mare with a soft gait, and, all things considered, he thought he'd been doing pretty well, even if his tailbone was beginning to hurt. But he was wishing Firefly were even tamer – if such a thing were possible. He wanted to be able to focus completely on the conversation and not have to give even part of his mind over to staying safe on a horse.

That clearly wasn't possible. The trail had begun to gain in pitch as it wound up into the mountains, and it was narrow as well as steep. But if he could only think clearly for a minute about how to proceed from here with his questions, he should be all right.

He wondered why Jake Blackhorse – when he'd been sidling up to Mallory – hadn't mentioned the reservation to her. It seemed odd to Jupiter, even suspect, that when Jake had said that a man he worked with drove back and forth to Wyoming, he'd neglected to mention that he drove right to the reservation where Mallory's fictional boyfriend supposedly was from!

Although he couldn't double-check with Mallory at the moment, Jupiter knew as well as he knew his own name that if Jake had mentioned the reservation as Travis Garrett's Wyoming destination, Mallory would have reported that.

So why, Jupiter wondered, had Jake mentioned the man but not where he went? Most anyone else would have said that he knew someone who drove to the exact place that Mallory said she wanted to go – and that maybe that someone could give her a ride.

But Jake hadn't. He'd kept it much more vague than most people would have.

Jupiter would have to put off consideration of that point until later, he thought. The important thing at the moment was to keep talking. In particular, he needed to keep playing dumb, which had been having quite good results with Travis. If he'd been acting more like himself, Jupiter thought he would have spooked Travis Garrett and the man would have shut down entirely.

"That's interesting that you get horses from the reservation," Jupiter observed. "Are they tame or wild?"

Travis laughed. "They're tame enough. Though as a matter of fact, there's a wild horse sanctuary on the res. A herd of wild mustangs. But no rodeos."

If there was going to be an opportunity for Jupiter to bring up Thomas Littlewolf, this was it. "I was reading about the Mustang Ranch – I mean your ranch, not the one on the reservation – "

Garrett interrupted him. "There's no ranch on the res," he repeated. "Just that herd of mustangs."

"Oh," Jupiter said, "Anyway, I read that

a couple of years ago there was a guy who worked at your ranch who tamed wild horses. They called him a horse wizard or something. You were working there, then, weren't you? Did you know him?"

Travis Garrett's shoulders stiffened. He was silent for a while, and the only sound Jupiter could hear was the shuffle of the horses' hooves through the chalky dirt and the sound of Pete and Bob laughing, somewhere behind him. He thought he'd pushed too far, or in the wrong direction − or, most probably, that he'd suddenly sounded a bit too smart for the persona he'd been developing.

When Travis finally spoke, his voice had lost its friendliness; it seemed gruffer, more hard-edged, even a bit surly.

"Don't remember no one like that," he said.

It was clearly a lie, and even though Travis didn't know that Jupiter would see through it, Jupiter decided that he needed to stop asking questions for a while, and think instead.

As they gained altitude the vistas were better, though the ground stayed dry and rocky. There were few trees − far fewer than Jupiter had expected − but after about ten minutes of silence as the horses plodded along in line, all of them following Travis Garrett, they emerged onto a plateau that looked both ways, back toward Redlands and San Bernardino and the flatlands, and off into the higher reaches of the San Bernardino National Forest.

Jupiter took a deep breath as he looked around. The air was hot and dry, but there was a sweet piney smell, and it did indeed seem cooler than it had when they'd started their trek. Off in the distance he thought he heard the sound of water − perhaps the Santa Ana River − and he was suddenly glad he wasn't talking. It was a very pretty scene.

He noticed a large bird, a raptor of some sort, floating on the thermals, barely moving its wings, and as it glided closer he saw, to his astonishment, that it was a golden eagle. It was a majestic bird, with a wing span of over six feet; its dark brown feathers seemed rimmed with gold in the bright light of day. He hadn't seen one since the beginning of summer the year before, when he and Pete and Bob had taken the trip to Yosemite, and now, he couldn't help but remember what Jimmy Littlewolf had told him about the Shoshone having a special reverence for the golden eagle.

As he looked up at the bird soaring above him, he wished for a moment that he actually *were* a golden eagle, and that he could have looked down, from his place in the sky, on that rocky upthrust near Lander, Wyoming, that day a little over a year ago, and had seen what had actually happened.

But since he wasn't, and he couldn't have, at least he could do something the eagle couldn't do — which was analyze the information he'd gathered and come to a logical conclusion. Human beings couldn't fly, and their eyesight was nowhere as good as an eagle's, but they did have larger and more supple brains.

Jupiter reminded himself, before he began, that scientific method — the best way to think logically — first required you to notice a pattern in what you were observing, and then to come up with a question you'd be interested in answering. The next step was to imagine a possible answer, or hypothesis, based on the available (but limited) evidence — a hypothesis which could form the jumping off place for further questions. After that, you needed to come up with predictions that would turn out to be true if the hypothesis was correct, and after *that,* you needed to test your predictions.

In terms of what had happened that day on the Triple X Ranch outside of Lander, how could Jupiter best apply the method he'd just described to himself?

If the question he was interested in was "Who killed Thomas Littlewolf, or who was present at the time of his death?", then one way to proceed would be to hypothesize that the answer involved the man who had shown up in Georgina Paxton's photograph – the man on horseback who had been leading the piebald stallion down the road in front of Dr. Paxton's veterinary clinic.

If the horse he had been leading had reared up and struck Thomas Littlewolf in the forehead with his hoof, then the man in the photograph would have been there at the moment it happened.

Of course, Jupiter reflected, that thought in itself contained several other hypotheses or guesses – the hypothesis that the piebald horse was, in fact, the savage stallion that Dr. Paxton had told his owner should either be put down or properly trained by someone like Thomas Littlewolf, and the hypothesis that Thomas had been riding that crazy stallion before his sudden death.

But at the moment, what Jupiter wanted

to think about was this: If the unknown rider – the man in the photograph – and Thomas Littlewolf had ridden together from somewhere on the Wind River Reservation to the upthrust from which Thomas had fallen, and if the other rider had been frightened by what happened – because, although he hadn't intended for it to happen he was afraid he'd be blamed for it – then why hadn't he ridden back to the reservation the way he'd come – taking the piebald horse with him? Why had he ridden down a public road on which he risked being seen, or even (as had actually happened) photographed?

Georgina Paxton had said that the road didn't have much traffic, but even so, it had to have *some*, and when Jupiter considered it, he thought that the chances of being seen and recognized were far greater on the road than they would have been if the man had ridden through the backcountry.

Therefore, he reasoned, the man in the photograph must have taken what seemed to Jupiter like the riskier route because it was in actuality *less* risky. Maybe because when the unknown rider and Thomas Littlewolf had ridden across the reservation, no one had seen them, but for some reason unknown to Jupiter, the man in the photograph knew that if he now went back the way he'd come, he'd be seen.

So what might have changed in the backcountry landscape in the hour or two since the unknown rider and Thomas Littlewolf had ridden over toward the Triple X Ranch from the reservation? What might have made it impossible for him to retrace his steps without risking being seen by someone?

Jupiter gazed ahead at Travis Garrett's back, which was streaked with sweat. The man rode easily, rising off the saddle and settling back down with his horse's rhythm. He was a cowboy, through and through. And then Jupiter thought about the word. A cow boy – someone who spent his days on horseback moving cows.

Jupiter didn't know all that much about working ranches, but he did know that they had herds of cattle that needed to be moved from place to place when the food or water ran out. What if the cliff from which Thomas Littlewolf had fallen was near an area of land that Emmett Morgan's cowboys had unexpectedly moved cattle into, after Thomas Littlewolf and the unknown rider had moved through it, heading west? What if some or all of the cowboys knew the unknown rider, and he knew he'd be recognized if he tried to go back the way he'd come? What if he'd therefore decided to take the (apparently) riskier route down the road instead?

The eagle had soared off, and the horses had moved on − a slow gentle ride that had leveled off for a while and now was climbing again. Jupiter took a sip of water from his canteen and let some of it dribble down his chin and onto his shirt where it felt cool and pleasant. The sky was a blue bowl overhead and seemed to bend down over the distant mountains.

Jupiter was pleased with his new hypothesis − that Emmett Morgan's cattle had been moved that day, forcing the unknown rider down the road with the killer horse − and he was determined to call Mr. Morgan as soon as he could to ask if, in fact, the cattle had been moved into the area near the upthrust around the time Thomas Littlewolf must have died.

If Mr. Morgan told him this had happened, then it seemed to Jupiter that the other guesses he'd made about the cattle would also have to be true − that the piebald horse Georgina Paxton had caught in her butterfly photograph had indeed been the savage stallion she'd once tended, owned by Billy Redsmoke;

that Thomas Littlewolf had been riding that stallion before his death; and that the man leading the horse hadn't meant for Thomas to be killed at all. If he had, he'd have planned a lot more carefully, Jupiter thought.

That was the great thing about logical trains of thought, Jupiter reflected. Once you'd gotten rid of everything that couldn't possibly be true, the explanation you were left with — even if it seemed far-fetched or unlikely — must be the truth.

Here was what Jupiter knew: There was a photograph of one man and two horses. They were riding away from the spot where another man lay dead and whose body would soon be discovered. The dead man was a horse whisperer, and one of the two horses in the photograph was a notoriously dangerous and difficult beast, known for rearing up and striking out with his hooves.

It was easy, from this evidence, to conclude that the two men had originally been riding the two horses, that the horse whisperer had been attempting to work his magic on the savage horse, that he had failed, that the horse had struck him on the forehead, leading to his death, and that the second man was now trying to get away without being seen, so as not to appear responsible for what had happened.

Jupiter also decided that, when he finally talked to Emmett Morgan, he would ask him if there was a second trail across the river — maybe several miles down from Dr. Paxton's clinic.

If that were the case, then the last part of the puzzle would be in place: The unknown rider had been heading toward another crossing that would return him to the backcountry of the reservation as quickly as possible — away from the cowboys who might have seen him, and off the road on which he might have been recognized by anyone coming along.

The trail had reached a steeper pitch, and, for ten minutes, all Jupiter could hear were the sounds of the horses' harsh breath and the dull clomp of their hooves on the dust of the trail. Each footfall sent up a miniature explosion. He was getting worried that they were straying too far from the ranch when the trail suddenly leveled off.

They'd reached the top of one of the foothills in the San Bernardino range, with more excellent views both ways — back down into the valley and across to the higher mountains. Bob had shown him pictures of the mountains in winter, the highest of which were snow-capped and forbidding. But now, at the height of summer, the mountains were free of snow and looked friendly and welcoming.

There were two groups of pines clustered together that threw some shade, and a rustic bench had been built under one of them. Travis Garrett dismounted and motioned to Jupiter and the others to do the same. It was a long way to the ground, but Jupiter managed to disengage his foot from the stirrup on one side, throw his leg over the horse, and lower himself without incident. He was glad to be on solid ground, but Firefly's motion had entered his body and for a while, even after he stood with both feet firmly planted, he felt as though he were swaying.

"Isn't this great?" Pete said, leading his horse by the reins. "I wish they had a ranch like this in Rocky Beach."

Jupiter smiled encouragingly but he was secretly glad there wasn't such an establishment. He'd stick to bikes, he thought. They were much more dependable and much less intimidating.

"Why don't the four of you park yourselves on that bench for a spell?" Travis said. "We'll head back down in a little while." He gathered the reins of the five horses and led them to the shade of the other pines. He fumbled an apple out of his pocket and then another, and with his pocket knife he cut off slices and fed them to the horses in turn.

Jupiter, Mallory, and Bob sat down on the bench, but Pete seemed too filled with energy to be still. He walked out into the sun and peered off at the mountains, then turned and walked back to look down on Redlands and San Bernardino.

"Boy," he said. "I can't wait to go on that raft trip. I mean, this is great, but that will be *really* great."

Jupiter was looking forward to seeing Branko again, and his family in Jackson, and he thought rafting would be a lot of fun. But right now he was just glad not to be on a horse. He felt as though his legs had been pulled apart, and the inside muscles hurt.

He looked up into the sky again, checking to see if the golden eagle was anywhere nearby, but it must have glided off to another part of the mountains. Jupiter wondered if he was the only one who had seen it. No one else mentioned it.

Travis was sufficiently far away that Jupiter knew he couldn't hear their conversation, but Bob kept his voice low anyway.

"How did it go, Jupe?" he asked. "Did you learn anything important?"

Jupiter shook his head slightly. "I might have deduced something," he said, "but not exactly learned."

"What do you mean?" Mallory asked in a voice that showed her surprise. She turned to Bob. "He learned that Garrett comes from a small town in Wyoming, about two hours from Lander and the reservation. His father owned a gas station but Travis loved horses and rode the rodeo circuit. Travis used to go to Lander every year, and he sometimes went to the reservation, since guys he knew from the rodeo circuit lived there."

"Like Jimmy's father," Bob said.

"Exactly," Mallory said. "And not only that. He said he still goes to the reservation because he sometimes picks up horses there and brings them to buyers in California."

"Yes, that's all true," Jupiter said. "But Travis's biographical information is of little use to us. The only important fact is that he drives back and forth to the reservation itself, and that he knows people who live there. Which made me wonder, Mallory — if Travis actually drives to the very place where your supposed boyfriend was going, why do you think Jake

Blackhorse merely mentioned that he drove to Wyoming? It's a big state."

"I have no idea," Mallory said. "But I noticed that, too. Most people would have said, 'Wow, I know a guy who drives right to where you want to go, and maybe he can give you a ride.' But Jake seemed to go out of his way to hide Travis's destination."

Once again, Jupiter was surprised at how alike his and Mallory's thinking was.

"Well, take a guess," he said. "What's your explanation?"

Mallory stared off into the distance as everyone waited for her response. Jupiter was aware that, if he had been the one thinking, he would have been pinching his bottom lip, but Mallory put her palms on her cheeks. Finally she shrugged her shoulders, just a quick up and down as if she were scratching an itch.

"There's only one reason I can think of," she said. "What if Jake has some secret information about Travis that he doesn't want anyone else to know he has?"

"Hmm," Jupiter said. "Go on. Keep your voice low."

Mallory looked up quickly, searching for Travis. Jupiter could see he was still with the horses.

"Maybe Jake is actually afraid of Travis for some reason," Mallory said, "but when we were talking in the casino he was more interested in impressing me. So he thought it would be cool to tell me he knew someone who could help me – but then thought better of it. On second thought, he came to the conclusion that it would have been better not to have mentioned Travis at all."

"I don't know," Pete said. "He doesn't seem that threatening to me."

"Maybe not," Bob said, "but what Mallory is saying makes a lot of sense. Jake blunders ahead without thinking, and then tries to backtrack. But he can't erase Travis's name, so he does the next best thing – withholds the most important piece of information."

"I agree," Jupiter said. "That makes sense. Here he comes."

Jupiter had been keeping an eye on Travis, and now he was heading back with the horses.

"O.K., you guys," he said. "It's time to get back in the saddle. We need to get going."

The minute Jupiter stood up, he realized how much his legs ached. He hadn't really thought of horseback riding as exercise, but clearly it was. Pete and Bob mounted quickly, and as Travis started out, back the way they had come, the two of them followed along. Jupiter and Mallory wound up at the back of the line this time, Mallory riding in front of him, which was fine with Jupiter. He wanted the chance to talk to Mallory. They fell back far enough so that they could talk without worrying about being overheard.

"So what do we do next?" Mallory asked over her shoulder.

"The first thing I want to do is to call Emmett Morgan in Lander. He's Georgina Paxton's neighbor – the guy who discovered Thomas Littlewolf's body. I have a question for him. It's too complicated to go into right now; I'll explain later. But I can't wait to get the answer."

"I'd also like to find out more about when Garrett made trips to Wyoming," Mallory said. "It would be good to know if he made a trip to the Wind River reservation at around the time that Jimmy's father went there to visit his sister. If they were both there at the same time."

"Yes," Jupiter said. "We should certainly try to cross off what a scientist would call the most parsimonious explanation for Travis Garrett's involvement in the situation."

"What's a parsimonious explanation?" Mallory asked.

"The explanation that requires the fewest number of details in order to make sense is the most parsimonious one," Jupiter said. "The one that hits the target most directly. In this case, it might indeed be the right one."

The sun was hotter now and Jupiter was feeling very thirsty. He took a drink from his water bottle, and as he lowered it and reattached it to his pommel, he caught a glimpse of Travis Garrett riding.

Because Jupiter was seeing Garrett from behind – at a greater distance and an entirely different angle than he'd had when he was right behind him – Jupiter noticed what a big man he was, how long his legs were, how tall he was. In fact, he suddenly saw – or at least imagined! – what he hadn't seen until now – that Travis Garrett looked a lot like the cowboy in Dr. Paxton's photograph of the monarch butterfly.

11

Freya Gets The Goods

On the trail ride down to the Mustang Ranch, Bob found himself third in line behind Pete and Travis Garrett. Although the ride up into the mountains had been slow and rather stately, the ride back seemed to take very little time – as though the horses were hurrying to their barn, looking forward to lunch. Did horses eat lunch? Bob didn't know.

But he and the others were hungry, and about a half hour after they thanked Travis Garrett and left the ranch, Worthington pulled the Flex into the parking lot at Buzzy's, a sandwich shop on the outskirts of Claremont. Everyone had thought it would be a good idea to have something to eat before going to Pomona College and meeting Dr. Yang.

Buzzy's was a busy place, but they managed to find a long picnic table out back under a pleasantly shady tree, big enough to fit all four of them and Worthington. As they waited for their food, Jupiter told them his theory about the cattle drive and how eager he was to find out if his hypothesis was correct.

As Records and Research, Bob had been given custody of the papers and reports that Chief Reynolds had handed to Jupiter, and now he took them out, found Emmett Morgan's telephone number, and programmed it into his phone. That way they'd be all ready for Jupiter to place the call after they'd finished lunch.

Bob was in a great mood. He'd really loved the horseback ride and had especially enjoyed talking and joking with Pete as they'd brought up the rear on the ride up into the mountains. And Buzzy's was just fine. But he was really not looking forward to taking part in this creativity research with Dr. Yang.

He was truly flattered that Hector Sebastian had thought him a suitable candidate for Dr. Yang's project, but he had serious misgivings.

He couldn't put his finger on just why. When Bob had talked to his mother about Dr. Yang's experiment, she'd said that, as an evolutionary biologist, she thought it was likely to lead to the discovery that certain types of creativity could indeed be linked to certain genetic markers.

She thought they might vary widely, and that what made one person inclined to write would be very different from what inclined another to paint or to compose music.

But the more Bob thought about it, the less he felt like he wanted his own creativity to be studied or examined. It felt secret and private to him.

When he sat down to write, sometimes it went well and other times it didn't. It was mysterious, and he liked the mystery — even though it was often frustrating. Once again, he thought that Mallory had been right when she'd suggested that, especially in the beginning of a project, it was a huge mistake to think too hard about it or to talk about it with other people.

After all, in those beginning stages, something was knitting itself together; something was coming forth from nothing, and shining a bright light on it could make it retreat into the darkness it had come from. Creativity was a tentative process, step by step.

The wrong word or response from someone else — even if meant to be encouraging — could knock you off course or stop you altogether.

Not that criticisms or suggestions were bad, Bob thought. Often, someone else could see something you'd missed. But in the earliest stages, you needed to be quiet and private in order to let the impulse develop. Hector Sebastian, who had written lots and lots of books and had achieved a great deal of success as a writer, might well feel confident enough to take the risk of having a scientist analyze his genetic makeup to see if there were any connections or resemblances to that of other highly creative people. But Bob understood that he was nowhere near confident enough to risk it.

He was still young and hadn't been writing for that long, and if, at the end of her analysis, Dr. Yang were to tell him that, as far as she could see, his genetic makeup didn't match the makeup of other creative people, it could easily derail him.

At the very least it would make him question himself – make him nervous and anxious, or even completely ruin his pleasure in what he was doing and his belief that he was doing it well.

And if the news from Dr. Yang were different – that she saw connections between his genetic makeup and that of other writers – what good would that do him? He already knew he loved writing and wanted to be good at it. The whole thing seemed – well, interesting, maybe, in the abstract, but it didn't really have anything to do with him personally.

Pete put down the remnants of a sandwich he'd almost devoured and looked at Bob peculiarly.

"What's going on?" Pete said. "I smell wood burning."

Bob smiled. "I was thinking about this experiment Hector Sebastian signed me up for."

"I bet you're looking forward to it," Pete said. "You must be really pleased."

Bob frowned. "Not really," he said. "I mean, I'm flattered that Hector thought of me, and everything, but I'm — I don't know. Of course I suppose it will be interesting, but — "

"I get it," Worthington said. "It's great to have your creativity recognized by someone like Hector Sebastian, but what's really important is to *be* creative, not to have someone else think that you are, or decide that you are on the basis of some sort of test. In other words, it's nice to be invited to the dance, but you don't have to go."

"Yeah," Bob said. "That's exactly right."

Worthington went on. "Of course, it's important that scientists find out whatever they can about the evolutionary origins of all sorts of human abilities and traits, and we're still at the beginning of genetic research. But I don't

think Bob ought to feel any pressure to participate in any particular experiment if he doesn't
want to."

He turned to Pete. "Would you want to
take part in an experiment trying to find out
why some people are so good at hacky sack or
baseball?"

"I don't know," Pete said. "I never
thought about it."

"But it wouldn't help you, would it?"
Worthington asked.

"No," Pete said. "At least I don't think
so."

"So maybe Bob should give this a miss,"
Mallory said suddenly. "After all, there will be
lots of people who'll want to participate in an
experiment like this." She smiled slyly. "But I
don't think they'll necessarily be the ones who
are the most creative."

Bob nodded. It was just like Mallory to
be able to put his feelings into words.

"I think Worthington's right," Jupiter
said. "From what I've been able to learn from
my reading, very creative people don't tend to
listen too carefully to other peoples' opinions
about their abilities. It's possible Dr. Yang will
have a harder time getting a proper sample for
this study than she imagines."

"So how ought she go about it?" Bob asked. "Do you think she's making a mistake by selecting people she's already decided are 'creative,' whatever that means?"

"She started with published writers, as I recall," Jupiter said. "Maybe the only way to do what Dr. Yang wants to do would be to take DNA samples from an entire, randomly chosen population. And then she'd need to give that population a standardized test."

"But what kind of a multiple choice test could ever determine creativity?" Mallory asked.

"Exactly," Jupiter said. "Standardized tests work well with mathematical or spatial or logical or verbal abilities, but I would think that creativity would be much harder to test for."

Worthington had been listening to the conversation with great interest, and he suddenly joined in again.

"I agree with Jupiter," he said. "The abilities those tests measure are somehow pure and distinct. But creativity is a hybrid, made up of lots of different parts, and pretty messy."

Bob felt as though a weight had been lifted from his shoulders. Being given permission by his best friends not to participate in Dr. Yang's research not only made him feel a great deal better, but also freed him to at least be polite to Hector Sebastian and Dr. Yang.

"I might as well check it out at least," Bob said. "After all, we're right here in Claremont. Pomona College can't be more than a few minutes away, and Hector said we'd all really like the campus. But first, now that we've finished eating, Jupiter should call Emmett Morgan."

Bob took out his cellphone and upped the volume, then hit the 'call' button. He'd already programmed the number of the Triple X Ranch into it, and the phone began to ring. He placed it carefully in the center of the table, and all five of them leaned close in order to hear.

On the fifth ring, a deep male voice answered. "Triple X," he said.

"Could I speak with Mr. Emmett Morgan?" Jupiter asked.

"You got him," the man said. "Who's this?"

"Mr. Morgan," Jupiter said, "my name is Jupiter Jones. I'm calling from California. I'm a member of a small detective firm investigating the death of Thomas Littlewolf. We know his son, Jimmy. I read in the sheriff's report that you discovered his father's body."

"I did," Mr. Morgan said. His voice sounded stiff and suspicious.

"I'm also an acquaintance of Dr. Georgina Paxton," Jupiter said. "I was talking to her yesterday. She spoke very highly of you and said that she was sure you'd help our investigation by answering a few questions."

"You know Georgie?" Mr. Morgan said. His voice had become a good deal friendlier. "Well, that's a different kettle of fish. Sure, I'll help if I can. Fire away."

Pete shot Jupiter a confident glance and gave him a thumbs-up.

"Thank you, sir," Jupiter said. "If you would, I'd like you to think back to the day you found Mr. Littlewolf. I was wondering if you remembered where your cattle were that day."

"That's over a year ago, son," Mr. Morgan said, "and my boys move the stock most every day. But I actually do remember, because that day was different. I still think the sheriff didn't get to the bottom of Tommy's death."

"That's what we're trying to do, sir," Jupiter said.

"So the boys moved the cows that day from the western fields down toward the river, to the east," Mr. Morgan said.

"Near to where you found Mr. Little-wolf's body?" Jupiter asked.

"That's surely right," Mr. Morgan said. "I was riding old Tumbleweed out to see how the boys were doing."

Jupiter smiled. Bob was amazed. How had Jupiter figured that out? Gosh, he thought. Dr. Yang ought to be studying Jupiter! After all, Jupiter had always been the really creative one – the one who could think his way through just about any problem.

"And I was wondering," Jupiter went on. "I was told there was a trail across the river there, near where you were riding. Is there another crossing up the road, maybe two or three miles further up?"

"Indeed there is, young feller. The north fork spreads out; the water's pretty shallow and you can get across it easy."

Bob thought that would be the end of the conversation, but Jupiter surprised him by asking a third question. "Mr. Morgan," Jupiter asked. "Have you ever heard about, or run across, a palamino belonging to someone who lives on the reservation? One with a white patch on his rump?"

"You surprise me," Mr. Morgan said. "I knew that horse right well. A savage critter, to-

tally untamed, and mean as hell. He belonged
to Billy Redsmoke, an Arapaho from Ethete
who worked for me one summer. Billy brought
that horse with him and about two weeks after
I hired him, Billy smashed a bottle of liquor at
the ground in front of the horse. It was already
a spooky critter, but that spooked him more
and he reared up and struck out at my boy
Clay with his front hooves."

Bob looked around at his friends. All of
them were listening attentively. Pete looked like
he had stopped breathing. Jupiter was nodding
slightly. Worthington frowned. Mallory's eyes
were wide.

"What happened?" Jupiter asked.

"Clay was all right," Mr. Morgan said.
"He jumped out of the way, but he fell over
backwards and landed on his behind, and it
was touch and go for a minute. But I fired
Redsmoke on the spot and told him to take
that dang horse and get off the ranch. That
was totally reckless, what he did, and I wound
up feeling sorry for a horse that would be
owned by someone like him. Why do you want
to know?"

"When I'm a little more sure of my
facts," Jupiter said, "I'll be happy to call you
back and tell you. But right now, I don't want

to say something I can't fully support. Thanks a lot for your time, and for being so cooperative. We'll definitely let you know how things go with the investigation."

Jupiter shut the phone and handed it back to Bob. Everyone sat in silence for a few seconds before they all burst forth, talking at once.

"That's it, then," Pete said. "I got to hand it to you, Jupe. You figured out what happened!"

"Maybe," Jupiter said.

"But if this Billy Redsmoke owned that horse," Bob said, "and hired Thomas Littlewolf to train him a bit, and the two of them went for a trail ride, then we know what happened, don't we?"

"If," Jupiter said, "is the operative word."

"So they got off their horses at the top of the cliff," Pete said, "the way we got down at the high point of our ride earlier. And this jerk breaks a liquor bottle in front of the horse — maybe just because he's a jerk! And this time, the horse rears up and knocks Jimmy's father unconscious, and he falls off the cliff and dies. I bet that Billy Redsmoke wanted to get away as quick as possible. He'd have had to avoid the cowboys on the cattle drive − after all, he worked on that ranch for two weeks! It all fits!"

Bob tried to remember what Georgina Paxton had said about the man in the photograph, but he was so excited he couldn't. He was surprised that Jupiter looked less pleased than he would have expected, and Mallory didn't say anything at all.

"I don't know," Jupiter said. "Georgina told us − "

But Pete was incensed. "Jeez," he said. "Why didn't the Lander sheriff talk to this guy? He's not on the list, is he, Bob? Even if he's not legally responsible for the death, he's morally responsible. I mean, he made the horse rear up!"

Bob pulled out the papers and checked. Pete was right. The sheriff had never interviewed Billy Redsmoke. As he put the papers away, he glanced at his watch. It was time to get to Pomona.

Bob and the others were all amazed at how beautiful Pomona College was. This was where Hector had gone to college? The buildings were constructed largely of white stone and had red tile roofs; the walkways were wide and, though it was summer, there were students on campus. All of them looked interesting and intense.

Bob felt completely at home, very different from the way he'd felt when they'd been on campus at the University of California Santa Barbara, which had seemed both too big and sprawling and too diffuse. This campus had a coherence he immediately understood.

Mallory, too, was impressed. "This is brilliant!" she said. "I can see how a bunch of easterners might have started it, but it's western, too, with the tile roofs and open courtyards. It's a cool mixture of the two, looking east and west at the same time. Very Janusian, really."

After asking directions, they found the building where the biology department was housed, and in a laboratory on the second floor, they finally met Dr. Yang. She was a petite woman, with long black hair pulled back into a ponytail, and she looked the four of them over – Worthington had remained with the car – with disinterested eyes.

She was wearing a white lab coat, and she seemed so cool and rational that Bob knew immediately that he'd made the right decision not to take part in her experiment. He'd like to be cool and rational, more like his mother, but he wasn't – he was more emotional, like his father.

Still, he surprised himself, and his friends, with his firm statement to Dr. Yang that, though he appreciated the opportunity, he'd decided not to take part in her study.

She looked slightly surprised but immediately accepted his decision. After telling her that he wished her all the best in her research, Bob turned to leave, followed by the others. No one said anything as they followed him down the winding stairs and back outside, and Bob felt relieved at having said no to something that he hadn't really wanted to do to begin with.

He felt a little sad to be leaving Pomona so quickly, but he hoped this wouldn't be the last time he saw the campus.

All the way back to Rocky Beach, the five of them talked about Bob's decision, and everyone agreed that, although genetic research was important, no one should ever feel pressured to give their DNA to the cause of science if they didn't want to.

"It's a basic matter of freedom," Jupiter said.

"I agree," Pete said. "I read a newspaper article about a guy whose DNA was stolen! Someone picked up a coffee cup he'd used in a cafeteria!"

"That's just plain wrong," Mallory said. Everyone agreed that it was immoral to use trickery to get DNA.

When they finally pulled into the Salvage Yard, Bob was surprised to see that Freya Haldorrson was there, sitting on the office steps, waiting for them.

"Look!" Pete said. "It's Freya!"

"She's probably come to tell us what she found out," Mallory said. "Jupiter and I never got around to telling you that we asked her to get some information from Jimmy. Remember at his house when we told him that Jake and Mackie Gupta had taken DNA tests together, supposedly as a joke? Jimmy was so startled he blurted out, 'But that was the summer that I took a − .' He got interrupted when Jake came home.

"Jupiter wondered how else the sentence could possibly have ended other than with 'a DNA test,'" Mallory added. "Freya was going to a chess tournament with Jimmy, so we asked her to find out what she could."

Bob hadn't seen Freya since the day she'd taken them to her house to meet Jimmy Littlewolf, and he found he was glad to see her. She looked very pretty, and the pink spots on her cheeks seemed pinker than usual.

"Hi!" Bob said to her. "How did you get here?"

"I hitched a ride with Leif and Magnus," Freya said.

"Have you been waiting long?"

"Well," Freya said. "I knew you'd want to hear what I found out."

Bob could see she was just about bursting with the information, and before she could come out with it, there, in the parking lot, he suggested they all go to the outdoor workshop to talk. She looked at him gratefully, and followed as he led.

They had barely settled down when Freya began talking. Bob found himself, somehow, in charge of the conversation, which he didn't mind a bit. He liked Freya's excitement, and he was very much looking forward to hearing what she had to say.

As it turned out, Freya wasn't just excited; she was also upset. The day before, at the chess tournament, Jimmy had been so flummoxed when she asked him about the test – and so impressed that The Three Investigators had somehow figured it out – that he'd told her everything.

"He took the test the summer after his father died," Freya said. "Not very long after.

He and his mom went back to the Duck Valley reservation in Nevada for the funeral. Where they'd all lived before they came to California. Somehow they'd gotten his father's body from Wyoming to Nevada. Jake didn't go. He had to work at the casino."

"Whoa, whoa," Bob said. "Slow down. We've got all afternoon." Freya had begun talking so rapidly that Bob was afraid he'd miss some of what she had to say. Freya smiled and took a deep breath and started again.

"Jimmy said he was so angry and so sad that when some friends of his asked him if he wanted to drink with them, he decided he would. He'd never done it before, after what his father had said about alcohol, but now his father was dead, and someone had thrown alcohol on him before he died, so Jimmy decided he didn't care."

"What happened?" Mallory asked.

"They had some beer and some wine and some whiskey, I guess," Freya said, "and before long Jimmy's friends were all staggering around and getting sick and laughing, and Jimmy didn't feel much of anything at all. He thought that was weird, because Indians weren't supposed to be able to tolerate alcohol. So when he got back to California, he told

Jake. And Jake said that wasn't surprising, because Thomas Littlewolf hadn't really been Jake's father, anyway."

"What?" Pete exclaimed. Bob felt shocked, too.

"That's what Jake told him. Supposedly their mother had — their mother had had an affair." Freya's cheeks grew even redder but her voice remained steady. "Fourteen years earlier, with some doctor who had worked at the clinic on the reservation."

She was proud to have told this straight, but also quite clearly embarrassed, Bob saw.

"Anyway, Jake went on to tell Jimmy that not only had their mother had an affair, but their mother's mother had too! Jake said he didn't know if the guy with their grandmother was Native American or not, but maybe the reason Jimmy didn't get drunk was because he didn't have much Native American blood at all!"

"That's terrible!" Mallory said. "Jake told him that?"

Freya nodded. "Jimmy said that Jake was always telling him crazy stuff, trying to put one over on him, and he might not have believed a word of it, but then he started thinking about horses."

"Horses?" Pete interjected. "What do horses have to do with this?"

"Jimmy doesn't like horses," Freya said. "He doesn't trust them, and he has no natural instinct for riding or for understanding horses. And he was always embarrassed about that, because his father was so great with them and had always been so proud of his skill and had actually made a living working with them."

"And because the Shoshone are famously such great horse people – " Bob started.

"Exactly," Freya said. "So the two things together – the fact that he had a hard time getting drunk and that he didn't like horses – kept nagging at him and made him think that maybe there was something in what Jake had said. And the worst thing was that, when Jimmy seemed down about this, Jake pushed the idea of a DNA test on him, saying he ought to take it so that he'd know one way or the other."

"So he took the test," Bob said.

"Yes," Freya said, "and when the results came back, they said that the donor was less than twenty percent Native American."

"And ever since," Mallory said, "Jimmy's been depressed and angry – at his mother, at his father – because now he thought he knew he wasn't who he'd thought he was."

"I knew that Jimmy wanted us to help him with something other than the death of his father," Jupiter said thoughtfully. "Now we know what is is."

"But," Freya said. "I'm sure Jimmy is just who he always thought he was. I'm sure that Thomas Littlewolf *was* his father and that Jake is a – " Her voice got very low and her cheeks flamed. " – a bastard who's just trying to mess with his head."

"What do you mean?" Bob asked – though he was beginning to get the idea.

"I'm sure Jake must have switched Jimmy's DNA test with someone else's – probably Mackie Gupta's."

When Freya triumphantly announced this, Bob realized that, though he might have been walking down the same logical path, she'd gotten there before him. She was frowning now, her blue eyes wide, her cheeks bright red, obviously both proud of herself and also enraged at Jake Blackhorse's cruelty toward his own half-brother.

Why would someone do something like that? he wondered. There was only one explanation. Jake was angry himself, though he wouldn't have put it that way. His anger was subterranean. He was jealous of how smart Jimmy was, and of the fact that Jimmy's father had been a man of substance who had stuck around to raise his son.

Bob was angry at Jake as well, but he was also impressed with what Freya had managed to find out and how she'd thought about it. Up until now he'd been slightly bothered by the idea that Freya Haldorsson had a crush on him, but he suddenly discovered he was glad she did. She was pretty cool, actually – and coolly pretty. Very pretty. She was smart and cared deeply about things.

And she was turning out to be a good friend to Jimmy Littlewolf. Bob was sure that somehow she'd help Jimmy learn that he needed to look clearly into his own past in order to move into his future – not dwell on the lies his brother had told.

Of course, even when he did that, he still wouldn't know what his future looked like, exactly. He wasn't the god Janus, after all! Still, at least he'd be able to imagine some interesting, decent paths.

Bob remembered what Jupiter had said about life and chess being somewhat alike, and all of a sudden he thought that life might be like chess in that you did well by not making too many bad moves.

He also thought that Freya would understand exactly what that meant!

12

Pete Sees What Really Matters

Though Pete was startled by Freya's deduction, he was even more interested in the expression on Bob's face. He'd never seen Bob look at Freya that way before – with a mixture of admiration and excitement and pleasure. He looked as though he was interested in her, and not just as someone with information for The Three Investigators. He was looking at her as a *girl.*

Pete found himself smiling so widely that the sides of his mouth hurt. For a moment he was on the verge of making a joke, but then thought better of it. Now was not the time to be a smart aleck. He was amused, of course, because Bob had complained more than once about the crush he thought that Freya had on him. It looked like Bob wouldn't be complaining any more.

Like Bob, Pete was impressed with Freya. Jupiter and Mallory had simply asked her for some information, but she had done a good deal more than get it. She'd acted like a real investigator! She'd gathered her facts and then used them to come to a conclusion that Jake must have switched Mackie's DNA for Jimmy's.

He could see that both Freya and Bob were incensed by what Jake had done, but he found he wasn't quite as upset. It was a rotten trick, no doubt about it, but he thought there was a possibility that Jake hadn't done it merely out of meanness. He was a dumb guy who didn't take anything very seriously, and he got his kicks by trying to come out on top in a world where he often came out far below that.

"I hope you told Jimmy what must have happened," Pete said. "I bet he was glad to hear it."

Freya looked at him a bit blankly, he thought. "No," she said, "I didn't tell him."

Pete was aghast. "Why not?" he said.

"I really, really wanted to," Freya said, "but it was just an idea I had. What if I'm wrong? I don't have any proof, and, anyway, I'm not one of you guys – or even a Special Consultant like Mallory. I really didn't feel I had the right to get in the middle of what you four are trying to do for Jimmy. I did my part by putting him in touch with you. And now I've told you what I found out and what I think."

"Wow," Pete said. "I guess I see what

you mean." He was *really* impressed now. If it had been him, he knew there was no way on earth he could have kept his mouth shut. Once he had figured out what he thought had happened, he was sure he would have told Jimmy – both because he would have been so proud of himself and also because he knew it would make Jimmy feel better. He wouldn't have been cautious or deferential, the way Freya had been.

And what if, as Freya said, the conclusion was wrong? What if Jake hadn't switched Gupta's test with Jimmy's? What if Jimmy really *was* only twenty percent Native American? Then Pete would really have stuck his foot in it. He needed to remember that Jupiter was always reminding him and Bob that suspicions weren't truth. Somehow Freya had known that instinctively.

She was quite a great girl, he thought, even though she wasn't his type. Which was funny, in a way, because up to this point in his life, he had pretty much liked all girls. But Freya, for all her good points, was just a little timid for him. He liked girls who were more assertive and lively. Freya seemed a little passive. He thought ahead to the raft trip that they'd be taking soon, probably right after they wrapped up this case. Maybe next week! He was pretty excited by the fact that Mallory had agreed that they should ask Califia García-Williams to be the sixth person on the trip.

While Pete had been thinking all these things, Jupiter, Mallory, and Bob had been talking, and Pete realized he'd been so deep inside his head that he'd missed a lot of the conversation. As he tuned back in, he heard Bob ask, "But what does chess have to do with it?"

"I don't know for sure," Jupiter said. "But it certainly is an odd coincidence."

"Wait a minute, wait a minute," Pete said, confused. "I think I missed something. I mean, I *know* I missed something. I was daydreaming there for a minute. What are you guys talking about?"

"Jupiter was wondering why Jimmy had started to play chess in the first place," Bob said. "It's not as though he learned it from his mother or father or Jake. And it would be even better if we knew when he started to play."

"He told me he started about a year ago," Freya said. "He's very good for someone who hasn't played for that long."

"In other words, Jimmy started playing not long after his father died, and soon after the results of the DNA test came back," Jupiter said.

"I don't see the connection," Pete said.

"Maybe that's because you don't know much about the history of chess," Jupiter said.

"You can say that again," Pete said.

"The earliest forms of the game come from the Gupta empire in northwestern India," Mallory said.

"Really?" Pete said, surprised.

"Really," said Mallory. "When it was first thought up, fifteen hundred years ago, it was based on Indian military strategy. It spread to Persia and then, after the Muslim Empire conquered Persia, it expanded into Europe. The rules and the game as we know it were put in place in the 19th century. But we're pretty certain that it started in India."

"And not only that," Jupiter said, "but in recent years an Indian man named Viswanathan Anand was the Chess World Champion five times. He became a sensation in India, and chess is a very popular game there now — probably because of the publicity around Anand."

"What Jupiter is suggesting," Bob said, "and it makes a lot of sense, I think, is that when Jimmy got the results of the DNA test, he was so flabbergasted he looked up what Indians from India were good at. He wondered if he might be good at chess."

"The false test," Mallory said, "I mean, the test that wasn't his − told him he was more than 50% Indian from India, rather than Native American, as he had always thought. And the sad truth is that when Jimmy discovered he *was* good at chess, he must have taken it as further proof that the DNA test was right."

"I wonder how Jake explained the results of that test to Jimmy," Pete said.

"He probably just told him that the man his mother had supposedly slept with was an Indian doctor who worked at the clinic on the Duck Valley Reservation. After all, a lot of doctors *are* Indian − Mackie's father is," Bob said.

"Anyway," Mallory said. "It must have been just more proof to Jimmy that he wasn't who he'd always thought he was. Now he had three pieces of evidence. He was good at chess; he could hold his liquor. And he didn't like horses."

"This just goes to show," Jupiter said, "how careful we have to be with our facts and our logic. Genetics can be so easily misunderstood and misused. The fact that Jimmy has no understanding of or affinity for horses has nothing to do with genetics – at least not in any kind of simple way. The Shoshone didn't have horses until they had dealings with the Spanish. Genetic changes take thousands and thousands of years, so even if there were some genetic link between the Shoshone and a love of horses, it wouldn't show up for centuries.

"As for chess, that also doesn't involve genetics – just a specialized kind of raw intelligence," Jupiter added. "Only Jimmy's ability to drink without getting drunk is relevant in this case, but as we know, there's a wide distribution of traits throughout a population, and on any bell curve there are tails at both ends."

Pete had absolutely no idea what tails at both ends of a bell curve were, but at the moment he didn't care.

As far as he was concerned, there were a lot of things more important and pressing to talk about than chess and horses and alcohol and genes, and he was determined to say so. It was all well and good to get caught up in theoretical discussions, but sometimes you just needed to be practical. Which was what Pete was good at.

He got to his feet in order to be more emphatic. "We need to tell Jimmy that we think Jake mixed up Jimmy's DNA test with Mackie

Gupta's on purpose. Even though we don't have total proof, it's our responsibility to tell him as soon as possible so that he can stop feeling bad about himself."

"Hmmm," Jupiter said. "Go on."

"Before he started doubting himself," Pete said, "he was probably very proud of the fact that he was the son of a full-blooded Eastern Shoshone man from the Wind River Reservation and a full-blooded Western Shoshone woman from the Duck Valley Reservation. And if it weren't for the lies Jake told him, he'd still be proud. But now he's embarrassed and ashamed and confused, and he's felt this way for a whole year! You yourself told us you thought that Jimmy wanted help with more than his father's murder. And now we can help him.

"And what's more," Pete continued. "Remember how Jimmy acted with his mother? Ever since his brother lied to him, he's thought *she* was the liar − that she'd slept with a man who wasn't his father. It's hurt their relationship a lot. Remember how sad she seemed? How painful it was to meet her with Jimmy there? Probably he and his mom were very close before Jake pulled his trick."

"You're right," Jupiter said. "We may

246

not know the absolute truth, but the explanation makes so much sense that it must be true. And to wait any longer to tell Jimmy — until we were sure sure sure — would be as immoral as what Jake did to him."

"I think it's also time to tell him," Pete went on, "that all the evidence so far points to the fact that his father's death wasn't a murder at all, but just an accident. An accident that was covered up, sure, but at least that's better than thinking that someone hated your father and wanted to kill him and got away with it."

Mallory was looking at him doubtfully.

"What?" he asked her.

She threw her hands up and shook her head. "I just don't know," she said. "In one way I agree with you, but in another way I don't. It's important to make Jimmy's life better — that's why we decided to take the case in the first place. But thinking things through carefully doesn't have to be opposed to being compassionate. Even though what we think is true would make Jimmy feel a lot better, it would be best of all if we could prove beyond a shadow of a doubt what happened."

"That's true," Pete said, "If we could prove what we think, that would be best. Just so long as it doesn't take too long."

"I think so too," Bob said. "But how can we do that?" He thought for a minute. "Mallory, you said that Mackie Gupta was really a good guy and that you liked him a lot better than you liked Jake. Maybe, if we talked to him, he'd be willing to take another DNA test so that we can prove the first one was his."

"Or maybe we could get Jimmy to take another test," Pete said.

"Not without explaining to him what we think," Jupiter said.

"You're right, Bob," Mallory said. "Mackie was a nice guy, and your idea might work, but it would also work if we could just get Jake to admit what he did. He undoubtedly has his faults, but I didn't think he was a total git, and if he were approached the right way, he might do that."

"What are you thinking?" Pete asked.

"Well, I talked to him the first time," Mallory said. "I'm willing to try again."

"To get him to confess?" Pete said. He thought of all the movies he'd seen with policemen in darkened rooms, and a suspect who sat under an unshaded light bulb as they threw question after question at him.

"The results of Jimmy's DNA test are one thing," Bob said. "But what about Thomas

Littlewolf's death? How are we going to prove who was involved with that? At the moment, our hypothesis is that the rider in Dr. Paxton's photograph was with Thomas Littlewolf when he died, and that he's the owner of the piebald horse."

"Actually," Jupiter said, "there's something I haven't told you yet. It happened when we went on the trail ride earlier. It made me really wish we could find out whether Travis Garrett was at the Wind River Reservation at the time that Thomas Littlewolf died."

"What is it?" Pete asked. "Why didn't you tell us earlier!"

"I hadn't found a good moment to mention it," Jupiter said. "On the way up the trail, I was right behind Travis so I could ask him questions. But on the way back, after we stopped at the top, I was last in line. So I got a very different perspective on Mr. Garrett. I was far enough back and saw him from a different angle, and I have to say that he looked a lot like the rider in Dr. Paxton's picture."

"Really?" Bob asked.

Jupiter nodded. "He's a big man, really tall, with broad shoulders. But, after lunch, when we called Mr. Morgan, we all wanted to leap to the conclusion that the man leading the piebald horse had to be Billy Redsmoke because of the story Mr. Morgan told us about him breaking the bottle of liquor at the horse's feet. After all, shards of a broken liquor bottle were found at the scene, and there was liquor on Thomas Littlewolf's clothing.

"But I've been thinking. If Billy Redsmoke was fired after that stunt, the story about him breaking the bottle in front of that stallion would have been all over. Travis Garrett would have heard it too. So we actually have two suspects – Travis Garrett and Billy Redsmoke – and Redsmoke might be considered the less likely of the two. After all, Dr. Paxton said that Billy Redsmoke was pretty short, with narrow shoulders, and that he always wore a hat with four eagle feathers."

"That's right," Pete said. "Dr. Paxton did say that. I remember now."

"Travis Garrett was wearing a plain cowboy hat today," Mallory said. "And the man in the photograph was too."

All this talking and thinking was great, Pete thought. But it *was* time for some action. While they were being careful, Jimmy was stewing in his own juice, as his father put it. There was nothing wrong about sharing their ideas with him. They could tell him they weren't absolutely positive yet.

"Can we please call Jimmy and ask him to come over?" Pete said. "We really can't wait to tell him the good news. I've been flip-flopping, I know, but I've made up my mind."

He felt passionate about this and now that he'd convinced himself, he wasn't about to be dissuaded.

Jupiter nodded. "All right," he said. "Let's do it. If everyone else agrees?"

Pete glanced around. Freya looked particularly happy at the decision and so did Bob. Even Mallory, who'd been the loudest voice for waiting, seemed to have become convinced.

Bob took out his cellphone and dialed Jimmy's number. He stood up and paced, waiting for someone to answer. Just when he was about to give up, he said, "Jimmy? Is that you? This is Bob Andrews with The Three Investigators."

He listened for a moment.

"No, we're all fine, thanks," he said. "We're back from the Mustang Ranch and our trail ride with Travis Garrett. Listen, we have some good news for you — really good news — but we'd like to give it to you in person. Can you come over to the Salvage Yard? You can? That's great! O.K. We'll see you in about twenty minutes."

He hung up the phone and smiled at the others.

"Twenty minutes?" Pete said. "I guess I can wait that long."

He looked up to see Leif Haldorrson approaching the outdoor workshop. "Hey, Leif!" he called. "Good to see you!"

"What's all the mystery?" Leif asked.

"We're getting close to the end of a case," Pete said, "and Freya really helped!"

Leif smiled and looked at his sister. "I'm sorry to drag you away," he said, "but Magnus and I are leaving, and we have to take you with us."

"Right now?" Freya said. "You can't wait twenty minutes?" She looked very disappointed that she wouldn't be there when Jimmy Littlewolf arrived.

"Sorry," Leif said. "We've got to go."

Freya groaned and got to her feet. "You have to tell me all about how Jimmy reacts when you tell him the news," she said to Bob.

"I will," Bob said. "You can count on it."

"Bye, everyone," Freya said, lifting her hand and giving a little wave. "Bye, Bob."

Pete watched her walk away. She was a

great girl. He glanced at Bob, who evidently thought so, too.

He turned back to the group. "O.K.," he said. "We can tell Jimmy what we suspect is true – and what we sort of know *has* to be true because nothing else explains the facts – but how are we really going to pin it down and prove it?"

"I have an idea," Mallory said. "After all, I'm the one who talked to Jake, and he sort of seemed to like me. He told me if I stopped by the Mustang Ranch some time, he'd introduce me to Garrett. I know he tried to back out of it later, but he did say that. Anyway, I could call him at the casino and ask if he wanted to meet me somewhere.

"I could tell him I've decided to take the bus to Wyoming, so I don't need to meet Travis Garrett after all. That should make him feel better. I can say I want to know more about the reservation and about Wyoming in general, so that when I manage to track down my ex-boyfriend I'll know more about how to win him back."

What would an ex-boyfriend of Mallory's look like? Pete wondered. Last year, Bob had been interested in her, but, unfortunately for Bob, that hadn't gone anywhere. Mallory had

253

been nice about it, and they'd wound up fast friends. Still, Pete couldn't quite imagine watch-ing Mallory attempting to win anyone back. She was confident enough to stand on her own, and she wasn't about to go begging.

"What would be best, of course," Mal-lory said, "is if the three of you could do what we did when Worthington talked to Jake – be close enough to overhear but far enough away so that he didn't suspect. So somewhere public, I guess, and somewhere fancy."

"We don't really need to overhear," Jupi-ter said. "You can report to us afterwards. It would be too likely that we'd be discovered, and your whole plan would be ruined."

"Well, it has to be somewhere I can get away easily, and where there would be some-one to help me if I needed help," Mallory said.

"It's not public," Bob said, "but I bet Hector would let you meet Jake at his house. And he could keep an eye on you and help if you needed it. You could tell Jake you'd met this rich mystery writer who was letting you stay in his guest house for a while."

"That's a great idea, Bob," Jupiter said. "Mallory could use the guest house and Mr. Sebastian could keep watch from the main house."

Now they were getting somewhere, Pete thought. "Mr. Sebastian would like to get involved in one of our cases," he said. "He's often said so."

"That will work," Mallory said.

"O.K.," Pete said. "But how are we going to get to the bottom of Thomas Littlewolf's death?"

"We can go down the list of people the sheriff interviewed and call them up again," Jupiter said.

"But we've pretty much narrowed it down, haven't we?" Pete asked. "We don't have any suspects other than Travis Garrett and Billy Redsmoke."

"That's right," Jupiter said. "And if they both come up empty, we're back at the beginning with no real way to try again."

Pete thought for a moment. "How about this?" he asked. "Georgina Paxton was Billy Redsmoke's vet at one time – at least until he stopped going to her. So she knows him a little. And she knows his horse. Maybe Dr. Paxton would be willing to go onto the reservation and confront him and see what he says. If she told him everything we tell her, and everything she knows, she could either get him to confess or to tell her what he knows about Travis Garrett."

"Good thinking, Second," Jupiter said. "I like that idea a lot."

Pete heard the sound of tires on gravel and he looked up to see a red Buick sedan with thick black racing stripes on the hood.

"Come on, guys," Pete said. "Let's go say hello!"

Jimmy got out of the car and stood there looking hopeful, blinking in the bright California sunlight.

"You've got good news?" he asked.

"Boy, do we!" Pete said enthusiastically. He felt very good about the two plans they'd devised and especially good about the excellent news they were about to give Jimmy.

"Let's go over and sit down, and we'll tell you all about it!" he said. As he walked by Jimmy's side, he thought of the moment in the casino in Highland when the man with the beard and the cowboy hat had suddenly hit the jackpot, and his luck had been announced with the noise of a screeching klaxon as coins poured past him to the floor. This was much, much better than anything like *that*; it was a moment when Pete and the other Three Investigators were going to give Jimmy the kind of riches that could last for the whole of somebody's life.

And although Pete and Bob and Jupiter had all played an important role in learning what was really going on in Jimmy's life, it was actually Mallory who was going to play the most important role of all when she tried to get Jake to admit what he'd been doing since Jimmy's father died. If it worked, she and Jimmy would have a pretty durable bond.

13

A Dial Canyon Triumph

Two days later, all the plans had been set in motion and Mallory was on her way to Phillipa Paxton's house by bike. She'd been thrilled by how excited Jimmy had been to learn that they were approaching what would be called, in chess, the endgame – but she was more than a little nervous about pulling off her part in it now.

After all, it was one thing to eat French fries with two strangers in a crowded casino burger joint, and quite another to talk in private with a guy who thought you might be interested in him as a guy, when what you actually wanted was to get him to admit he was a liar. She'd managed to reach Jake at the casino when he was on a break, and he'd agreed to meet her at Hector Sebastian's today.

At first he'd been suspicious. "I thought you were living down here in Highland," he'd said. "How did you meet someone up there?"

"He's a friend of a friend," Mallory said. "What do you care how I met him? He's got a pool and a big house and he's letting me stay in his guest house for free."

"Sounds pretty cool," Jake said.

"So you'll come?" Mallory had asked, feeling a little breathless. Though this wasn't the first time she'd played a role in order to help with a Three Investigators case, it was the first time she'd had to keep up the ruse.

"Yeah," Jake had said. "I can do that."

Since it was too far for Mallory to ride her bike to Dial Canyon, she'd made plans to meet Phillipa at her house in Rocky Beach, after which Phillipa would drive her to Hector Sebastian's.

She and the boys had decided that their original impulse had been right, and that they shouldn't be anywhere nearby if Mallory's plan were to have its best chance of success. When Jake came to call on her, the only people around would be the owner of the house and his friend Phillipa Paxton. That way the story that she'd been invited to stay in Hector's guest house would hold water.

Later that day, after Jake had left — hopefully after having told Mallory all about how he'd switched Mackie Gupta's and Jimmy's DNA tests — Pete's plan would go into effect. Worthington would bring Jupiter, Pete, and Bob out to Dial Canyon so that they all could take part in a second call with Georgina Paxton.

Dr. Paxton had agreed to ride onto the reservation to talk to Billy Redsmoke. She'd learned that he was working with a crew doing some buck and rail fencing on the reservation, and her plan was to catch him and talk to him there, with other people around.

She had a smartphone, and she planned to take it with her; hopefully she'd be able to stream video of her conversation with Redsmoke so that Mallory and The Three Investigators, almost a thousand miles away, could see and hear the conversation. She'd also record it if they needed confirmation of what Redsmoke had said.

Mallory was now several blocks from Phillipa Paxton's house, and as she rode, she remembered how happy Jimmy had been at all the news they'd given him two days ago, and how happy she'd been to take part in giving it to him.

Jimmy had labored under a delusion for a full year. It had shaken him badly – had made him doubt himself and the major relationships in his life. Still, he had managed to begin building what seemed to him a new life with courage and dedication. Jimmy was very special, she thought – deeply sensitive and soulful, and very smart.

She was also thinking about how Pete saw so clearly and argued so forcefully that even if they were *never* able to tie up all the loose ends in the case, what really mattered was Jimmy's feelings. After all, from the day she and Bob had met Jimmy at Freya's house, she had sensed that there were a lot of mysterious things other than his father's death that worried him. Now she knew what they had been, and The Three Investigators had been able to dispel them, to reassure Jimmy, to give him back his confidence and his sense of himself.

In the beginning, this had seemed like an impossible case. The sheriff of Fremont County, Wyoming hadn't been able to figure it out, and he'd been on the spot soon after it had happened. How could The Three Investigators discover anything about a death that had taken place over a year ago and in a different state? But somehow they'd put their heads together and gotten to the bottom of it.

As Mallory thought about Jupiter, Pete, and Bob, she was suffused with a sense of pleasure. Jupiter was so smart and so good at thinking a problem through, so while Pete was practical but also so sensitive to other peoples' feelings and needs. That's why he was such an excellent matchmaker – and why it looked like he was going to have another real success with Hector and Phillipa.

And Bob was not only solid and dependable and a great climbing partner. He was also an intuitive and tireless researcher and a talented writer – one who understood how complex and variable human nature could be. That was one of the things you needed to know in order to be a good writer, Mallory thought. How no one was all of a piece. How everyone was full of contradictions.

Mallory remembered how, just the other day, she'd held back from telling her mother she'd decided she wanted to stay in the United States – even though it might have been cruel to keep her in suspense. But she hadn't wanted to blow her own (and her mother's) chances for this to come out happily. She knew how contrary she herself could be – how often she felt the need to act against expectations – and she'd been afraid that if she committed too early to staying in Rocky Beach, she'd have so much time to worry about her decision that she might change her mind.

She thought of Bob and the conflicted

way he felt about taking part in Dr. Yang's research. On the one hand he'd been flattered that Hector Sebastian had asked him – but on the other hand, he'd felt a bit resentful at having been forced to make a decision. He liked steadiness and continuity, and he didn't like the boat to be rocked.

He also didn't like to stand out all that much from the crowd. That was why the bobcat was a perfect avatar for him – or a perfect spirit animal. Actually, all three of the animals they'd chosen for the new Three Investigators logo were perfect, Mallory thought. For the first time, she wondered what her spirit animal would be, if she had one. That would take some thinking and she didn't have time right now. But as she pedaled into Phillipa Paxton's block, she suddenly had an idea about the new Three Investigators Headquarters.

She still wasn't certain about a lot of aspects of the design, but from the very start she'd had the idea that HQ2 should have two entrances – with glass French doors on the side of the building that opened to the outdoor workshop, to make it easy to carry things in and out, and a single wooden door with a glass top panel in the building's front, facing the main gates. That would be the entrance their clients would use when they came to consult.

Now Mallory had the sudden idea that they should commission an artist to design a wooden sign to hang above that door. On the sign would be the words *The Three Investigators,* curved in an arch – perhaps with a dot at either end of the words – and tucked under the words would be the chimera logo that Connor O'Malley had designed, curved as well and brightly painted.

It was a great idea, she thought, but as she pulled into Phillipa Paxton's driveway, she shoved it aside for the time being. She had barely dismounted before Phillipa came to the door, waving, and told her to put her bike safely in the garage. Ten minutes later they were on their way to Dial Canyon.

After some friendly small talk, they fell into a companionable silence. Mallory assumed Phillipa was thinking about the two plans that Mallory and the boys were unfurling that afternoon – one of which starred Phillipa's sister. Mallory was thinking about how much she liked Phillipa and how easy it was to be around her, especially since their adventure in Castello Serreno in Napa at the beginning of the summer.

But she was also thinking about human creativity, and how surprising it was. There she'd been, biking along, thinking hard, and her train of association had taken her from Jimmy and the current case, to how much she liked Jupiter, Pete, and Bob, to the nature of a good writer. Which had brought her to Bob's avatar the bobcat, and The Three Investigators logo — and then the burst of inspiration that had resulted in her idea for the sign over the door. She smiled. You never really knew when an idea would break upon you. You had to be ready and receptive.

Hector Sebastian obviously had had his eye out for them, and he came down to the driveway to meet them as soon as they'd parked.

"You're here!" he said. "I was getting a little worried. What would I have done if that young man had shown up and Mallory wasn't here?"

"Don't worry, Mr. Sebastian," Mallory said. "I told him to be on time, and we still have a half hour."

"That's good to know," Hector said. "But let's not stand around dawdling." He peered at Mallory. "You look quite well put together for a runaway," he said. "And not too malnourished."

The three of them walked off across the

property, past the pool, to the guesthouse. He flung open the door and Mallory walked in. It was small, she realized; it looked bigger from the outside. It was barely twenty feet wide by twenty-five feet long — not much bigger than the new Headquarters she was planning. It had a small kitchenette and a pull-out sofa, very comfortably furnished. She looked around approvingly.

"This is great," Mallory said, "but I think it would be best if Jake and I talked outside, on the porch. You can keep an eye on us from the house that way."

"Are you going to record the conversation?" Hector asked. "I have a small handheld digital recorder you could use."

Mallory thought about that for a second and then rejected it. "No thanks," she said. "I'm sort of afraid I might fumble it."

After all, this wasn't a sting operation, and she didn't want to do anything too obvious or that would make Jake suspicious.

"We'll just sit on the porch and talk," Mallory said. "I think the best approach is to make Jake feel comfortable. I hope my instinct is right — that he's been feeling guilty about what he did and that he'll be relieved to admit it and set everything straight."

"I hope he does," Phillipa said, "and you can bet we'll keep an eye on the two of you while he's here."

"When he gets here, we'll come out to meet him, just to play along," Hector said. "Then we'll go into the house and you and he can sit out here on the porch and talk. Come along to the kitchen and I'll give you some lemonade you can give to him."

"Tart and sweet," Phillipa said to Hector. "Just like you."

Wow! Mallory thought. Pete had really hit the bull's eye this time.

She followed them across the lawn and patio and into the main house. Hector had already arranged a small tray with two glasses and a pitcher of lemonade, filled with ice cubes.

"Here you go," he said. "As I told you, we'll keep an eye on you through the window in the living room. When you want the meeting to be over, for whatever reason, why don't you give us a signal?"

"That's a great idea," Mallory said. "Why don't I stretch both of my hands as high over my head as I can? That should be pretty visible."

"That's perfect," Phillipa said. "We'll be on the lookout."

The three of them went out onto the patio to wait for Jake, and he didn't take long to arrive. He was driving the same battered blue pickup she'd seen when she ran away from Jimmy's backyard the day Jake had appeared unexpectedly. Today the back was stacked high with bales of hay.

Phillipa and Hector ducked back into the house, and Mallory went down to the truck to meet him.

"Hi, Jake," she said. He was wearing a heavy metal t-shirt, faded jeans, and cowboy boots. He looked like an urban cowboy – more dangerous than he'd looked when he was dressed in his casino uniform. His mirrored glasses reflected the sun.

He took off his sunglasses and planted them carefully on the top of his head; then he crossed his arms and smiled at her, friendly but edgy – as though he expected something, Mallory thought.

"Hey there," he said. "You certainly landed on your feet. This is quite a place. Quite. A. Place."

He was looking past her at the pool house and the pool and the landscaping.

She was a runaway, she remembered. She'd been living on the street. She was homeless. Her Indian boyfriend had dumped her and deserted her.

"Yeah," she said. "I'm not staying in the big house." She pointed to the small guesthouse. "That's where I'm staying."

"Still," Jake said, "it's all part of the same package."

Mallory squinted at him. "This guy Hector Sebastian is pretty rich and sort of annoying," she said, "but he's not all bad. He leaves me alone, and this certainly beats anywhere else I've stayed in several weeks."

"I bet it does," Jake said. He unfolded his arms. "Well, let's go."

He was headed toward the guesthouse when Mallory stopped him. "I think you ought to meet Mr. Sebastian before we go talk," she said.

"Why?" Jake asked. "He's not your father."

"No, he's not," Mallory said. "But it would be polite."

"All right," Jake said. "Fair enough." His tone suggested that politeness was not his strong suit.

Mallory brought Jake around to the patio and opened the French doors into the living room. "Mr. Sebastian?" she called. "My friend's here."

Hector appeared immediately, as though he'd been waiting just outside the room, and came to the door. Mallory suddenly saw him as she would have had she actually been a homeless runaway – a bit stuffy and formal. He'd abandoned his jeans and cowboy boots and was wearing gray slacks, a blue blazer, and tasseled loafers.

"This is Jake Blackhorse," Mallory said.

Hector looked Jake over, then extended his hand. "Nice to meet you, young man," he said. "I'm Hector Sebastian. How old are you?"

The question clearly surprised Jake. "I'm – I'm twenty," he said. "Almost twenty-one."

That wasn't true, Mallory thought. Jimmy had said that Jake was twenty-four. He was downplaying his age because she was so young.

"Hmmm," Hector said. "Welcome to my home." He turned to Mallory. "Is there anything you need, Mallory?"

"No, thanks, Mr. Sebastian," she said. "We'll just go talk now."

"Enjoy yourselves," Hector said. He nodded and closed the French doors behind him. Mallory wasn't sure where things with

Jake would lead, but she felt safer knowing that Hector and Phillipa were watching and that they'd be over in an instant if anything unexpected happened.

She led the way across the yard to the guesthouse.

"I didn't expect the second degree," Jake said.

"I thought you had to be twenty-one to work in the casino," Mallory said.

"I'm twenty-four," Jake said. "But he didn't need to know that."

"Do you lie a lot?" Mallory asked.

"Yeah," Jake said, with a big grin. "Too bad I didn't bring my swimming trunks."

Jake wasn't the only one who lied, she suddenly realized. She was lying too, of course – pretending to be someone she really wasn't. She was hit by a wave of guilt at the trickery she was engaged in. But even as she thought that, she knew it was pretty silly. The lies Jake had told Jimmy were both far more elaborate and worse in every way – intended to hurt, while Mallory's were an attempt to help Jimmy. But the way her mind was pulling her in two directions at once – lying was always bad vs. lying could be good if it served a higher purpose – made her think of Janusian creativity.

Almost without thinking, she said, to her own amazement, "Have you ever heard of Janus? Or the Janusian process?"

Jake's mouth fell open. "The Janusian what? It sounds like something you'd find in a hot tub."

Mallory laughed. She couldn't help noticing that Jake seemed to keep suggesting that the two of them should be doing something other than talking.

"The other day Mr. Sebastian mentioned this ancient Roman god named Janus," Mallory said. "He pulled down a book and showed me a photo of how the Romans pictured him. He had two faces, looking both backwards and forwards, into the past and the future at the same time. The process that's named after him is about trying to see two things that are total opposites at the same time."

Jake was looking at her in astonishment. Clearly he hadn't expected anything like this. They'd reached the porch of the guesthouse where there was a small round filigreed metal table and two metal chairs. The tray with the lemonade and glasses sat there, sweat running down the sides of the pitcher. Mallory could see that most of the ice cubes had already melted.

"Want some lemonade?" she asked.

"Sure," Jake said, "unless you got something stronger."

Mallory ignored him. "I think love can be like that sometimes," she said. Now Jake looked even more astonished. She was getting a kick out of surprising him. "I mean, you can love someone and hate them at the same time, can't you? I feel that way about my mother a lot, and I think my ex-boyfriend felt that way about me, too." She had poured two glasses of lemonade and pushed one across the table toward the chair where Jake was sitting.

"Thanks," he said. He picked it up and took a sip.

"Do you have any idea what I'm talking about?" Mallory asked. She searched his face to see if he was even really listening. She was pleased to see that he was. "Have you ever loved someone and hated them at the same time?"

Jake frowned and put down his glass. He looked at Mallory intently.

"Yeah," he said. "I have." His eyes narrowed. "I had a stepfather for a while – he died about a year ago. He got me the job at the ranch. I felt that way about him a lot of the time. My own father was a real jerk, not good at anything but drinking and breaking things. He left me and my mom when I was very little."

"I'm sorry," Mallory said.

"Anyway, my stepdad was good at a lot of things – talking, fixing engines, horses. He was magic with horses. I should have liked him a lot but he made me angry, and he made me feel weird and jealous."

"Wow," Mallory said. "That sounds tough."

Jake nodded. "Not only that," he said, "but he and my mom had a son, my half-brother. I was sure my parents liked him better than they liked me. Plus, he's real smart and always did real well in school. I didn't. I screwed up a lot. So I've always been a dick with him. He's a good kid and all, but I sort of hate him. After my stepdad died, I started being really nasty." He shook his head. "I'm not even sure why."

"I know what you mean," Mallory said. "After my father died, my boyfriend started saying really cruel things – like he wanted to hurt me more. I was already hurt, but he just couldn't seem to stop being mean."

Before she'd spoken, Mallory had had no idea that she was going to say this – something true about how she'd felt after her father died, all mixed up with something she'd made up about a nonexistent boyfriend. But the moment she said it, she realized that this was the way a good story got told — you mixed up deeply felt truths with something you made up, as a way of getting at the truth.

Mallory hadn't known how she'd get Jake to talk about Jimmy but she seemed to have lucked into it right from the start. She was clearly on a roll, and she didn't want to stop the momentum.

"How were you mean to your brother?" she asked.

Jake looked a bit uncomfortable. "I lied to him about our mother," he said. "And about our grandmother. I told him things that weren't true. I've been feeling bad about it for a while now. Ever since I told him, he's been mean to our mom, and the two of them aren't getting along. She's been pretty unhappy."

Jake stared out across the pool and Mallory didn't say a word. He was clearly caught up in what he had done and was ready to talk about it.

After a while, he said, "And that's not all. I fooled him into thinking that his father wasn't really his father. That threw him for a loop. And I've really been sorry about it because I got a friend to help me, and he's a great guy – a lot nicer than I've ever been. Anyway, he doesn't know anything about what I did, so now, whenever I see either of them, I feel guilty."

"That's good in a way," Mallory said. "If you feel guilty, it means you know what you did was wrong, and sooner or later you'll make it right. I can see you're not a bad person."

Jake smiled at her, a tentative little smile. "Thanks," he said.

Mallory was feeling both relieved and triumphant. She'd gotten all the information she needed from Jake – perfect confirmation of the theory she and The Three Investigators had come up with. She was sure that, once she reported this to Jimmy, Jimmy would confront Jake and the truth would come out and some harmony would be restored to the Littlewolf Blackhorse household.

It was ironic, she thought, that Jake's meanness had stemmed in part from the fact that Jimmy was smarter than he was, and now his impulse to torture Jimmy had, in a way, returned to bite him. If Jimmy hadn't come to believe that his father was an Indian from India, he might never have learned to play chess at all. As a result of Jake's cruel game, Jimmy had discovered a hidden talent that might otherwise have stayed hidden. Jake was going to have to live with that, because Mallory got the strong impression that Jimmy was destined to keep getting better and better as a chess player.

She was done now, so she stretched her hands as high as she could above her head and yawned.

"What's the matter?" Jake asked.

"Suddenly I can't keep my eyes open," Mallory said. "I feel like I could fall asleep sitting here."

"But we haven't even talked about what you wanted to talk about," Jake said. "You said you were taking a bus to Wyoming and needed to learn about the res."

"I know," Mallory said. "I got sidetracked." She glanced across the yard to see that Hector Sebastian and Phillipa Paxton were walking quickly toward the guest house.

"Whoa!" Jake said. "What's going on?"

"How is everything?" Hector asked Mallory when he arrived on the small porch.

"Fine," Mallory said. "I'm just suddenly very tired."

Hector turned to Jake, his voice friendly but firm.

"I'm glad that Mallory has found a friend," he said. "But I'm going to have to ask you to leave now. As Mallory knows – perhaps she forgot to mention it to you – a social worker will be here shortly to interview her."

Jake shot to his feet in alarm. Clearly, Mallory saw, he had some knowledge of social workers. "O.K.," he said. "I had to be going anyway."

Mallory walked with him down to his truck. Jake looked at her suspiciously, obviously not very pleased with how everything had turned out.

"You're one weird chick," he said. "I hope you find your boyfriend."

"I'm sorry," she said. "I forgot about the social worker." She made her voice sound whiny and peeved. "I had to agree to talk to her in order to stay in the guesthouse."

"When are you leaving for Wyoming?" Jake asked.

"Any day now," Mallory said. "I know we didn't get to talk about the reservation, but it was still really helpful to me to talk about that other stuff."

"Yeah," Jake said. "Well – " He put his sunglasses back on, and Mallory could see her tiny reflection in them.

"Thanks for coming," she said. She watched as he fired up the engine, backed out, and started down the gravel drive toward Dial Canyon Road. She was just about to go back up to the house when she saw that the Ford Flex had turned into the driveway and was headed toward her.

That was a close call, she thought. But the end result had been excellent – a Dial Canyon triumph. She'd gotten to the truth by a devious path. She couldn't help but think that she'd been quite creative, even Janusian, in her approach.

Creativity certainly was complex, she thought, and had many more than two faces. She thought it must have hundreds of thousands – all different, all interesting, all staring into a future that hadn't yet come into being. As Worthington parked in front of Hector Sebastian's house and Jupiter climbed out of the Flex, she waved at him.

14

Dr. Paxton and Billy Redsmoke

Jupiter was surprised but pleased to see Mallory out in the driveway, waving madly, as he emerged from the cool of the backseat of the Flex. He assumed from the jauntiness of the wave that Mallory's plan to get Jake to confess had worked like a charm. And he was right. As soon as they'd all gotten out, Mallory said, "You just missed Jake! And boy, did he spill the beans!"

"Was that him in the blue pickup?" Pete asked. "We saw it leaving the driveway just as we were getting close. He really told you what he'd done?"

"He sure did," Mallory said. "But maybe we'd better go inside so I can tell Hector and Phillipa at the same time. Plus, we don't exactly know when Dr. Paxton will call from Wyoming, and we should probably be ready."

Mallory led the way inside, and after hellos all around, Hector and Phillipa led the way to Hector's study where there again were chairs set up in front of Phillipa's laptop. At that point, Hector and Phillipa both said to Mallory, "So tell us!"

As she did, Jupiter nodded, smiling slightly, highly satisfied that Mallory had managed to confirm what The Three Investigators had hypothesized about Jimmy and the DNA test. There could be no question now, and Jupiter was sure that Mallory was right in thinking that once Jimmy confronted Jake with what he'd told her, Jake would confess to Jimmy, too.

But although Jupiter was pleased at how well that part of the mystery was likely to resolve itself, he had to admit he'd feel even better if the next part of their plan went as smoothly.

He wasn't at all sure that it would. It involved technology – the video feature on Georgina Paxton's smart phone – and Jupiter thought that just about anything could go wrong. Georgina had told him and the others that she would be riding onto the Wind River reservation, by a back trail, to surprise Billy Redsmoke where he was working. She would have her phone with her and she hoped to be able to live stream the whole conversation without him knowing about it. The strength of the signal was just the start of the possible problems.

Mallory had just finished telling everyone about Jake, and everyone had congratulated her both for her idea and for her success at putting it into practice, when the call from Wyoming came through.

"Hello, hello," Georgina Paxton said. "Are you there?"

Jupiter thought Dr. Paxton had come up with a very clever way to film her conversation with Billy Redsmoke. She had a small blue shoulder bag, about seven inches high and five inches wide, with a zip at the top, and designed for keeping a wallet, a cellphone, and a set of car keys when you went running.

She'd cut a few small holes in the front of the bag and had found a way to fasten the smartphone securely inside so that its camera was positioned directly in front of one of the holes. When Phillipa said they were all there and ready, Georgina showed them how she planned to strap the bag to her abdomen, just above her belly button, so that she could film hands free.

"O.K.," she said. The picture wobbled and streaked. "I'm just putting the phone into position now."

Jupiter could see a stretch of desert bounce on the screen.

"Testing, testing," Georgina said. "I'm riding onto the reservation now. Is the sound all right? Can you see?"

It was quite disorienting, Jupiter thought – a disembodied voice and a herky-jerky video that jolted around with no rhyme or reason. Jupiter caught glimpses of a rock, the sky, some clouds, tumbleweed, what looked like the back of Dr. Paxton's horse's head.

"You're coming in, Georgina," Phillipa Paxton told her sister. "We can hear you fine. The video's a little – a little jumpy."

"You try filming with a camera from the back of a horse," Georgina Paxton said. "At least you're getting the video. You are, aren't you?"

"Yes," Phillipa said. "But it's somewhat impressionistic."

"As long as the picture's coming through," Georgina said. "I fastened the phone with duct tape, and since the bag's made of some sort of plastic, I was hoping this would work. When I get to where Billy is fencing, I'll get down off the horse. When the camera is stationary, the video should be better."

"The good news," Jupiter told her, "is that the sound and the video both seem to be working. I assume you can hear us too. Which reminds me to say that, here on our end, when you start your interview, we'll have to keep very quiet."

"Yes, indeed," Georgina Paxton said. "Or else he'll quickly know that something's up. Either that, or he'll think he's hearing voices."

"How long until you reach him, Georgina?" Phillipa Paxton asked.

"It won't be too long now," Georgina said. "By the way, I wanted all of you to know that I looked carefully again at that photograph I took — the one of the monarch butterfly with the two horses in the background. Quite honestly, I still think the man on the first horse doesn't look like Billy Redsmoke. Although I'm almost positive that the horse the man is leading was Billy's horse."

Jupiter suspected the same two things, but he didn't say anything aloud in response. As Dr. Paxton brought her horse to a trot, the camera was jostled even more violently, transmitting a kaleidoscopic, almost deranged blur. The images switched from one to another so suddenly and quickly that Jupiter could not pick out anything in particular — just colors and motion and the sound of the wind.

Then the horse slowed down and Jupiter began to be able to identify various things again – the horse's ears, a patch of blue.

"I'm almost there," Dr. Paxton said, her voice a bit softer now. "I can see the buck and rail fence that the crew is putting up. There's Billy. There's no one else here at the moment. That's good, actually. I want to talk with him alone, at least at first."

The horse was walking now and Dr. Paxton was rocking in the saddle. "O.K.," she said, even more softly. "He sees me. I'm getting off the horse now."

As she swung one leg over the saddle and dismounted, the camera's images were blurred again. Jupiter thought he could pick out the pommel, the saddle, the horse's flank, and then, suddenly, a man with a felt cowboy hat and four feathers sticking from it. Now Dr. Paxton was walking toward him.

She stopped about ten feet from him, with just the right amount of distance and perspective so that Jupiter could see him fully. He was shorter than Travis Garrett, by a good six inches; Jupiter could see how Dr. Paxton could easily distinguish between them in a photograph. He wore buckskin pants and a chambray shirt; he had hard eyes, and his mouth looked like he had just tasted something sour.

"What are you doing here?" he said to

Dr. Paxton. His voice was clearly hostile. In front of him he held a long-handled shovel with a glinting steel blade.

"I wanted to talk to you," Georgina Paxton said.

"Well, I ain't wanting to talk to *you*," Redsmoke said. "I told you I didn't ever want to see you again after that time you said I should put Teton down."

The audio was a little fuzzy, but Jupiter could still hear every word, and the video was much sharper than Jupiter had expected it would be.

"Yes," Dr. Paxton said. "I remember. I thought he was dangerous. I did recommend you put the horse down, but only if you couldn't find someone to train him properly. Did you ever find someone like that? Did you even try?"

"How is this your business?" Redsmoke said harshly. "You didn't trek all the way out here to see if I'd gotten Teton trained." He picked up the shovel and thrust it down, hard, its blade cutting into the ground. "Why you here?"

"I heard some talk in town," Dr. Paxton said, "that you did try to find a trainer. I also heard that a vet from Dubois finally put the horse down."

Redsmoke scowled and stared at Dr. Paxton. He looked as dangerous as that horse of his, Jupiter thought. He hoped that they hadn't put Dr. Paxton in jeopardy by asking her to interview the man. Redsmoke turned his head to the side and spat.

"Listen, lady," Redsmoke said, his voice a growl. "You better get lost or I'm gonna get angry."

Dr. Paxton didn't budge. She was really brave, Jupiter thought. Instead of responding to his hostility, Dr. Paxton kept her voice steady and mild, without anger or recrimination.

"Listen," she said. "It's been a year now, and I've been wondering. I heard from a number of clients on the res that you hired Thomas Littlewolf to train Teton, not long before Littlewolf was killed. Is that true?"

Redsmoke stared at her blankly, but his face changed. Jupiter could see that he was surprised by the new direction the conversation had taken. He opened his mouth and closed it again, without saying anything.

"I know that you knew Littlewolf when both of you were a lot younger − before he got married," Dr. Paxton said. "After he died, one of my Arapaho clients told me she'd seen Thomas riding Teton on the very day he died. She said she only caught a glimpse of him but knew who it was because of the beaded hatband on his cowboy hat. And she said that Teton was pretty hard to mistake."

Redsmoke began kicking at the shovel's blade as though there were something in his way that he wanted to get rid of. His hands grasped the handle tightly. He was staring at the ground, but as Dr. Paxton talked, he glanced at her, sneering, his lips curled.

"You don't know nothing," he said sharply. "Who you talking about? I bet I never heard of her."

Again, Dr. Paxton ignored him. "She told me that Thomas wasn't alone. He was riding Teton, but there was another horse with him, and you were riding it."

"That's a lie," he shouted.

"She said you were riding west, toward the Triple X Ranch and the outcrop that Thomas fell from. What do you have to say about that?"

Redsmoke was getting increasingly enraged. The muscles in his face were clenched and his expression was darkening. Without warning, he wrenched the shovel from the ground and hurled it in Dr. Paxton's direction.

It was a heavy-duty tool; when it landed, its blade kicked up a spray of dirt. Dr. Paxton's horse whinnied and stepped backwards.

"Steady, girl," Dr. Paxton said.

Jupiter glanced around him. Everyone in Hector's study was keeping quiet, as Dr. Paxton had asked them to, but they were all extremely worried. Pete had gotten to his feet with his hands clenched. Phillipa Paxton looked very pale.

"Oh, no," she whispered. "I should never have encouraged my sister to do this."

However, as far as Jupiter could see, her sister was utterly unperturbed by the outburst and remained calm even as Billy Redsmoke threatened her. She spoke softly to her horse, patting her on the neck.

"You get the hell out of here now," Redsmoke said. "You turn that little sissy horse of yours around and go back where you came from. If you don't, I swear − I swear − " He walked toward her and retrieved the shovel. "I'll hit you over the head with this." He brandished the tool. "And if you die, I'll dig a big hole with it and bury you in it."

Jupiter was amazed that even under this threat Dr. Paxton remained calm. "You haven't changed a bit," she said. "I can see

289

that pretty clearly. You still like throwing things at horses' feet. You're lucky you didn't break the shovel the way you broke the bottle of whiskey you threw in front of Teton the day Emmett Morgan fired you from the Triple X."

"What's that got to do with anything?" Redsmoke yelled.

"Up until recently I thought it was strange that the sheriff found broken glass from a whiskey bottle at the top of the cliff Thomas fell from. But I don't think it's strange any more. You were with him, weren't you? You threw that bottle at Teton's feet and the same thing that happened at the Triple X happened again. Teton reared up and struck out, but this time he hit something. Didn't he?"

Billy Redsmoke had gone stock-still. He had jammed the shovel's blade into the ground again and he stood there quivering with rage. When he spoke, his voice was low and ugly. "That's a dirty lie," he said. "A filthy stinking lie. And if you say it again, I *will* kill you."

Suddenly he wrenched the shovel free and held it like a baseball bat, the blade aimed at Dr. Paxton.

Jupiter could see he had lost his temper entirely. When people were in the grip of passions that extreme, anything could happen. He gripped the armrests of the chair he was sitting in so tightly his fingers hurt.

"You ought to know," Dr. Paxton said coolly, "that I've been recording this entire conversation, and if anything happens to me – "

"You think I care?" Redsmoke yelled defiantly. "I'll bury your phone with the rest of you."

"Maybe not," Dr. Paxton said. "I've not just been recording our talk. I've been filming."

Redsmoke stopped and looked at her suspiciously. "What do you mean?" he said.

"I mean that I'm streaming you, right now, live, to some very reliable friends who have been watching and hearing everything. They're miles and miles away from here, watching on a computer. Whatever you did, you could never get away with it."

Redsmoke was suddenly less sure of himself. He lowered the shovel, planted its blade in the ground once more, and leaned on it. Most of the sting had left his voice. He sounded tired and defeated.

"You got it all wrong," he said. "I haven't done nothing to you, and I didn't do nothing to Thomas Littlewolf neither."

"I'm listening," Georgina Paxton said.

"That wasn't me riding that day with

him, when he was on Teton," Redsmoke said. "That was a guy named Travis Garrett who buys horses off the res sometimes. Garrett and Littlewolf came by my place that morning. I've known both of them for years."

"And?" Georgina Paxton said, encouraging him.

"I told them I was close to having Teton put down," Redsmoke said. "I couldn't do nothing with him. He was even wilder and crazier than he had been. Like a demon horse. Even *I* was a little scared of him."

"He should have been put down years ago," Dr. Paxton said.

"Yeah?" Redsmoke said, with a touch of the old fire. "That's easy for you to say."

"So what happened?"

"Travis was trying to rile Thomas up. He kept saying how he thought Thomas was so great with horses and could tame the wildest bucking bronco that ever was. Thomas asked me about Teton and I told him. Travis kept saying stuff like, 'Come on. What are you? Scared of a horse?' Then he told me I should let Thomas Littlewolf try and tame my horse.

"I told Littlewolf he could take Teton for a ride if he wanted to. He didn't look like he wanted to, but he wasn't going to take any guff

292

from Travis. He said he didn't hold out much hope after what I told him, but maybe he'd see if Teton could be saved.

"Well, I saddled him up and off the two of them went, and later that afternoon Travis came back, with Teton on a lead. Thomas wasn't with him. Travis said Thomas had ridden off on his own and that Teton had come back without him. He swore he didn't know where Thomas was.

"I believed him. I told him that if the horse had showed up riderless, Thomas was probably dead. That horse was a killer. I said we both should keep our mouths shut or we'd be blamed for Thomas's death. And sure enough, he turned up dead."

He looked almost plaintive, Jupiter thought. He was a blowhard and a bully and probably very bad with horses, but he certainly hadn't wanted anyone to die.

"That's the whole truth," Redsmoke said. "I swear." He held his hand up as if he were in a court of law. "But what business of yours any of this is I don't know."

"It's my business because Thomas Littlewolf's son, Jimmy, wants to know what happened to his father," Dr. Paxton said. "And he deserves to know. So did that vet in Dubois put

Teton down?"

Redsmoke stared at her hard and nodded.

"Too late, I'm afraid," Dr. Paxton said. "I'm leaving now, but I'm sure I'll see you again."

She mounted her horse with a sudden blur of images and color, and took off, back in the direction from which she'd come. Billy Redsmoke was no longer visible, but Jupiter could imagine him standing there on the Wyoming desert, tongue-tied and feeling desperate.

As Georgina Paxton bounced along in the saddle in Wyoming, everyone in the darkened room in California started to talk at once.

"Dr. Paxton," Pete said. "That was amazing. I can't believe how brave you were."

"You can say that again," Bob said.

"Oh, Georgina," Phillipa Paxton said. "I'm so sorry. I can't believe we sent you out there all alone."

Georgina's voice was serene when she answered. "I knew he wouldn't hurt me. The six of you were with me, at least in spirit. And in addition to you, I had a trusty friend with me." She did something they couldn't see, and then they were suddenly staring at a wicked-looking little black handgun with a bright red sight.

Jupiter blinked in surprise.

"Wow!" Pete said, as it vanished again.

"It's a .38 revolver," Dr. Paxton explained, "lightweight and compact. I keep it in my pocket when I'm in the backcountry. It wouldn't protect me from a grizzly, but it would certainly protect me from someone like Billy."

"You're like Annie Oakley," Pete crowed. "Can we see it better?"

"Sure," Georgina Paxton said.

The next minute, the gun was back. It was so small it looked almost like a toy, Jupiter thought, but it clearly meant business.

"Do you shoot tin cans with it?" Pete asked.

"I usually shoot at the gun club," Georgina said, "though sometimes I'll practice in the back part of my yard."

The gun was gone again now, replaced by images of the trail back to her property.

"I didn't think I'd need to pull the gun out," Georgina said. "I thought just knowing he was being filmed would be enough to make Billy back down. But you can tell from what some people are willing to do — even when a policeman's body camera is on — that cameras alone won't always stop people who are really intent on doing damage. To make them back down you need a firearm. All in all, people are really *much* more dangerous than grizzly bears."

Jupiter hadn't thought a lot about guns or gun ownership. Ever since that guy had broken into the Salvage Yard the previous summer, his uncle had talked about buying a gun to protect the place, but so far his aunt had talked him out of it. There were a lot of restrictions on guns in California, which, from what Jupiter had read, had the strictest laws in the country. He knew that it was illegal to carry a loaded gun in the state. So – since Georgina Paxton's pistol had clearly been loaded – it was good that what had happened between her and Billy Redsmoke had happened in Wyoming, not in California.

"Anyway," Dr. Paxton said. "I wasn't too worried about Billy Redsmoke. I've known him a while, and he talks loudly but carries a small stick."

Jupiter smiled.

"He's a nasty sort," she went on. "But from what I can see, he's not legally responsible for Thomas Littlewolf's death – even if he's morally responsible, in a way. He should never have let Thomas get on the back of that murderous horse. And of course he's responsible for Teton's death. That horse was salvageable, I think, if he'd had a better and different owner – one who'd worked with him when he was a colt. I'm going to turn the phone off now," she added. "I'm running out of juice."

"Thanks so much for everything," Jupiter said. "You were great. Jimmy will be very happy – well, not happy, I guess, but relieved – to finally know the truth, at least once we get to the bottom of it with Travis Garrett. We could never have done any of this without your help."

"Boots on the ground," Georgina Paxton said. "You can't see me, but I'm tipping my hat. I'm glad to have helped and glad to have found out what really happened. I'll sleep better now. Phillipa, I'll call you later! Over and out."

The screen went black.

It seemed strange to be in Hector's study, in a Tudor-style home in California, when minutes before Jupiter had been riding a horse on the Wyoming desert.

When he stood up, his muscles ached. He hadn't noticed how tense he'd been, how on edge. But part of it could be left over from the ride with Travis Garrett.

"This is so great," Pete said. "I don't know how we did it, but we solved a mystery

that happened over a year ago in another state
– one that the local sheriff couldn't solve."

"Yes," Jupiter said, "though there are some details we still don't understand. Like why Travis Garrett had a bottle of liquor with him when he and Thomas Littlewolf riding, or how it ended up at Teton's feet."

"Still," Mallory said, "we're close to the end. And it sure feels different from the end of other cases we've been involved in."

"We were never in any danger at all," Bob said. "But it was awful to know we wouldn't be able to help if anything went wrong."

"Boy," Mallory said. "I was almost hyperventilating."

"Me, too," Phillipa said. "It's a miracle of sorts, but live video, happening somewhere and being streamed to somewhere else, is a very mixed blessing. You can watch things happening, but you can't interfere with them or have any effect at all. Everything in me was screaming to go to my sister's aid, but we were a thousand miles apart."

"Yes," Jupiter said. "It flies in the face of human instinct."

"And we need to remember," Mallory said, "that though we may never have been in danger during this case, Jimmy was. It was a different kind of danger, but real just the same. Not physical danger so much, but he was in danger of staying miserable for the rest of his life if he'd never learned the truth about his past."

"Now he'll be able to put it behind him," Bob said.

Jupiter was glad of that – very glad. He remembered the great sense of relief, of freedom, he'd experienced the summer before when he and his friends had unraveled the secrets of Jupiter's past. Not his own past so much as the past of his parents. Learning about their lives had meant a great deal to him, even if he had never really known them. They were real to him now in a way they never had been before.

The danger of not knowing the truth was really a danger for everyone, Jupiter thought. For a while on this case he had wondered if they were simply wasting time they might have better spent elsewhere, but he was now very glad that Freya Haldorsson had met Jimmy Littlewolf. It was strange, but all of a sudden, this summer, both Pete and Bob seemed to have gotten interested in a girl – and unless he was very much mistaken, the girls in question were also interested in them.

But although Jupiter, too, was interested in a girl — and had been ever since he'd met her at the Next Chapter Bookstore in Grass Valley — his own interest, he thought, was of an entirely different nature. He was interested in how they were both alike and different, and he was interested in noticing things about her in the same way she noticed things about him. This case had had the two of them working together unusually well, he thought.

Though actually the last case had also seen that happen. And with all the talk about creativity that had been floating around, Jupiter suddenly started to wonder if there was something about having Mallory with the firm which had made him more creative as a thinker — or more willing to follow his intuition, or something. After all — as he'd sometimes told the others — intuition was just reason speeded up.

Now, as he, Bob, Pete, and Mallory got ready to leave Hector Sebastian's house and head back to the Salvage Yard, Jupiter asked if Phillipa could make a copy of the live-stream of Georgina's trip onto the reservation. He said he wanted to have it to show to Jimmy. But while that was true — he did — it was also true that when Dr. Paxton had been on the way to meet Billy Redsmoke, and the camera had been jumping around, showing pictures of earth and sky, Jupiter had thought, for an instant, that he'd glimpsed a golden eagle.

It would be cool if he'd really seen that — and now he remembered the moment in the San Bernardino Mountains when he'd seen the golden eagle riding the thermals. As he'd looked at the bird soaring above him, he'd wished for a moment that he actually *were* a golden eagle, and that he could have looked down on that rocky upthrust near Lander, Wyoming, the day Thomas Littlewolf had died.

He still didn't know exactly what had happened, but he was fairly sure it had been an accident, not murder, and he hoped that if Travis Garrett were given the chance to explain it to Jimmy, he'd be willing to do just that.

15

A Janusian Jackpot

Four days after Georgina Paxton's encounter with Billy Redsmoke, Bob was sitting in the outdoor workshop at the Salvage Yard with Jupiter, Pete, and Mallory. They were waiting for Jimmy Littlewolf, who'd called Bob the night before to see if he could meet with the four of them because he had something to give them.

"Any hints?" Pete asked. "About what it could be? I say it's a present."

"I bet you're right," Bob said. "But whatever it is, he can't stay long. He and his mother are getting ready to do something together later. He said he'd be here for half an hour, tops."

"I'm glad to hear that things are better between Jimmy and his mother," Mallory said. "When we met her, the two of them were barely talking."

"Yes," Jupiter said. "It's amazing how knowing the truth can change your attitude entirely."

"If Jimmy's bringing us a present, I feel bad we don't have anything to give him back, as a way to remember us," Pete said.

"Maybe we do," Mallory said. "The day we first met Jimmy, I told Bob and Freya about a set of chessmen found in Scotland, on the Isle of Lewis in the Hebrides. The real set – the original – is carved from walrus tusks and dates to about 1110. But earlier this summer Jupiter's uncle bought a reproduction set, and I liked it so much I've kept it in my shed.

"It's made of red and yellow soapstone, and I'll bet Jimmy has never seen anything like it. The king has a full beard and is holding a scroll. The queen and the other figures all have really expressive faces. And the castles aren't castles, as we know them – they're called warders and they're carved to resemble Viking berserkers."

"That sounds perfect for Jimmy," Jupiter said, nodding approvingly. "Why don't you go get it?"

Mallory jumped to her feet and dashed away. When she got back, she took the pieces out of their wooden box and arranged them in ranked files the way they'd look on a chessboard. Bob picked up one piece after another, admiring it, feeling its weight in his hand. The figures' features were so distinctive that Bob imagined they could open their mouths and start talking if they wished to.

While he was examining them, Jupiter went to find his uncle and returned with the very good news that he and Aunt Mathilda would be happy to make a gift of them to Jupiter and his friends, seeing as they were going to give the set to Jimmy Littlewolf. Bob wondered whether Aunt Mathilda would have parted with the set quite as easily as Uncle Titus had, but as it turned out, Jupiter had told Uncle Titus a little about the case, and he said he would explain things to Aunt Mathilda if the matter ever came up. Which he didn't think it would.

After Mallory's conversation with Jake Blackhorse at Hector Sebastian's guesthouse, she, Bob, Pete, and Jupiter had met with Jimmy again, and Mallory had told him that Jake had more or less confessed, and that what they'd told him a few days earlier had now all been confirmed − that Thomas Littlewolf was indeed Jimmy's father, that Jake had lied about Jimmy's mother and grandmother, and that he'd switched Jimmy's DNA test with Mackie Gupta's. She'd also assured him that Jake was feeling bad about what he'd done.

Already, Jimmy seemed like a different person. Bob thought back to the brooding, somber young man he'd met eleven days before at Freya's house. At the time, he himself had been feeling a little downcast, too – partly because he'd still been wishing that things had worked out differently with Mallory, and partly because he'd been thinking that, even though he admired science fiction and fantasy, he'd never be able to write them.

It was amazing what could happen in just eleven days. When all of this had started, Bob had been reading the novel *We* and had been in the mood to envy the way writers like Yevgeny Zamyatin extrapolated from the world that really lay around them to the world they *might* live in if things went either totally well or horribly badly. But as of now he felt really good about the prospect of just trying to set Jimmy's story down on paper. His ambitions as a fiction writer could wait a while.

After all, Jimmy had been transformed by what had happened. He was happy – really happy for the first time since they'd met him, no longer weighed down by the lies Jake had told him. It was as though he'd been poisoned and now he'd been cured. All his anger and resentment and self-doubt had vanished. Bob couldn't have been more pleased. Of all the clients they'd ever had, Jimmy Littlewolf seemed the most changed by what they'd done for him.

Bob had been afraid that Jake would be defensive and arrogant and refuse to admit that he'd done anything wrong when Jimmy confronted him, but from what Jimmy had said, Jake had truly been sorry. Jimmy hadn't exactly forgiven him − in fact, he'd knocked him to the ground − but in time Bob assumed they'd reach an understanding.

So that had all come out really well − and so had Bob's feelings about Freya. He'd gone from embarrassment that she liked him to pleasure and to liking her back − partly because, just like Mallory, she'd played a vital role in figuring out what was going on between Jimmy and his brother.

Now, as the four of them sat waiting for Jimmy to show up, Bob was making a few notes about the case in a file open on his laptop. Before Jupiter agreed to tell Jimmy what had happened to his father on the Wyoming desert, he'd called Chief Reynolds and asked if he could help confirm what they'd learned from Billy Redsmoke − that Travis Garrett had indeed made a trip to the Wind River reservation at the same time that Jimmy's father had gone to visit his sick sister.

The chief had contacted several horse shipping companies, and he'd found the one

that Garrett worked for. Travis Garrett had indeed been in Wyoming the day Thomas Littlewolf died.

"So what do we do now?" Pete had
asked.

"Couldn't we just tell the Lander sheriff?"
Bob had suggested. "Or have Chief Reynolds
call and tell him?"

It had seemed to him that there was
plenty of evidence for the sheriff to act on –
that it might be possible to charge Travis Garrett with manslaughter or something. To that,
Jupiter had said that he thought they should
leave it up to Jimmy to decide what to do with
the evidence. Maybe it would be enough for
him to know what happened. Maybe it would
be too upsetting to go through a trial – especially one that would totally disrupt his life and
that of his family.

Jupiter had been right, as he usually was.
Jimmy had decided that what would be best
was for him to confront Travis Garrett the
same way he'd confronted Jake – to get the
whole story and an apology. The Three Investigators had been so helpful with everything, he'd
said. Could they help him with this last thing?
So Jupiter had called Travis Garrett at the
Mustang Ranch and told him what they sus-

pected. He suggested Garrett should drive up to Palisade Point and meet with Jimmy, unless he wanted the information relayed to the Fremont County sheriff. Two days ago, Travis had driven up from Redlands, had told Jimmy the whole story, and apologized. And that had been that.

Now as they waited for Jimmy, Bob asked the others to help him with his initial case notes by talking over what Travis had told Jimmy – and what Jimmy had told *them*.

"We knew that Travis had been a rodeo rider," Mallory said. "He told that to Jupiter during our trail ride. We might have guessed that the rodeo circuit was a fairly small world and that that's where he met Jimmy's father."

"But even if we'd guessed that, we couldn't have known that Travis resented Thomas because he was a better rider," Jupiter said.

"I wouldn't say he resented him," Pete said. "He was jealous of him, and he got even more jealous that summer they were both in Nevada at the Silver State Stampede."

"And not about horses," Bob said. "Travis had been interested in Jacinta. But it was Thomas she fell for."

"So there was a lot of history between

them," Jupiter said. "A lot of frustration on Garrett's part. Then, on the day that Thomas died, they found themselves on the Wind River Reservation at the same time and in the same place. It's odd to think how many things could have changed the course of that day, but there they were, talking to Billy Redsmoke."

"Poor Thomas," Mallory said. "Maybe he didn't even know that Travis had been in love with Jacinta. Travis would have kept that a secret so his pride didn't get wounded. And then Thomas started talking about Jacinta, and how much he missed her, and how happy he was with his family, how proud he was of Jimmy."

"If I'd been Travis Garrett," Pete said, "not married and with no kids and listening to this other man who'd won the woman I'd loved – that really could have made me angry."

"And jealous all over again," Bob said, typing.

"So it was like a fire that had already been built," Jupiter said, "and there was Billy Redsmoke with the match."

Travis Garrett had already begun drinking. He had a bottle of whiskey that he offered around, and though Thomas Littlewolf turned him down, Billy Redsmoke had a swig or two.

They were talking about horses, and when Billy Redsmoke mentioned that he had a stallion named Teton that he hadn't been able to tame and that he was thinking of putting down, Travis had begun taunting Thomas.

Put him down? he'd said. When you're in the presence of a famous horse whisperer?

What do you mean? Billy had said.

Why Thomas, here, can make any horse do anything. He could probably make your horse recite the Bible, Travis had told him. I bet he can tame your horse. He does magic. What do you say, Thomas?

Thomas had said he didn't think so, but when Garrett had pushed him, saying it was either him or a gun to the horse's head, Thomas had relented.

"So Travis goaded Thomas," Jupiter said. "And besides that, Thomas was probably hoping he could save the horse. He took the challenge and the two of them rode out toward the Triple X Ranch."

"And Jimmy's father actually handled Teton," Pete said.

"From what Travis told Jimmy, it was a miracle," Jupiter said. "Travis admitted that he kept drinking from his bottle the whole time they were riding, even when they ran across the cowboys from the Triple X who were moving cattle. By the time they got to the cliff on the border of the reservation, the bottle was three-quarters empty."

"He must have been very drunk," Bob said.

"I would presume so," Jupiter said. "And also very angry. Every time he came up against Thomas Littlewolf, he lost. At the rodeo, with Jacinta, and now in his taunt about Teton. He didn't know what Thomas had done, but Teton seemed like a different horse – gentler and easier to handle. In his rage he remembered the story about what had gotten Billy Redsmoke fired at the Triple X Ranch, and there Travis was, holding a liquor bottle."

"So when they had both dismounted, and Thomas Littlewolf was feeding Teton apple slices, Travis Garrett threw the bottle at Teton's feet, just the way Billy Redsmoke had," Pete said.

Bob shook his head. It was awful to imagine – the horse that somehow Thomas had gentled now suddenly rearing up, eyes wild, lashing out with his hooves and catching Thomas Littlewolf on the forehead, Thomas staggering backwards, losing his balance, and falling to his death.

"Even really drunk, Garrett was so stunned by what he'd done – so ashamed and so guilty – that he quickly grabbed Teton's reins, got back on his horse, and got out of there," Jupiter said. "But now he had another problem. He had to avoid the cowboys from the Triple X. If they saw him with Teton, they'd know something had happened to Thomas. So he had to go out of his way, down the road, and cross back into the reservation further down."

"And that's how Dr. Paxton caught him in the photograph she was taking of the monarch butterflies," Mallory said.

"So he took Teton back to Billy Redsmoke," Pete said, "and lied to him."

"That's right," Jupiter said. "He told him that Thomas Littlewolf had ridden off by himself, that Teton had come back riderless, and that Travis had gone looking for him but had found nothing."

"Billy Redsmoke believed him," Mallory said, "for what that's worth. But he thought Thomas Littlewolf was probably dead because that horse was a killer. And he told Garrett they both should keep their mouths shut and not tell anyone about any of it."

"At least Jimmy said that he thought

Garrett was really really sorry about what had happened – and also about hiding the truth the way he did," Pete said.

"Well," Bob said, as a way of trying to bring their discussion to a close before Jimmy arrived, "I think the case turned out pretty well. Considering what we were up against."

"Yes," Jupiter said, nodding his head. "One of our oddest cases and one of the most satisfying. At first, I doubted we'd be able to find out much about something that had happened so far away in both space and time."

"But you know," said Bob. "It actually wasn't all *that* odd. I mean, it was a good reminder that – "

There he had to stop, because just then, the red Buick pulled in and Jimmy got out. He looked taller than he had before. He walked with a bounce in his step, and he seemed, to Bob, about to take to the air. His face was wreathed in a smile, and his eyes flashed with good humor. He was cradling something wrapped in buckskin.

"Hello," he called, waving with his free hand.

Bob could see that everyone's eyes were on what Jimmy was carrying. Soon he was sitting with them in the outdoor workshop, looking very happy and pleased with himself.

"Would you like something to drink?" Jupiter asked politely.

"No, thanks," Jimmy said. "I've got to be going soon. But I wanted to give this to you."

He put the buckskin-wrapped package on the table where he and Jupiter had first played chess.

"Four days ago," he began, "when you first told me about what you thought had happened to my father, I called my aunt in Wyoming – the sister he'd gone to visit. I told her I wanted to give you something to thank you for what you'd found out. She has a small crafts store on the reservation, things she makes herself – beadwork and jewelry made with turquoise and silver and reed baskets, that sort of thing."

Bob looked at the package. It was bigger than any of the things that Jimmy had mentioned.

"I told her about your logo," Jimmy said, "and I mentioned the eagle and the sheep and the bobcat. I asked her if she had anything that was Shoshone and that might make you think about your spirit animals. Well, here it is."

He pushed it away from him on the table, and it sat there for a minute, the object of everyone's fascination.

"Pete," Jupiter said. "Why don't you do the honors?"

Pete carefully removed the buckskin wrapping.

"Oh, wow!" he said in a hushed voice.

Jimmy's aunt had made them a wooden plaque, with the words THE THREE INVESTIGATORS and their logo at the top. She'd gone to their website and copied the design. Below it was fastened a soft leather medicine bag. Jimmy explained that it contained the claws of a bobcat. Below that was some beadwork in the shape of the horns of a bighorn sheep. Jimmy explained that the real horns would have been much too large and too heavy, so his aunt had selected this representation with brown and gray beads and a stream of red beads down the middle to represent the blood that was a horn's living core.

As a final, finishing touch − and on either side of the chimera − Jimmy's aunt had hung real golden eagle feathers, their shafts wrapped tightly with leather.

"Because golden eagles are a protected species, it's illegal to own these feathers unless you're an Indian," Jimmy explained, "but these particular feathers were actually found on the reservation, from a golden eagle who'd lived a long and natural life in the wild. And anyway, my aunt said that if the subject ever came up in conversation, you should tell whoever wanted to know that we aren't actually giving you the plaque outright − just lending it to you for the next thousand years or so!"

He walked over to Jupiter and shook his hand. "I'll never forget what you did for me," he said. "The way you imagined that the veterinarian might have photographed something other than monarch butterflies that day, and then you put together the events of the afternoon my father died just by trying to see the scene in your mind's eye − totally amazing."

He turned to Pete and Bob. "You were both incredible, too, but the three of you weren't mistaken when you decided that the golden eagle was Jupiter's spirit animal. You should know that there's an old Shoshone story, passed down through the generations by the tribal elders, that the golden eagle was a particular gift to the tribe."

Bob could tell that Jupiter was embarrassed but also pleased − but he was a little concerned that Mallory might be feeling left out by the nature of Jimmy's gift until Jimmy reached into his pocket. He drew out a small bird, carved of wood, and painted black.

He smiled shyly at Mallory. "I didn't know what your spirit animal might be, and it probably isn't a raven," he said. "But I thought you might like this anyway. Ravens are very important in a lot of Native American cultures – and I understand they're also important in Scottish stories."

Mallory looked touched to the heart, Bob thought.

"Gosh, thank you, Jimmy," she said. "Really, thank you."

"We have something for you, too!" said Pete. "Mallory found it in the Salvage Yard, and Uncle Titus said we could give it to you. It's a reproduction of a set of chessmen made by some Vikings almost a thousand years ago."

He handed Jimmy the wooden box, and when Jimmy opened it, his jaw dropped in astonishment.

"These are amazing!" he said. "What are they again?"

"They're called the Lewis Chessmen," Mallory said, "after the place where they were discovered. In the Outer Hebrides in Scotland. The originals are in the British Museum. They think chess originated in India, then made its way to Persia, somehow got to Norway by 1100 and then through Norway to what is now Scotland. It's too bad the Spanish didn't bring chess with them when they took California from the Chumash!"

"Maybe they did," Bob said. "Maybe the French or English brought chess to the Plains Indians, and maybe Jimmy's descended from some ancient Shoshone who was a chess wizard. There's always something new to learn about history."

Of course, he didn't think that that particular bit of history would have gone unnoticed if it had happened, but even so.

"Gosh," Jimmy said, "Thank you so much. I'm sorry I have to go so soon, but my mom's waiting for me."

"That's fine," Mallory said. "Though I hope there'll be a next time."

With a big smile and a wave – and holding the box with his new chess set – Jimmy was off.

"Boy," Pete said. He turned to the table where the wooden plaque and the carved raven lay. "I don't know about the rest of you, but I think this might be the best memento we've ever gotten."

Bob thought Pete was right. All the mementos they'd collected reminded them of the specifics of their cases, and a lot of them — most of them, really — were gifts from someone they had helped. But the plaque was the only one that had been made specifically for them as a thank you.

"That about wraps up this case," Pete said. "Soon you'll be writing it up, Bob. I was thinking — since we're up to 'J,' right? Maybe it should be the Mystery of the Jealous Something or the Something Jealousy. After all, what both Travis and Jake did was out of being jealous of Thomas and his son."

"That's not a bad idea," Bob said, "but don't you think it's pretty negative, given how well everything seems to have worked out for Jimmy? I'd rather name it something positive. Maybe something using Jackpot. A little while ago, Jupiter said this case had been one of our oddest, and I was starting to say that it actually wasn't all *that* odd just before Jimmy got here."

"That's right," said Pete.

"I was thinking about the case with Daman Duwalia, last summer. That one also revolved around jealousy — and in that one, too, we were never in physical danger," Bob said.

But though Bob had a lot more to say

on the subject, he suddenly felt tongue-tied. If he'd kept talking, he would have said that in most Three Investigators cases, there was an actual bad guy, but in both the Maduri Singh case and this one, there really hadn't been. Just fallible human beings who'd felt awful when they'd gone too far in trying to hurt someone. And who afterwards had wanted to make things right.

And though it seemed to be a natural human desire to punish evildoers when they had done something really bad, a case like this one could remind you that people were people, in the end. They envied other people, got angrier than they ought to, and then got scared they'd be punished if they got caught.

Indeed, although The Three Investigators had seen some real villains in their recent cases, there'd been something reassuring about both this case and the one Daman Duwalia had hired them about. In a way, they'd made him feel that although a dystopian future might indeed lie ahead for the human species – because too many human beings were too power-hungry or too stupid to stop their reckless rush toward doom – when you saw men like Jake Blackhorse and Travis Garrett (and a woman like Madhuri Singh) take responsibility for their actions and learn from them, it made you think that maybe humanity might survive, after all.

Since Bob really *couldn't* think how to say all of this just now, instead he said, "So why don't we call this case 'The Mystery of the Janusian Jackpot'? When that klaxon went off in the casino, I thought it was so sad that the man who'd won the jackpot seemed to think he'd done something amazing, when all he'd done was pull down the arm of a slot machine. Compared to that, the four of us and Jimmy really *have* hit the jackpot."

"What do you mean, exactly?" asked Pete.

Bob thought for a minute.

"Well, Hector Sebastian told us that Janusian creativity involved being able to think two things at once — two things that contradicted each other — and then making use of the clash between them to come up with a brand-new idea. And though everyone can probably do that at least a little, the four of us have to do it a *lot*. It's what makes us good at what we do — and what makes Jimmy such an excellent chess player."

Once again, he stopped and thought.

"I mean, human beings really *do* inherit a lot of things," he said. "Our sex and our height and our maximum life span are all programmed into our genes. So is some of our intelligence, and probably some of our creativity. But even so, everybody has creative talents. It's just a matter of finding out what yours are and then using them. In this case, Jimmy found out about one of his in a very unusual way. Because he wrongly believed that he had special genes for playing chess, he discovered he was actually very good at it."

Everyone agreed that 'The Mystery of the Janusian Jackpot' was an excellent title, and as Bob said goodbye and headed to his bicycle, he was thinking about his decision not to take part in Dr. Yang's experiment. He would never be as smart as Jupiter was at deductions and hypotheses and retaining complex information, and – well, a *lot* of things – but he knew, from his writing, if nothing else, that he was quite creative, and if he'd been trying to write down Jupiter's thoughts on the subject under discussion, he'd have had Jupiter say that although human beings were all born with potential individual talents – and even certain fixed proclivities – they also had the freedom to choose what they would do.

Bob himself would put it a little differently. He'd say that while it might be useful to understand that your genes had a lot to do with who you were, there was no reason to let them limit what you tried to succeed at.

As long as you hung onto your ability to hold two contradictory ideas in your head at the same time – for example, the idea that you were a person who had inherited a lot of your talents and inclinations, and also a person with free will and the ability to do anything you wanted – you would be able to live a really productive life. In fact, Bob thought, if you kept those particular two ideas in your head at one and the same moment, you might say that you'd hit the Janusian Jackpot.

The ride home seemed shorter than it usually did, and when he jumped off his bike Bob was smiling.

ABOUT THE AUTHORS

Elizabeth Arthur

Elizabeth was born on November 15, 1953 in New York City. She is the daughter of Robert Arthur, the creator of The Three Investigators series. She was educated at Concord Academy in Concord, Massachusetts, the University of Michigan in Ann Arbor, Michigan, Notre Dame University of Nelson, British Columbia, and the University of Victoria in Victoria, British Columbia.

Before she started working on the New Three Investigators series in December of 2018, Elizabeth spent most of her life writing for adults. *Island Sojourn* – a memoir about building a house on a wilderness island in northern Canada – was published in 1980 by Harper and Row. A second memoir, *Looking For The Klondike Stone*, was published by Knopf in 1992. She is also the author of the novels *Beyond the Mountain, Bad Guys, Binding Spell, Antarctic Navigation,* and *Bring Deeps.*

Elizabeth's writing has received fellowships, grants, and awards from the Bread Loaf Writer's Conference, the Ossabaw Island Project, the Vermont Council on the Arts, and the

Indiana Arts Commission. She twice received fellowships from the National Endowment for the Arts and was the first novelist ever given an Antarctic Artists and Writers Operational Support Grant from the National Science Foundation.

Her novel *Antarctic Navigation* was chosen by the New York *Times* as a Notable Book, received a Critics' Choice Award from the San Francisco *Review of Books*, and was chosen as a Best Book of 1995 by *A Common Reader*. In 1996 the novel received the Ohioana Book Award for Fiction from the Ohioana Library Association.

Elizabeth has also taught creative writing at Miami University in Oxford, Ohio; the University of Cincinnati; and Indiana University/Purdue University of Indianapolis, where she directed the creative writing program. She and Steven Bauer met in 1980 at the Bread Loaf Writer's Conference and have been married since June of 1982.

Steven Bauer

Steven was born on September 10, 1948 in Newark, New Jersey. He was educated at Hanover Park High School in East Hanover, New Jersey, Trinity College in Hartford, Connecticut, and the University of Massachusetts in Amherst, Massachusetts. In 1970 he received a B.A. with Honors in English from Trinity, and in 1975 he received an M.F.A. in English from the University of Massachusetts.

Steven is the author of three books for young people – *Satyrday*, 1980; *The Strange and Wonderful Tale of Robert McDoodle*, 1999; and *A Cat of a Different Color*, 2000. His book of poems *Daylight Savings* was published by Gibbs Smith in 1989 and won the Peregrine Smith Poetry Prize.

Steven's work has received fellowships from the Bread Loaf Writer's Conference and the Fine Arts Work Center in Provincetown, Massachusetts. In addition, he has been given grants and awards from the American Library Association, the Parents' Choice Foundation, the Ossabaw Island Project, the Massachusetts Arts Council, and the Indiana Arts Commission.

From 1979 to 1982, Steven taught literature and creative writing at Colby College in Waterville, Maine. From 1982 to 2009 he taught at Miami University in Oxford, Ohio where he directed the graduate and under-graduate creative writing programs. In 2010 he established Hollow Tree Literary Services, an independent editing business.

www.ingramcontent.com/pod-product-compliance
Lightning Source LLC
Chambersburg PA
CBHW021221310726
48971CB00006B/1646